To: Denny

CHARLES C. BROWN

Hope you enjoy #10!

JUSTICE
AS PROMISED

Charles C. Brown

D1716010

Dedication:

To my niece and her husband, Lynette and Ryan Giovinco. Wishing we lived closer and could get together more often.

Chapter One

Murray McCartney was having trouble focusing on the argument the two women were having. One of them had mentioned the name James Hartman, and the thought that kept going through his mind was: *If I had kept my promise, the son-of-a-bitch would have been taken off the streets years ago.*

The two of them had walked into his office minutes earlier, both of them slender brunettes of a little more than average height, and they looked enough alike that they were obviously related. The office was toasty warm from the electric heating units along the baseboards, and both of them removed their quilted jackets quickly. The younger one was wearing skinny jeans and a top that fit like a second skin. The older one wore similar attire, but hers was quite a bit more modest.

Murray had stood up from the chair behind his desk, introduced himself and gestured toward the oak armchairs that faced it, and they had taken seats. He had sat back down.

"What can I do for you?" he had asked, and the older of the two had answered.

"My daughter is being stalked and harassed by one of Huntingdon's finest," her tone made the word an insult, "and I want it stopped."

1

Murray had nodded and asked, "Could you give me this officer's name?"

"Hartman," the mother had said. "James Hartman." And that was when Murray's mind went numb. Darkness pushed in from his periphery until there was only a small circle of light left, and the women's voices suddenly began to sound like they were talking into a barrel—all echoes and far away.

"We shouldn't have come in here," the younger woman said, standing up, her eyes taking in Murray's gray hair and the shabbiness of his suit coat. "We're wasting our time and his. It looks to me like he doesn't even know what planet he's on."

"Sit down, Janie," her mother ordered. "Something has got to be done, and we can't do it ourselves."

"I'm sorry," Murray said, coming out of his trance. "I didn't mean to zone out on you like that, but the name you mentioned… it has a… a special significance to me. Let's start over. I'm Murray McCartney, and you are…?"

"Janet Hockenberry, and this is my daughter Janie."

Murray did his best to smile and nodded. "And may I ask who recommended me to you?"

"Nobody recommended you," Janie said, her tone somewhat hostile. "We were just driving by when my mother saw your little sign and decided to drop in."

Murray pursed his lips, nodding his head and letting that sink in. "And you are being harassed by Officer James Hartman?"

"Yes."

"How long has this been going on?"

"About two years," Janet Hockenberry said, "and it's way past time to put a stop to it."

"Two years," Murray said, nodding and taking a notepad and pen out of a drawer in his desk.

"Do you have a weak neck or something?" Janie asked. "Why do you keep nodding?"

Murray looked up and smiled. "No, I don't have a weak neck. I'm just trying to be agreeable. If it bothers you, I'll stop. Tell me about the first time you met Officer Hartman.

"He pulled me over up by Juniata College a couple of days after my father's funeral."

"Your father's funeral?"

"My husband was Deputy Sheriff Russell Hockenberry," her mother supplied. "He died when his pickup went off the road up on Warriors Ridge one night two years ago. I imagine you read about it in the *News*."

"I believe I did," Murray said and caught himself beginning to nod. "I'm sorry for your loss. But back to the problem at hand. When Hartman pulled you over the first time, were you speeding? Driving recklessly?"

"No, I wasn't doing anything wrong. I asked him why he stopped me, and he said because I cut my hair funny and dyed it purple. I was living in California when my father died, and lots of women have unusual hairstyles out there. Anyway, I told him my personal appearance was my own business and none of his. He seemed to think that was funny. He asked me if maybe we could get together some time, the two of us, go out to dinner or for a drink. I told him it don't never get that cold down there. I don't know what he would have done next. A bunch of students came down the street and were giving us funny looks, so he decided to let me go."

"And there have been other incidents since then?" Murray asked.

"About every couple of months," Janet Hockenberry said, "sometimes a couple of times a month. Just about any time she has to drive through town. It's like he keeps looking for her."

"Has he ever asked you out again?" Murray asked.

"A couple of times," Janie answered, "but usually, he just writes me a warning about speeding or double parking or whatever. It's like he wants me to know he's still out there, and it's all bogus. I avoid going through town as much as I can, but sometimes I have to. I work as a bartender at the American Legion in Mount Union sometimes, or at the VFW down there. If I get started on time, I go up toward Alexandria and catch Route twenty-two. But if I get started late, through town is the shortest route to work."

"But he went too far yesterday," her mother said. "Tell him, Janie. Tell him what happened yesterday."

"I was going out Penn Avenue when he started following me a couple of blocks before I got to the courthouse. I figured he would turn off after a couple of blocks like he does sometimes, but he kept following me, and he turned his flashing lights on. I ignored him until he hit his siren. Then I pulled off at that used car place across from the park that went out of business. I just stopped and sat there, waiting for him to walk up and ask for my license and registration like he usually does. When he walked past the back end of my car, he used something to smash my taillight, and then he wrote me a ticket because my taillight was broken."

"Because your taillight was broken," Murray repeated, a statement, not a question.

"That's what I said." Her tone suggested she was about to lose all patience.

"I'm sorry," Murray apologized, "but what you said just now maybe shed a little light on an incident that happened to someone else five years ago. But that's another matter."

"Anyway," Janet Hockenberry took over the conversation again, "with the cost of parts and labor to replace the taillight and with the fine because the taillight was broken, we're going be out more than four hundred dollars! We don't have that kind of money just lying around! I work in the kitchen at J. C. Blair Memorial, and Janie works as a bartender wherever she can find a shift. My son, Russ Junior's wife just had a baby and there were complications. The bill was horrendous, and his insurance only paid eighty percent, so we've been helping them out financially. On top of that, we're trying to get the homeplace livable so we can move back out there. The roof needs to be tarred, and the place needs to be painted, among other things. Until we get some of that done, there's rent on the apartment here in town and bills to pay. We can't be paying for damage Hartman does to our cars."

"I agree," Murray said and caught himself about to nod his head, "and I'll take care of the problem for you."

His answer brought a frown to Janet's face. "We don't really have the money to pay a lawyer."

"But you saw my sign and stopped in because you need my help. I don't have anything pressing at the moment, and I'll do it *pro bono*."

"You will?"

Murray was busy scribbling on his notepad and answered with a single, emphatic nod. "What kind of a car do you drive?" he asked without looking up.

"A two thousand nine Malibu," Janie told him, her tone a bit more polite.

"And is that the vehicle you are driving today?"

"No," Janet said. "We haven't got the taillight fixed yet. We're in my Nissan."

"Would it be too much trouble for you to bring the Malibu in and let me have a look at it, say later today or tomorrow, whatever is convenient for you?"

"We could do that." Janet looked at her daughter, and the young woman nodded. Murray saw it out of the corner of his eye and smiled to himself. Maybe someone else was developing a weak neck. He asked for and made notes of each of their phone numbers and their address, correctly assuming they shared an apartment.

"Okay," he said and stood, and both women left their chairs. "I'll go have a look at the spot where this incident took place. Out on Penn, across from Blair Park, right?"

"Yes," Janie nodded again, "On the right-hand side of the road where that used car place was just before you get to the creek."

"Plaza Motors?" Murray suggested.

"Yes, I think that's it," Janie agreed.

"I'll be in touch." Murray offered his hand.

Janet Hockenberry took it immediately and smiled tentatively. Janie seemed a bit hesitant but finally gave it a slack-fingered shake, her eyes downcast, and muttered, "Thank you."

Murray stood until the two of them had shrugged into their jackets and left. Then he sat back down in his chair and tilted it back. He laced his fingers together on the top of his head and stared at the ceiling, thinking about the day five years ago, a cold dreary day much like the one the city was having now, when his son had died by the hand of one James Hartman. *He smashed her taillight, probably with a telescoping baton*, he thought. *Most likely, that's how the taillight on Randall's pickup got broken, too. Something to think about.*

Chapter Two

Five years ago

Murray McCartney was sitting at his desk in the law offices of Baker, Yocum, Oppel and Ramsey, doing the usual scutwork that gets dumped on an associate who hasn't made partner yet, when he heard the phone ring on the receptionist's desk up the hall. Miss Dickens's answer came down the hall as a feminine murmur, and then she was at the door of his office looking concerned and glum.

"Mr. McCartney, you need to get to the hospital. Your son has been in an accident."

Later, he would not be able to remember leaving the office, getting into his car and driving to J. C. Blair Memorial. The shock of what he found in the emergency room there wiped much of the day and much of the following days from his memory. His son had been shot to death by an officer of the Huntingdon Police Department and had arrived at the hospital DOA.

He called his wife Vicki at the insurance office where she worked and told her she needed to come to the hospital. Their son Randall had been in an accident. She accused him of making a bad joke, went into hysterics when he was able to convince her that it wasn't a joke, and screamed at him over the phone. She was incapable of driving, she said. He had to go and pick her up and take her back to the hospital. She sat against the passenger door of his Chrysler and sobbed into a fistful of tissues. When he tried to comfort her with a hand on her shoulder, she jerked away.

He let her out at the door of the emergency room and parked the car. By the time he got back inside to join her, she had been shown into the room where their son's body lay on a gurney, covered with a sheet, the top of which was saturated with blood.

"Pull back the sheet," she was saying when he walked in, and the nurse was trying to talk her out of it. *"Pull back the sheet!"* she yelled, and the nurse did so, just as Murray came up beside her. It was immediately clear to Vicki, and would have been clear to anyone else, that their son's death had been no accident. His shirt had been cut away, and his left forearm had an extra bend midway between his wrist and elbow where a bullet had passed through it and shattered the bones. Much of the blood had been cleaned away, and the bullet holes in the left side of his chest and neck, his left cheek and temple were too obvious to be mistaken for anything except what they were.

Vicki McCartney gasped, her eyes rolled back, and she began to fall. Her husband felt like he had been stabbed through the heart, but he managed to catch her before she hit the floor. The nurse rang for help, and moments later, an orderly pushed a second gurney into the room, and the three of them together managed to get Vicki lifted onto it. The orderly pushed her out into the hall, and Murray turned back to his son.

"How did this happen?" he asked, and the nurse answered as best she could.

"I understand it was a traffic stop gone wrong."

"A traffic stop?" He choked on a sob. "A *traffic* stop? My son didn't drive fast. He didn't run red lights or drive recklessly. Why would a cop stop him and do this?"

"I really can't say." The nurse sounded a bit apologetic. "You'll have to ask the policeman or read the police report."

* * * *

It would be awhile before he could do either. The Police Department closed ranks and refused to release any information about the incident. Mayor Banks claimed not to know anything about anything. Murray filed a lawsuit, and Judge Blakemore ordered the Police Department to produce a copy of the report and the appropriate footage from the police unit's dash cam. Both would prove to be enlightening. And what they showed would turn Murray's life upside down, never to be righted again.

According to the police report, Randall McCartney had been pulled over because his pickup had a broken taillight. When Officer James Hartman (Murray finally got to know the name of the man who had murdered his son) approached the vehicle, the subject in the driver's seat informed the officer that he was carrying a firearm. Officer Hartman drew his own weapon immediately and instructed the subject to place his hands on the steering wheel. The subject complied, but moments later, he took a hand off the wheel and reached for his weapon. Hartman, concerned for his own safety, emptied his clip into the subject in self-defense. Then he called for backup and an ambulance.

The dash cam footage that was released to Murray bore out the police report—mostly. It clearly showed Officer Hartman approaching Randall McCartney's pickup on the driver's side. It showed him drawing his weapon and practically shouting, *"Hands on the wheel! Hands on the wheel!"* After that, his voice was less audible, and about the only thing anyone watching the footage could hear were seven gunshots that came so close together that some of them seemed to overlap, the sound muffled somewhat because the barrel of Hartman's weapon was inside the victim's pickup.

Murray watched the video so many times he began to see it in his sleep. Vicki read the police report but refused to watch the dash cam footage even once.

"So, it's *your* fault our son is dead," she railed at her husband. "*You* talked him into getting that concealed carry license, and *you're* the one who bought him the gun."

"I didn't talk him into anything. He wanted to take the class and get the license, and he was over twenty-one, old enough to do pretty much anything he wanted to do. And I bought him the automatic because that's what he wanted for his birthday. If anyone's responsible for his death, it's the man who pulled the trigger and shot him seven times."

"Well, what are you going to do about it?" Vicki wanted to know. "Sit on your hands and let the bastard get away with it?"

11

"What do you think I'm going to do? I'm going to do everything in my power to get justice for our son, to see that his murderer is taken off the streets, at the very least. It's just going to take some time to get to the bottom of it all."

And take some time it did, more than Murray ever thought possible. The Police Department remained buttoned up to protect its own. The thinking seemed to be: Let one of our number be convicted of a service-related death, and other members of the department would fall like dominoes. Besides, Officer Hartman had just been doing his job, the same job as everybody in the Department, which was to protect and serve. If the "subject" (using the victim's name tended to make him seem more human) had followed orders and kept his hands on the steering wheel, he would still be alive and well, having suffered nothing more than having to pay a fine.

Murray went to the mayor and the city council and demanded that an independent investigation into the shooting be made by someone from outside the Police Department and the Borough of Huntingdon. The mayor and the council refused his request and made a cursory investigation of their own. Murray was informed of the results of said investigation at one of their regular council meetings.

"Our investigation has concluded," Mayor Banks informed everybody present, "that in the April fourteenth incident involving Officer James Hartman and one Randall McCartney, Hartman was justified in using his service weapon. The subject admitted being armed, failed to follow instructions, and the officer was in fear of his life."

"You have got *to be kidding!"* Murray exploded. "In fear of his life from someone who had a broken taillight? How does that justify emptying his clip into a twenty-two-year-old man? What put him 'in fear of his life'? My big, bad, five foot six, one hundred-and thirty-five-pound son? *Look* at the man!" and then addressing Hartman himself, "What are you? Six-three and two-fifty?"

"'Bout that," Hartman answered, a smirk on his face.

Murray just stood there, staring at the man for more than a minute, taking in his barrel chest, his shaved and glistening head. Everybody in the room was so quiet that one could have heard the proverbial pin drop.

"What was the last thing you said to my son before you drew your weapon and emptied it into him?" Murray asked.

Hartman shrugged. "What difference does it make?"

"It might make a whole hell of a lot. What was the last thing you said to him?"

"I had to guess, I'd say it was, 'License and registration'."

"And my son took his left hand off the steering wheel, and you put a bullet through his arm."

"So?" Another shrug from Hartman.

"Randall wasn't reaching for any weapon. He was reaching for his wallet. That's where his license would have been, and he carried it in his left hip pocket. He carried his automatic at the small of his back, and if he had been reaching for it, he would have been reaching with his right hand."

"That's all news to me," Hartman said, "and it doesn't change anything."

"You aren't fit to wear the badge and the uniform," Murray told the man. "At the very least, you should be taken off the streets."

"That ain't gonna happen anytime soon," Hartman assured him.

"Oh, but it *will* happen," Murray told him, "Sooner or later, and for the safety of the residents of Huntingdon, I believe it should be sooner."

"Is that a threat?" Hartman asked, rising from his seat.

"No," Murray told him, "It's more like a promise."

"That's quite enough!" someone said. Murray and Hartman were in a staring contest, so he never did know or never could remember who it was. "I believe the information you came here for has been provided, whether or not it meets with your approval. So, security, please escort Mr. McCartney out."

Someone grabbed his arm from behind and turned him around. He stumbled but didn't fall, jerked his arm out of the hand that held it and left the building without looking back. The next day, he filed a wrongful death suit, naming James Hartman, the Chief of Police, the mayor and the members of the City Council individually as defendants and requesting the sum of ten million dollars from those responsible for the death of his son.

* * * *

The suit dragged on for a year and a half and produced some unfortunate results. Shortly after he filed it, Murray was fired from his position at Baker, Yocum, Oppel and Ramsey. There wasn't enough work to warrant employing him any longer was the reason given for his termination. The stacks of papers on his desk waiting for his attention gave the lie to that. Truth be told, and he knew it, all of the partners were either friends with the mayor or had friends on the Council, and the city manager threw business the firm's way occasionally.

"So, what are you going to do now?" Vicki McCartney asked. "Lay around the house all day while I go to work and make a living for the both of us?"

"I don't really know," her husband admitted. "Maybe get a job sacking groceries."

His wife looked at him like he had lost his mind and left the house. "Well, *I* have to go to *work. I*'ve already *got* a job."

Murray spent part of the day getting familiar with the inanities of daytime television. The rest of it was taken up with sleep brought on by depression. When Vicki got home a few minutes after five, she found him sitting on the sofa in a daze, red marks on his face where it had been pressed against a throw pillow. She gave him a stare that was meant to embarrass and went back into the kitchen. He got up and followed her as far as the archway, leaned a shoulder against the woodwork, hands in his pockets.

"So, how did your day go?" he asked.

"How do you think it went?" she asked in turn. "Word is getting out about what you're doing. My boss has friends in the Police Department and on the Council. I might be out of a job before long, and then what are we going to do?"

Tears welled up in her eyes and began to stream down her face. Murray went to her and tried to take her in his arms. She batted his hands away and shoved him back.

"Don't touch me! Leave me alone!"

He backed away stunned. "I'm sorry."

"Well, you should be, making us pariahs all over town. Go sit in the living room, and I'll heat up some soup."

He did what he was told, and some twenty minutes later, Vicki brought in tomato soup laced with Worcestershire sauce in bowls that had handles on the sides. She handed him one and took a seat on the far end of the sofa with hers. She picked up the remote and turned the television on. They sipped their soup and watched Fox News until she got bored with it. Then she surfed the channels and settled on reruns of the *Family Feud* with Steve Harvey. Their evening together lasted about another fifteen minutes and ended when Vicki burst into tears and ran to the bedroom, apparently upset by the happiness the families on the television were enjoying—happiness that she and her husband and son would never know.

Murray thought about going after her but was still smarting a little from her rejection in the kitchen earlier. Eventually, he muted the television, took off his shoes, stretched out on the sofa and let depression take him into a deep sleep again. He was awakened sometime later by the sound of running water—Vicki taking a shower. He waited until the water was turned off and he heard her going back into the bedroom. Then he got up and headed to the bathroom to take a shower of his own. When he climbed into bed in clean briefs, the red letters of the digital clock on the dresser read 10:48. Vicki was lying with her back to him on her side of the bed, as far away from him as a person could get in a queen size bed. He lay on his back and stared at the dark ceiling until he drifted off to sleep. Sometime later, the bed shaking with his wife's sobs woke him up. He rolled toward her and put an arm around her waist in a futile effort to calm her. She threw his arm and the covers back at the same time, got up and ran out of the room. He heard the guestroom door open and close, and he lay there in the middle of their bed, shaking his head.

* * * *

It would prove to be the beginning of the end of their marriage. The following evening, Murray left the house at about four-thirty. He went to McDonalds and loaded up on chicken sandwiches, chicken nuggets and whatever else he could think of that would spare Vicki having to make a meal for them that evening. He got back to the house about fifteen minutes after she had gotten home and found her transferring all of her clothes to the closet and the chest-of-drawers in the guestroom.

"What are you doing?" he asked.

She passed him with an armload of clothing. "What does it look like?"

"Vicki, we can get through this! There's no need for us to split up! All we have is each other!" He realized his tone was somewhat pleading.

"And whose fault is that?"

Her answer silenced him, as it was intended to do.

17

For several minutes, he just stood and watched her flurry of activity. Then he remembered the food.

"Well, come on in the kitchen and eat. I brought us some stuff from McDonalds so you wouldn't have to cook tonight."

His wife carried one more armload of clothes into the guestroom and threw them on the bed. She turned and gave him a look that seemed intended to incinerate him on the spot. "I'm not hungry," she said and slammed the door in his face.

By the end of the second week, Murray began to suspect that the rift between them was permanent. He knew beyond a shadow of a doubt that it was when, on what he came to think of as their final Friday, she told him, "I've had enough, and I'm sick of looking at you. Go live with your mother until you get your lawsuit settled."

Chapter Three

Present Day

The beginning of the end, Murray thought, tilted back in his office chair in his office and staring at the ceiling. *At least she could have let me stay in the house until the judge ruled on the wrongful death suit, and I had the money to buy this place, the dump that it is. But it had been nice, enjoying Mother's home cooking again.*

He won the lawsuit, sort of. He had been given a choice of getting the full amount of the suit over quite a number of years or accepting a much lesser amount and being done with it. He had accepted the second choice and signed a non-disclosure agreement. He had violated that agreement only once, revealing the amount awarded to Vicki after making her swear not to repeat it, ever, to anyone.

"That's *it*? You think that's all our *son's life* was worth?"

He was stunned by her vehemence. "It was take what they would give us or let it drag out for years!"

"What do you mean *us*? There's no *us*! I don't want any of your *blood money*. Just take it and go buy yourself someplace else to live! Your mother must be sick of you being underfoot by now! Just take your blood money and go have yourself a nice life."

Sitting in his storefront office now, Murray shook his head and smiled—a smile that never quite reached his eyes. That hadn't lasted very long. First, she had to quit her job because her boss was being mean and unreasonable, she said, and some of the customers were looking at her funny. Murray set her up an account and put a sum of money into it every month for more than two years. Then, she couldn't stand to live in the house they had shared since early in their marriage. It was the house they had brought Randall home to when his jaundice had been brought under control, and he was allowed to leave the hospital. Randall's spirit was haunting her, she said. His offer to move back into the house with her brought a laugh that was close to hysterical.

"Okay," he had told her, "find a place that suits you and let me know what you need to buy it. We'll put the house on the market and split whatever it brings."

In hindsight, he realized, he should have set a limit on what she could spend on a different place. *And maybe how long she could go without finding another job?* he thought now. But at the time, he still loved her and harbored a hope that Vicki might discover she had similar feelings for him, that she would come to her senses, and the two of them might live in the new house together. The new place had set him back nearly half a million. She left the house where they had raised their son sitting as it was, bought all new furniture with the money he was putting into her account and then complained that she didn't have enough money to buy food. The drain on his funds—and any hope of a reconciliation—came to a stop when he found out she was engaged to and had moved in with Harvel Yocum, one of the senior partners in his old firm whose wife had died of ovarian cancer. Vicki was sporting a rock the size of a dime when he ran into her in Walmart and asked her where she got it. If a face could get red enough to burst into flames, hers would have done it.

"Harvel Yocum," he had repeated when she told him where it had come from, "the Harvel Yocum from my old firm? Harvel Yocum, the senior partner who canned me when I won our lawsuit against the city?"

"It wasn't *our* lawsuit, it was *yours*," she answered, and her tone added, *if it's any of your business.* "And yes, *that* Harvel Yocum.

"What is he...?" Murray had asked, "... about half again your age? He was getting a little tottery and senile the last time I talked to him. How's he doing now?"

Her answer was a twist of the head and a shrug that essentially said once again, *as if it's any of your business*, and she had turned and hurried away.

Sitting in his storefront office now, he remembered thinking at the time, *how many ways can one man get screwed over?* But there was more still to come.

He had gone from Walmart to the bank, where he closed out the account into which he had been putting money for her. While he was there, he learned that she had not sold their old place but, in fact, had taken it off the market and was renting it out. He got the deed to the property from their safety deposit box and started the process to have her name removed from it. From the bank, he went to the old place and told the family

21

living there—a man and his wife and three children—
that they would be paying their rent to him from now
on and gave them the address where they could mail or
drop off the check. Just to keep them happy, he
lowered their rent by a hundred dollars. His practice
had grown by a few clients, and he had simplified his
life until he didn't need much.

Three months later, the man of the house had
gotten transferred to Georgia and taken his family with
him. Murray moved back into the house he had shared
with his ex-wife and his son, and things had come full
circle, except, of course, that he no longer had a wife
and there was no longer a Randall Mason
McCartney—and there never would be again.

* * * *

Murray shook his head and stood. No point in
wasting any more time dwelling on the past. He had a
job to do. He lifted his black overcoat off its hook,
shrugged into it, locked the office door behind him and
walked down to the parking lot on Penn where he
always left his fourteen-year-old Honda Civic. His
Chrysler had died years ago, and he had bought the
cheapest replacement he could find. Parking spaces
were scarce near his office, and he wanted to leave
them free for potential clients. The Honda still had
fairly low mileage since he seldom left Huntingdon,
and his hopes were that it would last him another ten
years. Besides, he needed the exercise, and he enjoyed
breathing the crisp March air.

From the parking lot, he headed east on Penn.
When he got close to Blair Park, he slowed down and

pulled up onto the blacktop where vehicles belonging to Plaza Motors had once been parked. What he had expected and hoped to find was there, glistening in the sunlight—pieces of red plastic that once had been the taillight of Janie Hockenberry's Malibu. He set his parking brake, got out and stepped to where the pieces lay; muttering a silent "Thank you" to whichever deity had kept Hartman from running over them with his squad car as he left. Squatting down, he picked the pieces up and fitted them together as best he could, holding all of them in two hands. They all shared a single point of impact where something small and round had hit them. Murray smiled to himself, pulled a sandwich bag from the pocket of this coat and dropped the pieces into it. Not until Janie brought her Malibu to him would he have all the pieces of what once had been a perfectly intact taillight assembly.

She brought it in the next afternoon, pulled it to the curb in front of his office and got out. Officer James Hartman was pulling up behind her, lights flashing, when Murray stepped out the door. He walked around the front end of her vehicle, opened her door and helped her out. Janie was already shaking, out of fear or anger, he couldn't tell. Hartman exited his unit and walked up to the two of them.

"You have business here, Hartman?" Murray asked.

"That's Officer Hartman to you," the man said. "I ticketed this vehicle for a broken taillight two days ago. I want to know why she's still driving it without taking care of the problem."

"She hasn't had the time or the money to take it by the dealership yet," Murray told him. "And as I understand it, the taillight wouldn't be broken if you hadn't whacked it with your baton."

Hartman's face got a little red, and he stepped forward until he and Murray were chest-to-chest. "Is that an accusation?"

"No," Murray said, looking up into the taller man's face. "I believe it's a fact."

Hartman glared but remained silent.

"Janie, do you have one of those phones that can take videos?" Murray asked and got a positive response. "Well, get it out of your purse or your pocket or wherever it is and make a video of this."

The young lady pulled her phone from a hip pocket and began doing as Murray had asked.

"Put the phone away," Hartman demanded, taking a step back, and when Janie didn't stop videoing, "You want to keep that phone and your freedom, you'll put it away."

"There's no law against videoing a policeman in the misconduct of his duty, Hartman," Murray informed him, "but you already knew that. I already intend to lodge a complaint against you with Mayor Banks and the City Council, so I would strongly suggest that you get back in your vehicle, shut off the lights and get out of here."

Hartman glared as he backed away. "This ain't over, McCartney. Both of you better keep your asses on the straight and narrow," and then with a smirk, "I'll see you on the street."

That being said, he got into his unit and followed Murray's suggestion. Janie kept videoing until the squad car disappeared around the corner half a block away.

"Go on into my office," Murray told her. "I want to check on something, and then I'll come in and make us some coffee." He watched her until she had closed the door behind her, and then he stepped to the rear of her car and took a look at what was left of the broken taillight assembly. As he had suspected, two pieces of the broken lens had gotten lodged inside it. He picked them out carefully and dropped them into the sandwich bag with the other pieces he still had in his pocket.

When he stepped into his office, she was sitting in the chair her mother had occupied a day earlier. "I'll have to go in the back to get the coffee going. Are you okay?"

She was kind of huddled in the chair, shoulders slumped, hands clasped between her knees. There was little sign of the belligerent young woman she had been the first time he had met her. She nodded her head but didn't look at him.

"Would you like some coffee?" he asked, and she answered quietly.

"Yes, please."

He went through the door behind his desk and all the way to the back of the building, thinking, not for the first time, that he needed to have the stacks of boxes hauled away and the bathroom moved closer to the front. The boxes had been there when he bought the building, and he had no idea what was in most of them.

Coffee on, he slipped back through the door into his office and found Janie sitting as she had been when he left her, except that she had taken off her quilted jacket and was holding it in her lap. He took a seat behind his desk, and she looked up at him with reddened eyes. He offered a smile.

"So? What do we do now?" she asked.

"Now, we wait until the coffee's done, and then we talk about what I'm going to do and what I want *you* to do. Is your mother doing okay?"

The question seemed to confuse her. "She's okay, I guess. Why?"

"Just trying to get your mind off what just happened out there for a little while. Your mother seems like a nice lady, and I think she has your best interests at heart. Do you and her get along okay?"

"Better than me and my dad ever did," Janie said.

"Hold that thought." Murray held up a finger. "The coffee should be done. I'll be right back." He disappeared through the door behind his desk again, was gone about three minutes and reappeared with two large white mugs of black coffee. "I forgot to ask, so I hope you like it black."

"Black is fine."

Murray resumed his seat behind his desk. "So, you and your father didn't get along?"

Janie took a sip of coffee and then shook her head. "He wanted his firstborn to be a boy. He was a hunter and wanted someone he could take hunting with him. Since I was a girl, he pretty much ignored me. In his opinion, girls couldn't or shouldn't do what boys do. Then Russ Junior was born, and I ceased to exist."

"You lived in California for a while?" He lifted his cup to his lips while he waited for an answer.

"I left the day after I graduated from high school and didn't come back until my father's funeral. Used the money I got for graduation and a little I had saved from babysitting and caught a bus. I don't think he ever even knew I was gone."

Murray caught himself nodding and smiled. "Were you a bartender out there?"

Janie rested her mug on the knee of her jeans. "I got lucky. Out there, you can't even get a job as a waitress unless you have experience. How can you get experience if nobody will give you a job? I met a guy that worked as a bartender, and he showed me how to mix drinks. It's about the only skill I have."

"So, you came back for your father's funeral, and shortly after that, James Hartman pulled you over."

Janie nodded, her coffee mug at her lips.

"Had you met him before?"

She lowered her mug and shook her head. "I had never even seen him before, as far as I know. He might have been there at my father's funeral. Why?"

"When he pulled you over the first time, you said he told you it was because your hair was cut funny and you had it dyed purple. It doesn't seem to me that he would have been able to tell all of that with you just driving by him in your car. How *was* your hair cut at the time?"

"I had it shave up to about here," she used her fingers to indicate about an inch and a half above her right ear, "and the rest was long, down below my chin. I had it bleached blonde, and the ends were dyed purple."

Murray considered her description, nodding. Was it possible Hartman thought she was... what... easy... because of her appearance?

Janie interrupted his thoughts with, "So, what do we do now."

27

"Now, I take these to Mayor Banks." He picked up the bag of lens parts and rattled them. "I tell him how James Hartman has been stalking and harassing you, and I tell him if such misconduct on his part should continue, I will file a lawsuit against the city on your behalf that will make you a very wealthy young lady, should the courts rule in our favor, and I think they will."

"What do you want me to do?" The Janie who asked the question seemed to be much different from the one who had come into his office with her mother only yesterday.

"I want you to have your taillight assembly replaced. Do you have a credit card you could use to do that?"

"No, Mom says credit card companies rip you off with interest."

"A savings account then? Or maybe cash you've been saving for something else?"

Janie shook her head. "I don't have a savings account, and I won't have enough cash until I work a couple of shifts somewhere."

Murray considered her answer, frowning. "I'll see what I can do. In the meantime, you should maybe follow the route you usually take up toward Alexandria and down Route twenty-two. If you have to go through town, have your cell phone ready, and if Hartman starts following you, make a video of it. I'll download it into my laptop and save it for the right occasion. Okay?"

Janie reached to set her empty mug on the edge of the desk, stood and put her jacket on. "How long do you think it might be until he backs off?"

"Oh, I think the process has already started. Just be patient. I'll give you a call when I know something definite."

Murray walked her to the door, opened it for her and the two of them stepped outside. Hartman and his unit were nowhere in sight. Janie got into her Malibu and drove away. Murray locked the office door and headed for the parking lot on Penn. There were some things in his safety deposit box that he needed to examine again, get his ducks in a row, before he paid a visit to Mayor Banks. He strode down the sidewalk in the cool afternoon air, smiling.

Chapter Four

To say that nobody in the mayor's office was happy to see him the following day would have been the understatement of the century. Murray stepped through the door and the receptionist, an elderly, gray-haired woman who had served several mayors, looked up, did an eye roll and snorted. The nameplate on her desk identified her as Stella Moffitt, not that Murray needed her to show identification. The two of them had butted heads on several occasions before.

"Nice to see you, too, Stella. How have you been?"

Stella answered with a statement. "You don't have an appointment."

"I don't need an appointment. He needs to hear what I have to say, and sooner rather than later," Murray informed her. "You get a chance; you might tell him that."

"Have a seat then," she said, her tone hostile. "He'll get to you when he gets to you, and that might be sometime tomorrow."

"Fine," Murray said. He slouched down in one of the upholstered visitor's chairs, settling in and making himself comfortable. Hands in the pockets of his overcoat, he crossed his legs and wrapped the tails of it around them. "I'll just sit here and admire this beautiful décor and this plush new carpet. What did it set the taxpayers of Huntingdon back? Couple hundred dollars a square foot? I just love those English hunting prints and those gold gilt frames. And is that a new desk? What happened to your old one? Get a scratch on it?"

Stella's reaction was swift. She shoved herself away from her desk, stood, stalked to the door of the mayor's inner sanctum and disappeared inside. She was back in a matter of minutes, the expression on her face suggesting extreme anger.

"The mayor's free," she said, resuming her seat at her desk and doing her best not to look at Murray. "You can go in now."

He smiled and thanked her, which only seemed to upset her more.

Arthur Banks, a semi-bald, portly man in his late fifties, was sitting behind a desk made of what looked to Murray like burled oak, and he didn't bother to stand when Murray walked in. "What do you want, McCartney?"

"What? No handshake?" Murray responded, taking in the silk tie and tailor-made suit, the two-hundred-dollar cotton shirt, and mentally picturing the Italian leather shoes that would be on the man's feet underneath the desk. "No 'How you been, Murray? It's been awhile since we've talked. I thought we should catch up?'"

"It hasn't been long enough, and there's nothing to catch up with. Just state your business and get on with it."

Murray got "on with it" by pulling the bag containing the broken pieces of the lens from Janie Hockenberry's vehicle out of his overcoat pocket and dumping its contents on the blotter on Banks's desk. The mayor's eyes got big and he pushed himself back.

31

"There's no need to be afraid, Arthur," Murray told him. "They don't bite. I thought about gluing them together, but I think they make a stronger statement when you can scatter them out. Don't you?"

"What is this?" Banks asked.

"These are the pieces from the left taillight assembly of Janie Hockenberry's two thousand-nine Malibu—the results of your favorite Huntingdon Police Department officer whacking it with what I imagine was his telescoping baton."

While he spoke, Murray was busy, putting the pieces of red plastic together.

"What? You're back on Hartman again?" Banks pulled himself back up to his desk and stared at the pieces of red plastic.

"I'm not 'back on' Hartman. I never got off the creep. Look at the spot where these pieces come together here near the center. That little dimple right there is where the little ball on the end of the man's baton made contact with the lens. He has been pulling the young lady over every time he catches her in town for the past two years now. The first time wasn't too long after her father's funeral, she says. She asked him why he stopped her, and Hartman told her it was because she had her hair cut funny and had it dyed purple. He asked her if they could go out for dinner or a drink, and she turned him down."

"And now she claims he broke her taillight?" the mayor's tone suggested disbelief.

Murray nodded. "Broke her taillight and then wrote her a ticket because it was broken. She and her mother came to me because they didn't know what to do."

"And you believe this nonsense?"

"I went out Penn Avenue to the spot where Janie Hockenberry said the incident occurred and found these pieces, right there on the blacktop that used to be Plaza Motors. There's not a doubt in my mind that she's telling the truth. Up until he pulled this, Hartman has been stopping her a couple of times a month, like I said, almost every time she has to drive through town, and was just writing her warnings about speeding, reckless driving, whatever came to mind, I guess. This was the first time he damaged her vehicle and wrote her a ticket. The family's funds are stretched thin, and they can't afford to have the vehicle repaired or to pay the fine. I want you to take care of the problem. Get the man off the street. Have them put him on a desk."

"James Hartman is one of the finest police officers we have," Banks countered. "He's an asset to our community. He's one of the reasons we have law and order in this town, and he..."

"And he what?" Murray asked when the mayor left his sentence unfinished. "And he what?"

"He writes his salary in tickets every month."

"Every month?" Murray was stunned. "And how many of those tickets do you suppose are bogus? How many are for broken taillights, for instance? I suggest that you check his ticket receipts and find out."

"We've never had any complains until you walked in here today."

"And I imagine that's because the man is so intimidating. Put him in a gray uniform with lightning bolt *S*'s on the collar and black, knee-high boots, and he would fit right in with Hitler's SS Troops."

"Now wait a minute... !" Banks started, but Murray wasn't finished.

33

"Or maybe he usually smashes the taillights while the vehicles are parked and waits until the owners get in them and drive off. Again, I suggest, very strongly, that you get hold of his ticket receipts and look for a pattern."

"Why are you so hung up on broken taillights?" Banks wanted to know.

"You remember back five years ago when Hartman murdered my son?" Murray asked.

"He didn't *murder* anybody. Your son was armed, and Hartman was in fear of his life."

"Hartman *murdered* my son," Murray insisted. "You remember how I had to file for a court order to get the police report and the dash cam footage released?"

"Yes," Banks said, "what of it?"

"Do you, by any chance, remember why Hartman pulled my son over to begin with?"

When the mayor refused to answer, Murray supplied one for him.

"Because his pickup had a broken taillight, the one on the left, driver's side."

"Now, wait a minute… !" Banks tried again.

"I got the dash cam footage the Police Department released to me out of my safe deposit box and watched it again yesterday. It took several viewings before I finally saw it. I was so messed up over Randall's death back then that it went right past me."

"What went right past you?" Banks prompted.

"The video was edited."

"Edited how?" the mayor finally began to show interest.

"I believe the part where Hartman smashed my son's taillight was erased. The video doesn't begin until he is almost even with the driver's door. If I had been thinking more clearly back then, I would have seen it. And I don't suppose you remember where my son's murder took place?"

"It wasn't murder!" Banks insisted.

"It was what it was!" Murray countered. "Do you remember where it all happened?"

Banks heaved a heavy sigh. "No, I don't recall."

"It happened out on Penn Avenue near Blair Park."

The mayor's eyes got wide, and then his brow knit in a frown. Murray gave the man some time to let it all sink in.

"I didn't even know where my son had died until I read the police report again. If I had known sooner, and if I hadn't been such a mess back then, I could more than likely have filled a bag full of pieces from Randall's taillight out there, don't you think? Right there on the blacktop where Hartman walked past the tail end of his pickup and whacked the lens with his telescoping baton."

"Okay, so there's a maybe there," Banks admitted, "but that incident happened five years ago. Let's get back to the one that happened more recently. What do you want me to do about it?"

"My first request would be for Hartman to be taken off the street, but you've already made it clear that you aren't interested in making that happen. So, back to the incident with Janie Hockenberry's Malibu. I want you to write a check, or have Stella out there write one, for the cost of the taillight assembly and the labor to make the repairs, and let's add a little extra for mental anguish and emotional distress. Let's round it up to, say, an even one thousand dollars. You could probably take that out of petty cash. And I want Officer James Hartman to be told in no uncertain terms that he is to back off where Janie Hockenberry is concerned. How does that sound?"

"A thousand dollars for a broken taillight? That's kind of high, isn't it?" Banks demurred.

"Not as high as the expense of defending James Hartman, the Police Department and the Borough of Huntingdon in general if I have to file a lawsuit over this incident," Murray told him, "and you know damn well I will if I have to."

Banks nodded. He began to sweep the pieces of the taillight on his desk into the palm of his hand, obviously preparing to deposit them in the trash.

"No, in here." Murray held the bag he had brought them in open, and Banks dropped them into it.

"Go wait in the waiting room and tell Stella to come in here. I'll have her write you that check."

Chapter Five

Murray McCartney couldn't help smiling every time he thought of the look on Stella Moffitt's face when she handed him the check. About the only thing he could imagine that might bring on such a pucker to her mouth—other than having to deal with him, of course—was the old girl biting into a green persimmon. He had gotten back to his office an hour ago, hung his overcoat back on its hook, and made a phone call to Janie Hockenberry. Was she free? Could she come in and pick up a check? She was and she could.

While he waited for her to show up, he called the Chevrolet dealership and asked about a taillight assembly for a 2009 Malibu. Yes, they had one in stock, but he would have to make an appointment to have it installed. He made the appointment, thanked them and hung up.

Janie Hockenberry arrived about fifteen minutes later. "You have a check for me?"

Murray picked it up from his desk and handed it to her. She looked at the amount on it, backed up and sat down in one of the armed, visitor's chairs with a plop. Uncharacteristic tears filled her eyes and threatened to spill over her lashes.

"You have an appointment with the Chevrolet dealership at two-fifteen tomorrow afternoon to have your taillight assembly replaced. They had one in stock. After this, you should have no more trouble with Officer Hartman. I imagine his focus will be on me now."

"How can I thank you?" Janie asked, wiping away tears with the heel of her hand. "This is more than I ever expected."

Murray found himself wishing he had tissues to hand her, but he smiled. "Just don't forget the appointment tomorrow, and when the repairs on your vehicle have been made, drive through town anytime you want or need to." *Having Hartman's blood boil when he sees you and knows he can't approach you is thanks enough* went through his mind, but he left it unsaid.

Janie promised to keep the appointment, stood and shook his hand and left. Murray tipped back in his desk chair, laced his fingers together on top of his head and stared at the ceiling—a pose he absentmindedly let himself fall into when he had nothing pressing to do.

So, what can I expect now? he wondered, and memories of a time three and a half years ago flooded his mind.

He had just won the wrongful death suit he had filed with the courts and accepted the lump sum the city had offered. James Hartman had come after him with a vengeance, vowing to get back every cent the city had paid, one way or another. In a six-month period, Murray had collected a pile of traffic tickets that nobody, not even an individual with the most blatant disregard for the law, would ever have collected in a lifetime, all of them written by Hartman. And with every pull-over, he was subjected to Hartman's foul mouth and derision. "When

38

ya gonna keep yer promise, asshole" or "I'm still on the street, dick face. I'm gonna be here awhile, and *that's* a promise." Once he even found a half pint of whiskey in his car, the seal broken and the bottle half empty, but was able to discard it before the next unwarranted stop. Hartman practically tore his Honda apart looking for it that same afternoon but had to let him go without a ticket.

Murray took the pile of tickets to the police station and presented them as evidence that he was being harassed. He was told that if he had a complaint, he should take it up with the judge at traffic court. Instead, he had gone to the mayor's office and threatened Banks with another lawsuit. Banks took the pile of tickets and said he would take care of it. The man had been as good as his word. Murray never had to pay out a penny, the fines were vacated, and for the next three and a half years, Hartman never stopped him again.

That was then; this is now? Murray thought. He couldn't imagine the man that was James Hartman not retaliating for the reprimand he was likely to get over the mayor's office having to write a check. *Best to be prepared.* With that thought in mind, he took his overcoat off its hook and slipped it on, locked his office door behind him and headed for the parking lot on Penn.

* * * *

Murray went to Walmart where he updated his flip phone with one that could take videos. He also bought a bracket the phone would clip into and that had a suction cup on the back that would fasten it to the dash of his car. The salesclerk gave him a quick course on how to get the thing started, and he paid for both items in the electronics department and was headed for the door when he thought about Janie Hockenberry sitting in front of his desk with tears in her eyes and not a tissue in sight. He turned around and went looking for paper products.

He located the tissues between the napkins and the plastic food storage bags on an aisle toward the back of the store. They came in a variety of boxes, and he stood for several minutes, contemplating his choices, before settling on the store brand. A hundred count box that was fifty-five cents cheaper than an eighty-count box of the name brand. *Fifty-five cents saved is fifty-five cents earned,* he thought. *Thank you very much Mister Franklin.* He picked up a box and turned to go, saw dishwashing detergent on the other side of the aisle and remembered he had emptied the bottle he had at home that morning. So once again, choices, and once again, he opted for a store brand that looked exactly like the blue stuff he had been using for years. *A penny saved is a... Get over it,* Murray told himself. *Your account is low, but not that low.*

On his way to the checkout, he detoured through the coffee aisle. Getting to sleep tonight was likely to take a while, given that he would be wondering how Hartman would retaliate, and he knew he didn't need caffeine. There was no choice to be made here. He liked good coffee and wasn't about to settle for any store brand. He picked up a small container of Folgers Decaf, thinking it would be his final purchase, but on his way to the front of the store, a box of Little Debbie cherry pies seemed to call out his name. So much for frugality.

His items scanned, bagged and paid for, he was almost to his car when he saw Hartman, still in uniform, get out of his black Dodge Ram and head his way. The man's face was a mask of fury, but Murray refused to be intimidated and stood his ground.

"You son-of-a-bitch!" Hartman started. "You got me suspended for two weeks without pay!"

"I'm surprised they took action so quickly," Murray told him, "and I'm totally *amazed* at the part about 'without pay', but *you* got you suspended, not me. Maybe you'll learn something from this. Conduct yourself the way an officer of the law is supposed to conduct himself, and maybe this will be your last suspension ever."

"I don't need to learn nothing!" Hartman said. "I know all I need to know already. And one thing I know for sure, I'll be back on the streets in two weeks, and when I am, your ass is gonna be in a world of hurt."

Hartman brushed past him, nearly knocking the bags out of his hands, and lumbered into the store. Murray watched him go and muttered to himself, "Why in the hell couldn't you have had your phone ready and videoed all of that?" Some days, everything goes wrong, he thought, and other days are worse.

When he finally got home with his purchases, his mailbox was stuffed with envelopes and magazines. He carried everything into the house and put it on the kitchen table and then went back for the mail—an advertisement for Direct TV, several catalogues for women's clothing (still coming all these years after the divorce), a catalogue of miscellaneous kitchen aids, trinkets and other junk, a water bill and an electric bill.

The water bill was for the same amount as always. With only Murray himself in the house, rinsing a dish now and then, showering at night and making the occasional pot of coffee, it was always the minimum. The electric bill, however, gave him pause. The house had to be heated in cold weather and cooled in the summer no matter how many people were living in it. With a bill here and one at the office, electricity was the biggest drain he had on his bank account. Looking at the amount on the bill and anticipating the one he would find at the office in the morning, he came to a conclusion. One of the places had to go, and the house was likely going to be it.

He tossed all the mail except the two bills in the trash and put his purchases away, leaving the box of tissues on a table in the living room to be taken to the office in the morning. He made himself a pot of decaf, kicked back in his recliner, sipped his coffee and spent the evening mentally planning the apartment he would have someone construct behind his office. Two rooms maybe? A large room that had a living room, kitchenette and small dining area, and a bedroom with a bathroom off it—a shower and vanity only, no tub. Get it finished and put the house on the market. But first, he would have to get someone to haul the stacks of boxes away.

* * * *

Murray got to his office the next morning excited about the prospect of having an apartment built in the unused space behind its back wall. He set the box of tissues on the corner of his desk nearest where Janie

42

Hockenberry had been sitting on her last visit, put his usual sandwich and bag of chips in a drawer, and hung up his overcoat. Then he went through the door behind his desk and, using a 25 foot steel tape he had discovered in the usual miscellaneous junk drawer found in most kitchens, he began measuring the space available—or that would be available once the stacks of boxes had been hauled away. From the back wall of his office to the back wall of the building, he discovered, was forty-six feet, more space than he ever imagined. The width of the building was twenty-one and a half feet. Why not twenty-two feet even? he wondered for all of two seconds and then got back to laying out his apartment.

He went back into his office, sat down at his desk and got a sheet of copy paper from the ream he always kept in a bottom drawer, a ruler and a pencil and began drawing floor plans. A wall set back twelve feet from the back wall of the office would give him plenty of space for the two rooms he wanted. And the ceiling would have to be lowered, of course. No sense heating and cooling space that wasn't necessary. By noon, he had the place pretty well drawn out—where the bathroom with its shower would be located, where a small sink and an apartment size stove and refrigerator would go—and then he realized he hadn't figured in a place to do laundry. Maybe a unit that had the dryer over the washer? Regardless, it would have to be placed near the bathroom because of the plumbing.

Satisfied that he had done everything he could for the moment, he went to the back of the building and started a pot of coffee. Then he sat down at his desk and took out his sandwich. Half-finished with it, he went to the back and got a mug of coffee and was dropping into his desk chair again when it hit him— heating and air conditioning. Electric base board units in each room for heat, simple enough, but for cooling? A small unit on the roof would require ductwork, but for several minutes, he could think of no other solution. Then the light can on, so to speak, window units set into the back wall. As small as the place would be, one-ten units would likely be sufficient. Problem solved.

He had been living mostly on the monthly retainer he got from Daniel Miller, a recent client. A thousand dollars a month seemed like a lot when all he did was collect the rent from the house the man owned here in Huntingdon and send it to him every three months. With that and the income he had from his small practice, Murray felt sure that he could afford all of it without completely depleting his supply of blood money, a term which always brought Vicki to mind, unfortunately. Then there would be the money from the sale of the house. Somebody would buy it eventually. He speculated that everything could probably be done in a week once a crew got started. It turned out to be not so simple.

To begin with, he discovered that there weren't very many crews willing to take on what they considered to be such a small job. And all of those who seemed willing to help him out were booked up for the better part of a month or more. They would get back to him when they could or if they had any cancellations. How about coming by and giving him an estimate? he asked and was told they would give him one before they started the job.

Murray put his floor plans in the drawer above the kneehole of his desk and turned to the task of getting the stacks of boxes hauled away. Finding someone to do that job turned out to be easier. A man and his son showed up the next day with a dump truck, and the back room was emptied out before the end of the week.

* * * *

On what Murray thought of as the tenth day of Officer James Hartman's suspension, a woman and her daughter walked into his office again. *A woman and her daughter just like Janet and Janie Hockenberry*, went through his mind, but there, all similarities ended. In this instance, both women were short and a little bit overweight, and the mother was the angry one. The daughter seemed cowed, and the left side of her face was covered with a dark bruise.

"Janet Hockenberry said you might be able to help us," this from the mother, who had on a modest dress and black athletic shoes with a white swoosh on the sides. Her long, gray hair was done up in a bun.

Murray stood up from behind his desk, introduced himself and told them to have a seat. When they had done so, he sat back down.

"And you are...?" he asked.

"I'm Joy Summers, and this is my daughter Cheryl," the older woman said.

"And how may I help you?"

"We want a restraining order taken out against Cheryl's husband."

Murray looked at the younger woman, who was

45

sitting with her shoulders slumped and her head bowed, staring at the floor. Her jeans were worn and frayed with holes in both knees, and her top was wrinkled and faded from many washings.

"Can you tell me what happened and why?" he asked.

"Her husband hit her with his fist."

"Was this the first time this happened?" Murray asked.

Cheryl simply shook her head and removed her jacket, held it in her lap. Her mother was more vocal. "No, it wasn't the first time. It's been going on practically since the day they married. But this had better be the *last* time."

"Please, tell me what happened," Murray said, and when the mother began to answer, he held up his hand and looked at the daughter. "When did he hit you and why?"

"Yesterday morning," the young woman said in a voice barely above a whisper. "He said his eggs were too runny and the bacon wasn't crisp enough. He threw them in the trash under the sink, plate and all, and when I told him not to break the plate, he turned around and punched me."

"And something like this has happened before?" Murray asked.

The young woman nodded. "When he's in one of his moods, anything can set him off. If he can't find his favorite socks because I haven't washed them yet. If the toilet paper doesn't tear straight, or if the weather isn't nice when he has to go to work. I try to stay away from him as much as I can, and *that* even makes him mad. I want a divorce, but I'm afraid to tell him."

46

Murray had heard enough and suggested a suit for domestic violence be brought against the man.

"Will they put him in jail?" Cheryl wanted to know and seemed not to like the idea.

"That's where he belongs," her mother said.

"It's a possibility," Murray answered. "So, tell me your husband's name and where he might be found."

Over the next half hour to forty-five minutes, he took notes and mentally prepared the suit he would file against one Barry John Knepp, sometimes known as B.J., for assault with intend to do bodily harm against his soon-to-be ex-wife. When he had all the information he thought he needed, he asked for phone numbers where they could be reached.

"You only need one," Joy Summers told him. "Cheryl will be living with her father and me until this is over and she's rid of him."

Murray made a note of the number she gave him and asked, "While I'm working on the domestic violence suit, would you like me to write up a bill of divorcement, also?"

"Whatever you can do to get her out of the situation she's in. We would really appreciate it."

He nodded agreement and walked them to the door. When he had closed it behind them and resumed his seat, he tipped the chair back, laced his fingers together on top of his head and stared at the ceiling for a while. Janet Hockenberry had told them he might be able to help them. Janet Hockenberry was a good-looking woman. She had been a widow for two years, and he had been divorced for almost three. He wondered if she was seeing anybody or if she might be willing to go out with him. *Never know until you ask her*, he told himself, *and you have her phone number.*

Smiling at future possibilities, he tipped his chair forward and wrote her number on a scrap of paper and slipped it into his wallet. No telling when he might build up the courage to ask her out. Then he picked up a legal pad and pen and began working on a domestic assault suit.

Chapter Six

Murray got the domestic assault suit and the bill of divorcement written up and printed out by late afternoon and decided there was enough time left in the workday to take them to the courthouse and file them. He locked the office door behind him and set off for the parking lot on Penn Street, thinking he would file the papers and then go home. There was nothing more that had to be or could be done back at the office until another client or a construction crew showed up. The weather was nice, the sun bright but the air cool, and he walked along at a fairly quick pace thinking, *four more days until he's back on the street and the harassment will start.* He couldn't have been more wrong.

The folder with the papers to file in his left hand and jingling his keys in his right, Murray slipped up between his Honda and the vehicle next to it and came to a dead halt. His left front tire had a four-inch slit in its sidewall. Backing up a bit, he discovered the same thing in the rear tire, and going to the other side of his vehicle, he discovered the tires on that side had been sliced open, too.

He got out his phone and took a photo of each tire, thinking as he did so, *I guess not being on the street in uniform doesn't mean not being on the street at all.* There was no doubt in his mind but that this was the work of one James Hartman, and an anger boiled up in Murray that might have been fatal to the man if he had been present.

"Cut and run, you son-of-a-bitch," Murray said out loud. "Cut and run."

At that very moment, the owner of the vehicle next to his walked up, keys in hand.

"You wouldn't have happened to see anyone messing around my car today, would you?" Murray asked the man.

"No," the fellow answered. "Is there a problem?"

Murray gestured toward his rear tire, and the man stepped around his vehicle and took a look. He let out a whistle when he saw the four-inch slit. Then he walked to the other side of the Honda and saw the slits in the tires on that side.

"All four? I'd say you've got somebody really pissed at you."

The two of them stood for several seconds, contemplating the situation. Then the man asked, "Can I give you a lift somewhere?"

Murray nodded. "If you don't mind, I could use a ride home."

* * * *

His evening did not go well, and the night was no better. Murray had trouble overcoming the anger he felt every time he thought about what it was going to cost him for a new set of tires, and his mind kept coming up with scenarios that would take James

Hartman off the streets permanently, coming up with and discarding them as too dangerous and too likely to get himself locked in a cell for the rest of his life. He wasn't about to let that happen, and the phrase "ain't worth killin'" kept coming to mind. Hartman had told him "your ass is gonna be in a world of hurt" when his suspension was over. That's where he wanted to put Hartman—in a world of hurt. But getting himself put in prison in the process was not acceptable. Four more days and the man would be back in uniform, back on patrol and menacing the citizens of Huntingdon, Pennsylvania, once again. He had to be stopped.

Nightmares kept waking him up throughout most of the night, crime scenes that involved blood spatter so vivid and realistic he could almost smell it. He would wake up in a cold sweat, expecting the authorities to come busting through his bedroom door at any second, handcuffs at the ready. Then he would realize where he was and that such a crime had not been committed—yet—and he would lay back down and try to go back to sleep. Morning came and his alarm went off. He turned it off and lay back down, woke up an hour later and knew he wouldn't be getting to the office on time. No matter, he had no appointments scheduled. He was free to get there when he got there.

He put on a pot of coffee—the real stuff this morning because he felt the need for caffeine—and started making calls to companies that sold tires and had a tow truck of the kind that winched a vehicle up on a sloping flatbed. There weren't all that many. When he finally found one that was willing to help him, he told them where his vehicle was and what kind of shape his tires were in. The man on the other end of the line chuckled.

"You must have really pissed somebody off."

"You don't know the half of it," Murray told him. He hung up and called a taxi.

He had the cab take him to the courthouse where he filed the two suits he had prepared and headed for the door. A young man and a young woman dressed in the uniform of the Sheriff's Department were sitting on a pew-like bench in the hallway. When he walked by them, he heard the young man say:

"I will always believe it was Daniel Miller... had to be."

"And I agree, Buckley," the female deputy concurred, "but how is anyone going to prove it?"

Murray did a right-face at the far end of the bench and took a seat.

From the corner of his eye, he saw Buckley purse his lips and give his colleague's question some thought. "I don't guess there's any way *to* prove it. But look at the situation. The three guys that raped Rosalynn Holder's daughter get murdered..."

"And one of the boys' fathers," his colleague interrupted.

Buckley nodded. "Then she robs Hillman's Jewelry at gunpoint, goes home, kicks back in her recliner and waits for the police to come and arrest her. They find the jewelry she stole, still in the pillowcase, on her kitchen table, along with the weapon believed to be the one used to kill her daughter's rapists, five empty cartridges still in the cylinder, her fingerprints on all of them, and a box of cartridges with five rounds missing sitting beside it. Rosalynn Holder is arrested and taken to jail where she dies and leaves Miller her house and everything she owns, including *two* Honda Accords, both of them gray. Why two cars that look almost identical if it wasn't so she could run around town in one of them and let people see her here in Huntingdon while he drove the other one to where the murders were committed?"

"I read the file just out of curiosity. How do you explain her fingerprints showing up on items at three of the murder scenes, in places that we can't prove she's ever been?"

No pause for thought this time. "She had him take those things—the lipstick, the compact and the credit card case with her prints on them—and leave them at the crime scenes just to cause confusion. She never left town, so that's the only way they could have gotten where they were."

"How could she have talked Miller into doing what he did?" the brunette asked.

"He and the daughter, Rose her name was, had been friends from the time they were four years old," Buckley explained. "When they got older, they were boyfriend, girlfriend, and would more than likely have got married when they graduated from high school, but she had a brain tumor that left her with the mind of a five-year-old."

"And then she committed suicide?"

"So they thought at the time," Buckley told her.

"And now…?"

"She supposedly swallowed a bunch of pills and washed them down with vodka. Question is: how would a girl with her mental capacity know what kind of pills to take?"

The female deputy nodded. "She wouldn't."

Buckley shook his head. "And they didn't find any alcohol of any kind in the house either. Lots of things about the case that confused us then seem obvious now."

"Like what, for instance?"

"Well, the boys that were involved were football players, and the Bearcats were supposed to have a chance of winning State that year. Then the three of them pick Rosalynn Holder's daughter up and... well, no need to go into all that again. The boys got put on trial, but it ended in a hung jury, and Rosalynn was pushing the DA's office for a retrial. When the girl died, all that ended, and the boys got off Scott free."

"Until someone took them out ten years later."

Buckley sat leaning forward, elbows on knees, and nodded his head. "Daniel Miller."

What might have been shared next went unsaid. A door on the other side of the hall opened, a woman in a business suit looked out and said, "Deputy Debora Hicks?" The brunette stood up and headed that way. The woman stepped aside so she could enter and then closed the door behind her. Murray sat there long enough to make it seem like he hadn't been eavesdropping on their conversation. Then he got up and left the courthouse, turning over and over in his mind what he had just heard. This new information cast a little light on why Miller was constantly changing his mailing address. Maybe making himself hard to find? No matter, he put the information aside for now and would think more about it later. He had more immediate business to attend to. Next stop the mayor's office once again.

* * * *

He had rehearsed what he intended to say the night before when his anger over the sliced tires had been at its height. What little sleep he had managed to get had mollified him somewhat, and the long hike from the courthouse to city hall, his mind on the conversation he had just heard concerning his client Daniel Miller, put a damper on it even more. Even so, the expression on his face must have been daunting when he walked through the door of the mayor's office. Stella looked up and frowned, pushed her chair back and went straight into her boss's inner office without saying a word. The door had hardly closed behind her when it opened again.

"You can go on in," she said, resuming her seat without giving him a second glance.

Mayor Banks was sitting behind his desk, as he had been when Murray had entered on his previous visit. Again, he didn't bother to rise or offer a handshake. His only greeting was a gruff question.

"What is it now, McCartney?"

For answer, Murray took out his new phone, manipulated it until he found the photographs of his sliced tires, and laid it down on the blotter on Banks's desk. Banks picked it up.

"Use your finger to scroll down," Murray said. "There are four of them."

"I know how to use a phone." Again, Banks's tone was gruff. "What am I looking at?"

"You're looking at the four-inch slits your golden boy put in each of my tires yesterday."

Banks's reaction was a slight tilt and bowing of

55

his head, a gesture that seemed to say, *Not his shit again.* He inhaled a deep breath and blew it out through his lips. "And you have proof that Hartman is responsible?"

"Proof that would stand up in court? No," Murray admitted. "But you tell me who else it could possibly be? Who else has a reason to do something like this to me? I ran into him at Walmart, and he blamed me for his two-week suspension, a suspension he brought on himself. Look at the punctures. The ones on the driver's side are in front of the rims; the ones on the passenger side in back of them. This was done by a left-handed person, and Hartman is left-handed."

Banks laid the phone back down on his desk and focused his attention on the opposite wall. "Well, until you can come up with irrefutable proof that Officer James Hartman did this, I'm not writing you a check. That is where this is going, isn't it?"

"Well, I damned sure didn't have four new tires at sixty-five dollars a pop plus tax worked into my budget, and the tow charge on top of that, but no. I didn't come here expecting a check. I just wanted to make sure you know what kind of a menace you're backing here. There's no way of telling what he might do from one moment to the next. The man is a loose cannon and a danger to the citizens of our city."

"So you've been saying for the last five years," Banks blurted, "but you haven't done anything about it."

His statement brought Murray up short. "What do you mean by that? Why should *I* have to be the one to do something about it? Why can't you? Why can't his superiors—Chief of Police Coder? The City Council?"

Banks glared straight ahead and refused to say anything more.

"Has he got something on somebody?" Murray demanded. "What? Who?"

Again, the inhale and exhale and nothing more. Murray stood looking at the man, trying to read his expression without success.

"You've known all along... you've known for *five years* that I've been right," Murray accused, "and *you* haven't done anything about it! You're the *mayor*! You're supposed to have authority over him, and you've done *nothing*! Now you put the blame on *me*? *I* haven't done anything about it?! I've done everything I could within the law, and I've got nowhere! What more did you expect me to do?"

Banks refused to answer, and for several minutes, a heavy silence hung in the air. Murray stood on the plush carpet at the corner of the man's desk and waited.

"Are we finished here?" the mayor finally asked without taking his eyes off the far wall.

Murray leaned over, picked up his phone, turned it off and slipped it into his suit coat pocket. "I guess we are, Mr. Banks," he said. "I guess we are."

* * * *

So, he had accomplished exactly nothing, Murray was thinking as he made his way toward his office. No compensation for the ruined tires. No possibility of Officer James Hartman being taken off the street permanently... unless he saw to it himself. And that could have repercussions that were unacceptable. He would have to give it some thought, but right now, he had other things on his mind.

He unlocked the door to his office and stepped inside. The air seemed stale, so he propped the door open with a wedge of wood he had picked up somewhere for that purpose. For a minute or two, he stood and wondered what to do next. Get the floor in the back room ready for when the carpenters arrived? He went to the door behind his desk and pushed it open. Now that the stacks of boxes were gone, he could see what a mess the floor was in, even with just the light coming through the doorway.

He took off his suit coat and hung in on the back of his desk chair. Then he rolled up his sleeves, went to the restroom and got the broom that had come with the building. Its bristles were bent and worn from use, but it was what he had to work with. He swept an area that was approximately fourteen feet wide measuring from the back wall of his office, piled up the dust and debris in the middle of it, then used a sheet of copy paper as a dustpan and deposited the mess in the trash can that he kept beside his desk.

"No doubt some of this is the ashes from the letter Rosalynn Holder left for Daniel Miller," he muttered to himself. "He wasn't back here long enough to make it all the way to the restroom," and that thought brought back to mind the conversation he had overheard between the two deputies at the courthouse. "Daniel Miller, the man who quite possibly took out four people and got away with it. Gotta talk to him soon, face to face, and see if he can't help me with my Hartman problem."

By late afternoon, he had mopped the area he had

swept using a bucket and mop that, like the broom, had come with the building. The black and white checkerboard pattern of the clean floor was not what he would have chosen for his apartment, but it was there, and digging up the tile and changing it would take too much time and create a mess. He stood looking at it and considering his options.

"It will be okay for the kitchen and restroom/laundry area," he told himself out loud. "Maybe area rugs for the living room and bedroom? I'll figure it out later. For right now, I've got other problems to work out—like how am I going to get home?"

And that's when Janet Hockenberry came to mind. He pulled the slip of paper with her number on it from his wallet and went looking for his phone. He dialed with trembling hands and hit send.

"Hello?" she answered on the third ring, and her voice sounded like music to Murray's ears.

"M-m-Mrs. Hockenberry?" he stammered, "this is Murray McCartney. I hope I'm not interrupting anything important."

"Who?" Janet asked.

"Murray McCartney, the lawyer."

"Oh... oh! Mr. McCartney! How are you?"

"Just Murray, please, and I'm fine, thank you, Mrs. Hockenberry."

"Janet, please."

"Uh, yes, Janet, could I ask a favor of you? My car is in the shop, getting new tires, and I was wondering if you could give me a ride home?"

"Yes! Yes! Of course. You're at your office?"

"I am."

"And what time do you want me to pick you up?"

"Oh, there's no hurry. Could you give me, say, thirty minutes to get cleaned up? And then I'll be waiting out front."

"I'll be there," Janet assured him and then hung up.

For several minutes, Murray stood there in shock. Every woman he had ever asked out, with the exception of Vicki, had turned him down. Now, he was to be ready to climb into a car with Janet Hockenberry within the hour. In the back of his mind, he heard his own voice say, *she didn't agree to go out with you, you idiot. She just agreed to give you a ride home.*

Coming out of his trance, he told the voice in his head to shut up, and he headed for the restroom at the back of the building. Supplies were limited, so he took off his shirt and used a roll of paper towels to wash and dry his arm pits. No deodorant available, and his suit coat would have to do to hide the sweat stains on his shirt. He combed his hair with water and studied his face in the mirror above the wall-hung sink, glad that his beard was so scant that he only had to shave once or twice a week and he had shaved just that morning.

"What are you doing, Murray? Have you lost your mind?" he asked his reflection. Then he turned off the light and headed for the front of the building.

She pulled to the curb while he was locking the door of his office. An omen? Perfect timing? *Don't get ahead of... of... of whatever*, he told himself. When he opened the passenger door and slid into the seat, she was smiling. She had apparently been at home when he had called. She was wearing jeans and a t-shirt type top, her hair pulled back in a ponytail.

"Where is home?" she asked.

"Well, before you drop me there, I was hoping you would take us across the river to Hoss's and let me buy you a rib-eye."

Her smile began to fade. "That would make me more beholden to you than I already am, wouldn't it?"

"I don't consider you beholden to me," Murray said. "I just want to get to know you better, for us to get to know each other better."

Janet turned her head to look through the windshield, her smile completely gone.

"What could it hurt?" he asked. "You told me that you and your family have been in a financial pinch lately. How long has it been since you've enjoyed a good steak? Let me treat you to one, and let's get to know each other better."

Janet turned her head to face him. "And that's all there will be to it? No strings attached?"

"If that's what you want when dinner is over," Murray agreed. "But I've got to tell you, I hope there will be more. I'm hoping that, at the very least, a friendship might develop. I seem to be kind of short of friends at the moment."

Her smile returned, although not quite as bright as it had been when she first drove up. She nodded, put the car in gear and pulled away from the curb.

Murray relaxed and sat back in the passenger seat, a smile on his face.

Chapter Seven

The hostess welcomed them to Hoss's and showed them to a booth. Murray waited until Janet took a seat and then slid into a spot across the table from her. Their server came, took their orders and left. They smiled at one another; Janet's smile somewhat tentative; Murray's smile bright enough to light up the room.

"So…" he said. "What shall we talk about? Janie tells me your husband was a hunter?"

Janet gave a snort of what anyone would have interpreted as disgust. "More like a guns and ammunition nut."

"Meaning what?" he asked.

She hesitated a moment and then answered, her tone angry. "There's probably two dozen or more guns out at the homeplace and enough ammunition for each of them to start a small-scale war. Plus, he had all the equipment to do his own reloading and a shed out back that has everything anyone would need to do their own butchering."

"And that upsets you?"

"What upsets me is that while he was buying more guns and more ammo and setting up his little butcher shop, the kids and I were doing without things we needed, and the house was falling down around our ears. His little butcher shop has a meat saw and an electric grinder, a stainless-steel sink, and a butcher block table. The kitchen in the house hasn't been upgraded since the place was built sometime around the beginning of the twentieth century, and all the furniture in the place we got at estate auctions and yard sales. Most of it is scarred up from use, and no two pieces of it match."

"Wow," Murray said, his smile gone, "and he worked for the Sheriff's Department?"

Janet's only answer was a nod.

"And he died in an auto accident?" he asked.

Another nod. "He was coming back from somewhere up towards Altoona in the wee hours of the morning and got caught in a snowstorm."

"I'm sorry for your loss," Murray said.

"It wasn't much of a loss," Janet answered. "I was in the process of filing for divorce. I had just found out he had a daughter about Janie's age with another woman."

Murray's brow furrowed in a frown and he let out a low whistle. "You've really been through it, haven't you?"

Their server brought their orders right then, and his question went unanswered. They both cut into their steaks and conversation was put on hold for a few minutes.

"What about you?" Janet asked.

Murray swallowed. "What about me?"

"Are you married? Do you have any children?"

"Was married; had a son," he answered.

"And?"

63

"My son was shot to death by a police officer five years ago, and his mother blamed it on me and asked for a divorce."

Janet went very still, laid her fork down and dropped her hands into her lap. She studied Murray's face, her brow drawn down in a frown. "And the police officer's name was James Hartman, wasn't it?"

Murray was in the process of cutting another chunk of meat off his steak. He speared it with his fork, then looked up into her eyes and answered with a nod.

"That's why you took our case, isn't it?" Janet asked.

Murray laid his fork down. "I know the man better than anybody in town, and I knew he was capable of doing just what Janie said he had done. I've known what it's like to be living on a shoestring, and I wanted to help. I've been trying to get him off the streets for the last five years with no success. But enough about me and my problems. Let's get back to you. I've met Janie and you've mentioned a Russ Junior. Do you have any other children?"

"Two was all we planned to have, and then eleven months after Russ Junior was born, Amanda Reann came along. After that, I had my tubes tied."

"Looking at you, it's hard for me to believe you've given birth to three children," Murray said.

"Well, thank you," Janet responded, and her smile was back.

"Where is this Amanda Reann, and when am I going to get to meet her?"

"Amanda and her husband are in Stuttgart, Germany. He's in the Army, and you will get to meet them in about two and a half years. He just started his tour over there."

"Do you hear from her often?"

"Not as often as I would like, and only in letters. Her husband is an enlisted man, and his mother is a widow. I think maybe he sends money home to her sometimes, so there isn't any for a smart phone. I miss her, but they'll get stationed back in the States eventually."

The rest of the evening went very well. They exchanged a few more details about their pasts and became better acquainted, as Murray had hoped they would. He even managed to make her laugh a time or two. The place began to fill up. The waitress brought their bill and he paid it. He slid out of the booth, dropped a tip on the table, and offered Janet a hand. She took it and slid out to stand beside him.

"Thank you," she said, "I don't know when I've enjoyed myself so much."

"We'll have to do it again soon," Murray suggested and let her go on ahead of him. She didn't respond to his suggestion in any way.

They left the building and walked to her Nissan. Murray opened the driver's door for her, but before she could slide behind the wheel, he looked over top of the vehicle and said:

"Aww, no."

"What is it? What's the matter?" she asked and then turned to look in the direction he was staring. Part way across the parking lot, James Hartman, in civilian clothes, leaned against the front fender of his black Dodge Ram pickup, his arms folded across his chest, a smirk on his face.

"What a bad way to end a wonderful evening," Murray said. "I think it's best if we just go."

Janet slid behind the wheel, and he closed the door for her, went around the car and got into the passenger seat. She started the engine and backed out of the slot, put it in drive and pulled out of the lot. He gave her the address to his house, and after that, neither of them said a word until they had crossed the river and were back in town.

"What do you think it all means?" Janet finally asked.

"I think it means that Hartman has a new target— you. Anyone I get close to has a tendency to get harassed. I'm sorry."

"Hey, it's not your fault, and like you, I've already had enough of this guy to do me a lifetime. I'll do what you told Janie to do, have my cell phone handy and make a video of whatever he decides to pull."

"It's another forty-eight hours until he's back in uniform, so you can relax until then. After that... well, we'll just have to wait and see."

Janet pulled to the curb in front of his house, and Murray just sat staring through the windshield for several seconds. Then he looked over at her and smiled, offered his left hand. She took it in her right, and they shook, on what, he didn't really know. Did it mean: *We're in this together* or *I like you and we should spend more time together*?

"Can I call you?" he asked.

Janet smiled. "I think that would be okay."

Murray returned the smile for a moment or two, and then his expression morphed into a frown. "Keep me posted," he said.

"I'll do that," she promised.

He got out of the car, stood on the sidewalk and watched her drive away.

* * * *

She had the forty-eight hours of respite that Murray had suggested, and then the harassment began. Officer James Hartman picked Janet's Nissan up as she was leaving the parking lot of her apartment on the west side of town at five-thirty in the morning and stayed on her bumper, lights on high beam, until she turned up the hill to J.C. Blair Memorial Hospital, at which point, he hit his flashing lights for a second and continued on down the street. She called Murray from work and told him about Hartman's stunt.

"I was so unnerved that I forgot to make a video of it," she told him. "I'm sorry."

"There's no need for you to apologize," he told her. "I think what you described would have unnerved anybody, a police car right on your bumper. We'll just have to get you prepared for the next time."

"You think there's gonna be a next time?!"

"Oh, I'm afraid he's just getting started."

But there was no time to get her prepared for "the next time" or to know when it would be. As it turned out, "the next time" came sooner than expected. When she got off work that afternoon, Hartman picked her Nissan up at the bottom of the hill on Warm Springs Avenue and followed her, again right on her bumper, out past the college, right up until she turned into the parking lot at her apartment. This time, he gave a chirp on his siren and kept going. She got into her apartment and made herself a cup of coffee, sipped on it until her hands stopped shaking and then called Murray at his office and told him what had just happened.

"I didn't get a video again. I'm sorry," she apologized.

"You have nothing to be sorry for," he told her. "We knew he would do something, but we had no idea what until now. They brought me my car today, with its four new tires, so I'm not stranded anymore. If it's alright with you, I'll come out to your place when I close the office, and we can get you prepared for tomorrow. I have something that I think will help."

She told him that would be alright with her, and he hung up smiling. It would be months before they realized that dealing with Hartman was an important factor in the two of them being drawn closer together. Whatever it took, Murray would say later, but at the moment, he was just glad for an excuse to see Janet again.

* * * *

The "something" Murray had was the gadget with the suction cup that a cell phone could clip into and that could be mounted on a vehicle's dash or windshield. When he got to Janet's apartment and knocked on the door, she opened it with a smile and invited him in for a cup of coffee.

"It's already made," she said, "and I imagine it's been a long day for you. Let's sit at the kitchen table with it."

Murray tacitly agreed and followed her into the kitchen, noting as they went the furniture in the living room. It was sparse and a little shabby, apparently not much better than the furnishings she had described as being out at the home- place. There was a sofa and an overstuffed chair, a coffee table and one end table that were chipped and scratched and did not match, and a small, flat-screen television which was sitting on a small chest-of-drawers and was off at the moment.

"Have you lived here long?" he asked, pulling out the chair she indicated and sitting down.

"Almost two years," Janet told him. "When I... left Russell, I moved in with Russ Junior, and his wife for a little while." She chuckled as she poured two mismatched mugs full of coffee and brought them to the table. "I guess you can imagine how that went, given the jokes people tell about mothers-in-law. Don't get me wrong. It wasn't too bad, but the kids hadn't been married long, and I felt like a third wheel. I found this place, bought a little furniture and a few dishes, and moved in."

"You didn't bring anything from the homeplace?"

She chose a seat to his left and sat down, offered a sad smile and shook her head. "I was still angry back then, and I didn't want anything Russell had ever used or touched. And what's out at the homeplace is no better than what I've got here, some of it maybe worse even. I go out there now and then to check on things or send one of the kids out. A place outside of town like that is an easy target for burglars, and I worry about Russell's guns. They're worth a lot of money, I think, and I'd hate for them to get stolen. Russ Junior doesn't seem interested in them. I suppose I should sell them, but I'm not sure how to go about it."

"Are they in a gun safe?" Murray asked.

"No, just in gun cabinets with glass doors," she told him. "Russell always said that anyone in their right mind would know better than to break into a deputy sheriff's house and steal anything, especially his guns."

"Well, Russell's attitude aside, if we could go out there and make a list of his guns, maybe I could help you get rid of them," Murray said.

"You would do that?"

He nodded. "*Pro bono.*"

Both of them smiled and took a sip of their coffee.

"By the way, where's Janie?" Murray asked setting his mug down.

"She's down in Mount Union working a double shift at the Legion. She seems to think she needs more money than she actually does. I don't know whether she's planning to buy herself a different car or take off back to California. She doesn't say much."

Murray gave her comments some thought and then pushed back his chair. "Thank you for the coffee, but I think maybe we should go out to our vehicles and install the something I told you about on the phone."

They got into her Nissan, Murray behind the wheel and Janet in the passenger seat. The old car's dashboard was too rough to hold the phone clip he had brought, so they had to install it on the windshield, just below the rearview mirror.

"Clip your phone into it before you even start your engine and start videoing before you ever leave the parking lot," Murray suggested. "If he's there in the morning, and I have every reason to suspect that he will be, all you will have to do is drive. On the remote chance that he *isn't* there, all you will have to do is punch your phone off."

"And what will you do with the videos if I get any?"

"I think they will be something Mayor Banks will need to see," he suggested, "not that it will likely do much good."

Out of the car and standing on the blacktop, they faced one another and smiled. Murray offered both hands, and Janet took them.

"Thank you," she said, "but now I'm in your debt again."

"No," he disagreed and let go of her hands. He went to his Honda and opened the driver's door. "You paid me with coffee. Call me in the morning and let me know what happens."

Pulling out of the parking lot, he glanced in his rearview. Janet was still standing where he had left her, staring after him, her fingers interlaced and her hands underneath her chin.

Chapter Eight

Murray's suspicions were not unfounded. Hartman was waiting when Janet left for work the following morning. She had done as Murray had suggested, clipped the phone into its holder and started the video before she put her car in gear. She made the right-hand turn out of the parking lot, and suddenly, a Huntingdon Police Department squad car was on her bumper, lights on high beam, so close that, if she had to stop suddenly, it would rear end her. Again, Hartman followed her until she made the turn up the hill to J.C. Blair Memorial, gave her a short burst of his flashing lights, and disappeared down Warm Springs Road.

Janet wasn't as unnerved as she had been the day before, but she would admit to Murray later that she was anything but calm. She didn't think to stop the video until she had parked and turned the engine off. Then she took the phone out of its clip and looked at what had been recorded. His high beams made it impossible to recognize Hartman behind the wheel, but that the vehicle behind her had a light bar could be clearly seen from the beginning, and the burst of light from that light bar at the end left no doubt. They had him… whatever that meant. She went into work smiling but waited until she thought Murray would be in his office before she called him.

"You were right," she told him. "He was waiting when I left the parking lot and followed me again."

"And you got a video this time?" Murray asked.

"And I got a video this time," she said, and he could hear the smile in her voice.

"Bring it by the office when you get off work, and we'll look at it together."

And so, the week went. Hartman picked her up at her apartment in the mornings and followed her to work, ending his pursuit with a flash of his lights. In the afternoons, he picked her up at the bottom of the hill and followed her home, leaving off with a chirp of his siren. The afternoon videos left no doubt about who was behind the wheel of the squad car. Even Mayor Banks had to admit that was his golden boy driving the vehicle when Murray showed him the videos on Monday morning of the following week.

This time, when he walked into the mayor's office, Stella glanced up, saw who it was and simply pointed. She was pushing a button on the intercom when he passed her desk. The man himself didn't bother to offer a greeting or even to look up. Murray started the videos and laid the phone down on his desk. Banks's face kept getting redder and redder, and the first chirp of Hartman's siren made him jump. He watched until the last video ended without saying anything. In fact, neither man had spoken since Murray had entered the room. Murray reached to pick up the phone and turned to leave.

"I'll take care of it," Banks said, and Murray stopped long enough to nod.

* * * *

Hartman's harassment of Janet Hockenberry ceased. Just what was said to the man or who said it, Murray didn't know and didn't care. As long as he and his friends were safe from the menace that was Officer James Hartman, life would be tolerable. Besides, he had other things to think about.

When he got to his office on Friday morning, he found a pickup parked out front with a logo on the door that read: **Wilson & Sons Construction**. Three men got out of the vehicle while he was opening his office door, all of them dressed in pristine gray workpants and shirts. When he swung the door open and turned, the older man spoke.

"I'm Ed Wilson, and these are my sons, Ed, junior and Ray. You called about wanting an apartment built?"

Ed, junior, was carrying a steel tape and he kept pulling it out a few inches and letting it snap back in. Ray was carrying an electronic device of some kind (a tablet?), and the two young men became Steel Tape and Tablet in Murray's mind.

"Yes," he said in answer to the older man's question, "in the space behind my office. Come on in."

He led them through the door behind his desk, picking up the sheet of paper with the drawing of his floor plan as he passed. He turned on the lights and handed the drawing to the older man, gave him a few minutes to look at it, and then began to explain what he wanted done.

"Doesn't sound too complicated," Ed said. "Might have to raise the floor of the bathroom to get the right pitch for the sewer outflow. That okay with you?"

"Whatever it takes to get the job done," Murray told him.

They discussed an estimate and Murray wrote him a check for half the amount the man thought it would require. Then Steel Tape began to take measurements and call out numbers to Tablet who punched them into his electronic device.

"Don't mean to suggest your numbers aren't accurate," Ed said. "He punches everything into that little gadget of his and comes up with how much we need of whatever materials we're gonna use. Makes things go faster. We'll get what we need to start ordered, and some of it will probably get delivered today, depending on how busy the building supply is. We should get something started before quitin' time, maybe have the walls framed out."

Ed stood with his arms folded and watched his two sons at work. Murray nodded agreement, went back into his office and sat down behind his desk. He laced his fingers together on top of his head, tilted his chair back and smiled at the ceiling. Things were moving right along. When they got his apartment finished and he could move into it, he would put the house on the market. When it sold, maybe he would use some of the money to make a trip down to Louisiana and have a visit with Daniel Miller, pick the young man's brain about how to solve his Hartman problem once and for all. Not that he wanted to kill the man, just to find a way to take him off the streets permanently.

From Hartman, his mind went to the videos Janet

had made and then to Janet herself. It had been a long time since he had been attracted to a woman the way he was attracted to her, not since Vicki, if he was being honest with himself. And Hartman had brought them together. That thought caused his smile to diminish somewhat, but only for a few seconds. Janet hadn't called yet this morning, and likely would not call until evening—if at all. On the days when Hartman was following her, she had called twice a day, and now Murray found himself missing her calls. Twice, she had come to his office when she got off work and showed him the videos she had taken. The two of them had stood by his desk, heads together, while they looked at the phone she held in her hand, their bodies so close together as to be practically touching. The second time, he had actually put a hand on her waist, and she hadn't objected. Thinking about it now, he smiled. A sign that there was a possibility of something between them in the future? He hoped so.

Ed Wilson and his sons trooping through his office brought Murray's mind back to the present, and he brought his chair forward and dropped his hands from the top of his head.

"Be back shortly," Ed told him. "Like I said, some of what we need should get delivered today. If it doesn't, we can still get some chalk lines popped."

Murray nodded and smiled. Every little detail was progress. He watched the three men get into their pickup and drive away. The thought that his apartment was about to become a reality kept his smile going, and his thoughts went back to Janet. Maybe he could talk her into going out to the homeplace over the weekend to make a list of the guns her late husband had left her. The homeplace, what would it look like? he wondered.

Only one way to find out. When she got off work, he would give her a call, maybe talk her into going to Hoss's or Wendy's for a bite to eat. Nothing ventured, nothing gained.

* * * *

He made himself wait until four o'clock, and her phone rang four times before she picked up.

"Hello, Murray," she said.

"How did you know it was me?"

"Come on, Murray," she chuckled. "You're a smart guy. Ever hear of Caller ID?"

There was a smile in her voice, and he laughed out loud.

"Is everything alright?" she asked.

"Everything is great," he told her.

"Then why are you calling?" Janet asked.

"Because if I didn't call, you wouldn't know that I will be picking you up shortly after five o'clock and taking you out to eat."

"Now, wait a minute," she objected. "You can't keep doing this, Murray. I feel like I owe you already."

"Yes, you do," he agreed. "You owe me the honor of seeing you sitting across the table from me when I sit down to eat this evening."

There was dead silence on the other end of the line for several moments, and then she spoke, "Shortly after five then," and she hung up.

He felt like he wanted to pump his fist in the air and say, "Yes!" Instead, he just sat there smiling.

Ed and his boys pulled up out front, and Ed came in to tell him the materials they needed wouldn't be delivered until the next morning. "About seven-thirty, I imagine," he said.

"On a Saturday morning?" Murray asked, objection in his tone. "I don't open the office on Saturday."

"Well, you better be here bright and early tomorrow," Ed advised. "Me and the boys are gonna take the rest of the afternoon off, but we'll be here at seven sharp Monday morning. See you then." He walked out before Murray could say anything more.

At straight up five, he locked his office door and headed for his Honda. She was ready when he knocked on her door at five-fourteen, but when she opened it, she wasn't smiling. On the way to his vehicle, he asked her where she would like to go, and she told him the choice was up to him. He took her to Hoss's, and the hostess led them to the same booth they had occupied before. *Another sign?* Murray wondered.

When they had slid into opposites sides of the table, Janet looked at him and smiled tentatively for the first time.

"Where is this going, Murray?" she asked. "You said 'no strings attached'."

He reached a hand across the table, palm up. She hesitated a moment and then brought a hand up from where hers rested in her lap and put it in his.

"This is going as far as we can get it to go, as far as *both* of us *want* it to go—just friends, good friends, great friends… somewhere beyond maybe? We're both alone. You're a widow. I'm divorced. I like you, and I think you'll find me a likeable guy if you let yourself get to know me."

"But I've got baggage, a son and two daughters and a grandbaby. Are you sure you want to get mixed up in that?" she asked.

"Whatever it takes if I get to spend a little time with you and then maybe a lot of time, as much time as you'll let me have." He covered the hand he was holding with his other hand and searched her face for answers that weren't there yet.

Her smile got a little brighter, she said, "Okay," and their server walked up and shattered the mood. Janet withdrew her hand, and they both sat back.

The evening went well. Murray got her talking about her grandbaby, and her smile shot up by several thousand lumens. Her first grandchild was a girl, and they had named her Madison Louise.

"That would have disappointed your late husband, wouldn't it?" Murray asked, and her smile diminished somewhat.

"I don't give a thought to what he would or wouldn't have liked anymore. In fact, I haven't given him much thought at all, ever since I learned he had an illegitimate daughter to a woman who used to be a dispatcher at the sheriff's office."

"You told me about that," Murray said. "What do you know about her?"

"She's about the same age as Janie. Russell let the girl's mother named her Leona, after his middle name which was Leon. Naming our son Russell Junior apparently wasn't enough of a legacy for him."

"You only found out about her just before he died? Had he been paying child support?" he asked.

Janet shrugged. "I don't have any idea, but he sure as hell wasn't spending much money on us. I only met the girl and her mother once, when they came to Russell's funeral. Mad as I was at the time, you can probably imagine how that went off. Janie and me sent them on their way before the service even started."

Murray didn't know what to say.

"Let's talk about something else, okay" she suggested.

"Okay," he agreed, and after a brief hesitation, "I'm having an apartment built in the space behind my office."

"An apartment to rent?" she asked.

"No, I'm going to sell my house and live there."

Now, it was Janet who didn't know what to say.

"I've been paying taxes on two places, paying two electric bills and two water bills, and it's been a drain on my savings account. Besides, I won't have to drive to work in the morning. I'll just walk through a door and be right there."

"That makes sense," Janet agreed. "Paying rent and utilities here in town and taxes and utilities on the homeplace keeps my checking account pretty slim. I've thought about turning off the electricity out there, but that would mean there would be no water either, and sometimes we need to use the bathroom when we go out there to check on things."

Murray took advantage of the opening she had given him. "Speaking of the homeplace, I was thinking maybe we could go out there sometime tomorrow and make a list of the guns you told me about. I have to have the office open at seven in the morning so building supplies can be delivered. After that, I'm free for the day."

"What would we do with the list?" Janet asked.

"I would put an ad in the paper and let hunters in the area know what was available. Or I could put them on eBay, or I could do both. From what you've told me, there might be a small fortune in guns and ammunition out there, and you could use the money you get from them to make repairs on the place. What do you say? Is it a date?"

She hesitated, possibly because of his use of the word *date*, but finally she smiled and asked, "*Pro bono*?"

Murray couldn't keep the grin off his face. "*Pro bono*."

They finished their supper, and she invited him back to her place for coffee. They were on third mugs when Janie came home.

"What's going on?" she asked.

"We're having coffee," Janet answered. "Pour yourself a cup and join us."

"Don't think I want any," she said. She gave Murray a dark look and disappeared into her room.

"Maybe I better go." Murray got up, rinsed his mug and put it in the sink, Janet at his shoulder, waiting her turn. "What time in the morning?" he asked.

"How does ten sound?"

"Like a dream come true." He waited until she turned to face him and offered both hands. As before, she took them, and they smiled at one another.

"Until tomorrow then," he said and pulled her in for a brief hug. She did not resist. He let her go and headed for the door without looking back. Another step taken toward the relationship he wanted, and he didn't want her to see the grin on his face.

* * * *

Murray's first glimpse of the homeplace put him into a silent shock. It looked like some of the old derelict houses he had seen falling down in pastures along some of the country roads he had traveled—structures of weathered gray, lap siding that looked like it had never seen paint, with rusty corrugated tin roofs, doors standing open, no glass in the windows, no longer habitable and left to decay. This place was different only in that its doors and windows were intact.

Janet seemed to understand what kind of effect his first look at the place was causing. She drove up the gravel lane much more slowly than he imagined she would have if he had not been sitting in the passenger seat. The field on either side of the lane was grown up waist high in dry, yellow grass. Saplings grew at random, wherever the wind had blown seeds. She stopped when she got to a spot opposite the end of the front porch. He scanned the place with his eyes, noticing that someone had replaced some of the boards on the near end of the porch floor and that the nearest porch post was a four by four and the others were lathe turned. Whoever had done the job had painted the repairs battleship gray, likely in an effort to make them blend in with the weathered look of the rest of the house, which only seemed to make them stand out more. The lower part of a frame in a second-story window had received the same kind of treatment.

"Who made the repairs?" he asked. "Your late husband?"

"Russell never bothered to repair anything that didn't have something to do with his hunting and fishing. I think it was one of the deputies he worked with at the sheriff's department. They weren't done until after his funeral."

"You don't know who?"

Janet shook her head. "They asked if they could send someone out here to look around, and I told them to go ahead, and told them where to find the key. The next time I came out here, someone had put new boards on the porch floor and set that new post. I don't know who did it, but I really appreciated it. The end of the porch roof was about to come down."

Murray sat and contemplated what she had said in silence for several minutes. The only sound was the hum of the car's engine.

"What do you suppose they were looking for?" he asked.

"I don't know for sure. They asked us if Russell had a laptop, and we told them we didn't think so. They thought he might have been mixed up in those two murders that happened just before his accident."

"But you don't think so?"

"I think Janie hit the nail on the head when she told them her father wouldn't kill anything that he couldn't have mounted and hung on the wall."

She put the car in gear and drove on around the end of the house and parked in a spot where two ruts were worn in the grass. On the back porch, she retrieved a key from under a flowerpot and unlocked the door. Murray noticed there was no storm door or screen door.

"The inside won't look much better than the outside," she said and went ahead of him through a mudroom that had coats hanging on one wall and a boot cabinet and a freezer against the other. Everything was dusty and kind of shabby, "This thing," she said, touching the freezer, "is still half full of deer meat. If you like venison, you're welcome to as much of it as you want. Me and the kids have eaten enough of it to last us a lifetime."

She led him through another door into a kitchen, and his jaw dropped. He had never seen anything like it. The floor covering was cracked and worn and, he was certain, made of a material that hadn't been manufactured in decades. A single tub, cast iron sink sat on a makeshift framework against an interior wall, its porcelain cracked and stained. A six inch, cast iron pipe and two smaller pipes ran up the wall next to it, serving an upstairs bathroom, Murray guessed. A washer and dryer sat to the right of the sink, the only semi-modern things in the room, and he found himself thinking, *Well, at least she doesn't have to use an old Maytag with a wringer like Grandma used to have.*

A scarred table and four mismatched chairs sat in the middle of the floor, and two Hoover cabinets sat against one wall. There were no built-in cabinets. The curtains on the windows were unbleached muslin and, he would learn later, had been handmade by Janet herself. She stood beside him and let him look his fill without saying anything. Then she walked ahead of him through and archway and into the living room.

The floor covering in the living room was of the same material as in the kitchen and just as worn and cracked but with a different pattern. The walls were covered with wallpaper, yellowed with age, that had a pattern of green vines with pale pink flowers. The main piece of furniture was an ancient sofa, its cushions frayed and threadbare. A coffee table sat in front of it and end tables that didn't match at either end.

What caught Murray's attention, though, were the mounted deer heads. They covered every spot on all four walls where there wasn't a door or window. When he had recovered the ability to speak, he muttered, "Wow."

"You haven't seen the half of it," Janet said, her tone a combination of resignation and disgust. "Let's go into the den. That's where the guns are."

She stepped through another archway, flipped a light switch and stood aside. Murray followed and felt like he had walked into a zoo. In addition to more deer heads, the room was full of mounted birds and animals—raccoons, squirrels, bobcats, pheasants, grouse, quail and doves.

"He killed all of these?"

"These and more. Some of the deer he killed were doe. If it moved, he wanted to shoot it. He made several trips to Colorado hoping to kill an elk and a couple to other states going after moose, came home angry and empty-handed, thank goodness. Where in either of these two rooms do you suppose he could have hung an elk head or a moose head? He boarded up the windows so he would have more wall space for his stuffed animals and put in his gun cabinets."

For answer, Murray just frowned and shook his head.

"Well, if we're going to get a list of these guns made before lunch, we better get started," Janet said and brought his attention back to the matter at hand. She took a key out of a drawer in a kneehole desk he hadn't noticed until then and opened the first gun cabinet door. It and the others that covered the entire wall were made of some kind of blonde wood, maple Murray thought, and were beautifully crafted, and he wondered again why there weren't any built-ins in the kitchen.

"What do you know about these guns?" he asked.

"Not much," she answered. "I know that you put a shell in them and when you pull the trigger, they all go *Bang!*, and a bullet comes out the barrel and makes a hole in whatever you're aiming at. Other than that, we'll just have to figure things out together."

Figuring things out took them to well beyond noon. When they had gone through all the doors of the gun cabinet, Murray had a list of twenty-five items on the legal pad they had brought with them. The late Russell Leon Hockenberry seemed to have had a thing for .30 caliber, lever action rifles and semi-automatic pistols, but bolt action rifles were also acceptable. In fact, it looked like any rifle that was legal for hunting was okay. Russell's collection even included a flintlock.

"I don't think this one has ever been fired," Murray said at one point. "It looks like some kind of commemorative gun, and it has a medallion with The Duke's face pressed into the wood part."

"If Russell wanted it, he bought it. He thought of some of them as investments."

"Great," he said. "If my suspicions are correct, you will likely get enough money from the sale of these things to paint this place and make any repairs that need to be made."

"So, we're finished then?" Janet asked.

"Let's make an inventory of the ammunition so

we can tell prospective buyers what we can give them as a bonus."

That done, they were heading for the backdoor when Murray stopped at the bottom of the stairs. "What's up there?"

"Three bedrooms and a bath in about the same shape as everything down here," Janet answered.

"Mind if I go up and take a look?" he asked.

She nodded and followed him up the stairs.

The first door on the right was the bathroom—ancient claw foot tub, small wall-hung sink like the one at the back of his building, commode with a cracked wooden seat. Second door on the right was the master bedroom, he thought; queen size bed, five-drawer mirrored dresser and a cheap metal wardrobe, window curtains of the same unbleached muslin he had seen downstairs. Not a very nice room for a married couple to share, but the room across the hall, obviously the girls' room, was worse. The bed had tall wooden headboard and footboards and looked like they would have been better suited to an elderly couple than a couple of teenage girls. It had exposed metal springs under an old cotton mattress. There was no closet or wardrobe. A length of three-quarter inch pipe hanging from the ceiling on chains held a dozen or so wire hangers. A wooden chest-of-drawers that matched the bed was the only other piece of furniture in the room. There was no mirror.

A monk's cell, Murray thought, *or a nun's*. Janet stood behind him and offered no comment. She had seen it all before. She had *lived* with it. He turned to face her and smiled, and she gave him a weak smile in return.

"Doesn't look like a very suitable room of young ladies," Murray suggested.

"Home décor was never my late husband's strong suit. The room looks a little better than it did when the girls lived here, thanks to the same man who repaired the porch floor and set the square post."

"How did he make it better?" Murray asked.

"The bedstead he brought in is in better shape than the metal one the girls used, and the chest-of-drawers isn't missing any knobs," she said and then fell silent.

He was still staring at the chest-of-drawers when she spoke again.

"We better go. It's past lunch time, and I'm a little hungry."

"To Hoss's then," he suggested.

"We were at Hoss's just last evening, Murray! Slow down! You've already taken me out to eat twice, and that's two more times than Russell ever did. We'll go back to my apartment and order in pizza or something, maybe pick something up on the way."

Chapter Nine

For one reason and another, the sale of Russell Hockenberry's guns got put on hold. Janet and Murray spent the most of Sunday afternoon together and then shared a supper of ham and cheese sandwiches and potato chips washed down with soft drinks and then coffee—all ingredients purchased by Janet. Janie, whose profession didn't allow her to work on Sundays, stayed in her room most of the time, coming out only long enough to make a sandwich and then retreating with it into solitude again. The couple passed another milestone in their relationship when Murray gave Janet a quick and very chaste kiss on the lips before heading out the door and going home.

On Monday morning, the Wilson's pickup was parked in front of the office when Murray arrived on foot, having left his vehicle in the parking lot on Penn.

"You walk to work?" Ed, senior, asked while he was unlocking his office door.

"No," Murray told him. "I park my car in the lot on Penn and walk from there. I like to leave the spaces in front of the office for potential clients."

Ed frowned. "You pay to park? Why not turn the space at the back of this building into a garage of sorts? I think there will be plenty of room left when we get your apartment built."

Murray nodded emphatically. "Why didn't I think of that? Let's get the apartment finished first, and then we'll see."

The doors got propped and Ed and his boys started carrying equipment into the backroom. The supplies that had been delivered on Saturday morning were stacked at the far back of the building—two-by-fours, two-by-eights, bundles of insulation, boxes of electrical wire, two pre-hung doors, and some kind of metal brackets and miscellaneous items Murray couldn't identify. From the size of the pile, he figured if Ed and his boys needed it to complete the job, it was probably there.

Murray sat at his desk and watched, too distracted to do much of anything else.

Their equipment toted in, the three of them got busy, and even with the door behind his desk closed, he could still hear them talking. An air compressor kicked on in the back room, and shortly thereafter, noises that sounded like a series of pistol shots followed. Murray realized there was no point in hanging around where he wasn't needed and where there was so much noise that he couldn't even think straight.

He stepped into the backroom to tell Ed he was leaving and was amazed at the progress they had already made. The framework of the back wall of his apartment lay on the floor, ready to be raised up and fastened into place.

"I'm gonna leave for a little while," he told them. "Go someplace where it's a little quieter. I'll be back by lunch."

They didn't seem to be concerned one way or another.

He spent the remainder of the morning at home, using his laptop to look up the value of the guns on the list he and Janet had made and jotting down the price each one might bring in the margin beside each item. Then he added them all up, and the total was amazing. He leaned back in his chair, laced his fingers together on the top of his head and smiled. If even a few of them brought in the kind of money the internet suggested, the homeplace could be made to look a whole lot better, and the old furniture in it could be replaced with new. He couldn't wait to tell Janet.

* * * *

He got back to the office in time to close it up while Ed and his boys went to lunch and was surprised to find them carrying their equipment out and putting it in their truck. Ed, senior, looked about ready to hit someone.

"What's going on?" Murray asked.

"We've been shut down," Ed, junior answered.

"You've been shut down? Why?"

Ed, senior, took over the conversation. "A police officer saw our truck parked in front of your office and the door propped open. He came in and wanted to see our building permit, and when we didn't have one, he ordered us to cease and desist. I told him we didn't need one to add walls in an existing structure, and he got mouthy, threatened to put us in cuffs. We got other jobs waiting, so give us a call when you get this shit straightened out."

"And I imagine the officer gave you his name?"

"Yeah, he said to tell you Hartman says, 'Hi.'"

CHARLES C. BROWN

Murray could do nothing but stand on the sidewalk and watch them get into their truck and leave. When they had disappeared around the corner, he went inside to see what kind of progress they had made. The framework for the back wall was up, and the ceiling joists were in place. Electrical wiring had been strung and light switches and receptacles were in place. He would learn later that Ed, junior, was a licensed electrician and brother Ray was a plumber. Anything the three of them needed done, one of them could do it. Murray's problem was that Hartman had told them they could do nothing, and the anger he felt sent him to the bottom drawer of his desk and a bottle of antacids.

He made the trek to City Hall and found out that Ed had been right. No building permit was needed to erect walls inside an existing structure. He bought one anyway, took it back to the office and taped it in the window, discovering in the process that the windows needed cleaning. There were no appointments on the calendar, so he got the ladder and cleaning supplies from the backroom and spent the better part of an hour taking care of that little chore. Working with his hands left his mind free to wander where it would, and it went back to his problem with James Hartman and the comment Mayor Banks had made: "… you haven't done anything about it." What could *he* do about it? The man's superiors didn't even seem to have any control over him. Something definitely had to be done, or Hartman would keep harassing him—and the citizens of Huntingdon—for the rest of his natural life. *When the apartment gets done*, he thought, *when the house sells, I'll drive down to Louisiana and pay*

92

Daniel Miller a visit, see if he can give me any pointers. Until then, everybody would just have to live with it.

He was putting the ladder and cleaning supplies away when he remembered the list and the good news he had to tell Janet, but even that didn't do much to diminish the foulness of his mood. He checked his watch and discovered it was a quarter past three. She would be off work and possibly already at home— naked and in the shower where she wouldn't hear her phone? *Keep your mind out of the gutter*, he told himself. Besides, what he had to tell her was too good to be told over the phone anyway. He waited until four o'clock, called and asked if he could come to her place. She told him she would put on a pot of coffee. She didn't ask why—another good sign? He locked the office early and walked to his car.

She opened the door on his first knock. He stepped inside and wrapped her up in his arms, his face against her neck.

"Murray, what is it?" she asked, pushing herself back gently. "What's wrong?"

"I need a distraction this evening. Will you be a distraction for me?" he asked.

She took him by the hand and led him to the sofa, a look of concern on her face. They sat down facing one another, still holding hands, their knees touching, and he told her what their nemesis had pulled and what he had done about it.

"You bought a building permit even though you didn't have to have one? Why?"

He shrugged. "I guess just to show him I could and that there's no way he can stop me from having an apartment built. But it's so frustrating. The guys that were doing the work went to another job and won't be back until sometime next week. He knew there was no need for a permit. This is just his way of letting me know he's still on the street. Well, he better enjoy it while he can because his day's coming."

Janet leaned forward, took Murray's head in both hands and planted a kiss on his lips that was just short of bruising. "How's that for a distraction?" she asked.

The look on his face was one of shock but slowly turned to a smile. "We're halfway there," he told her. "One more distraction, and then we better have some coffee."

They spent the evening together, holding hands and watching television. They took a break from that, and Janet made them spaghetti for supper. Neither of them could remember when they had spent such a pleasant time in someone else's company.

Murray was helping her wash the dishes and putting them away when he finally remembered the list. "Oh, I've been meaning to tell you. I've been working on pricing our list of guns, and I think if we get even, let's say, half of their value when we sell them, we should bring in something over twenty thousand dollars."

"What?! That much?"

Murray nodded. "That one with John Wayne's face on it sells for almost two thousand alone."

"This is great news!" Janet said. "You've been here for... what... two hours, and you're just getting around to telling me?

He tossed the dishtowel on the counter and pulled her in for another of those kisses. "I've been distracted," he told her when the kiss ended, and both of them chuckled.

He took her hand and led her back to the sofa. The television was still on, a different kind of distraction, and they spent the rest of the evening in front of it. Neither of them had cause to go outside or to look out the window all evening, so they didn't see the black Dodge Ram circling the parking lot. And if they had done so, they wouldn't have been able to see the smirk on the face of the man behind the wheel when he found Murray's Honda parked next to Janet's Nissan. Off-duty didn't necessarily mean off the streets.

* * * *

The work on his apartment would not get started again until Thursday of the following week. Murray tried not to think about why progress had come to a halt. There was nothing he could do about it, so why let it cause stress? He kept the door behind his desk closed when he had to go to the office and did as much of his work as he could at home.

He wrote a last will and testament for an elderly couple who were bitter because they felt their children—there were five—had all abandoned them. The fact that all of them now lived in California and Mom and Dad refused to move out there didn't seem to matter. They had given their children the best years of their lives, and now that they were in their declining years and needed help, they felt the ungrateful brats should be willing to do whatever it took to provide it. If their adult children had to uproot their families and relocate back to an area they had moved west to escape, so be it. It was their duty. None of them were willing to do so. To retaliate for such a lack of appreciation, Mom and Dad's intentions were to leave all of their worldly possessions to charity. *At least your children all survived to adulthood, unlike my son who died at twenty-two,* Murray thought, but he kept it to himself. He thought about Janie Hockenberry's reason for taking off to California right after graduating from high school and wondered if maybe there was a similar reason why all five of their children had gone out there. No matter, he wrote the will, and they left his office as happy as they were ever going to be.

Before the week was out, he picked up two more divorce cases. One involved another abused woman. The other involved a couple who had simply decided that they were no longer in love with each other and wanted to be freed from their marital contract. Murray had been recommended to both couples by a friend of a friend who was friends with Janet Hockenberry, which, of course, made him smile. He didn't like the thought that he just might be becoming the county's busiest divorce lawyer, but clients were clients, whatever their legal needs might be, and the fees he charged them paid the bills.

When there were no appointments on the calendar and no clients pressing him for help, he did whatever he could find to occupy his time. Some of it he used to work up an ad for the sale of the late Russell Hockenberry's guns and ammunition. He and Janet had talked about it, and his intentions were to put the ad in the local paper and several others in various areas of the state. She was eager to get rid of the guns and looking forward to having money to paint and make repairs on the homeplace. The two of them were spending most evenings together now, either at her apartment or at his house, and so far, their relationship remained platonic.

On Monday evening, one week to the day following the shutdown, Murray took his Honda to a carwash and cleaned it, inside and out. He was down on his knees, head stuck under the steering wheel, using the vacuum to suck up the grass and gravel that had accumulated over the last six months when Officer James Hartman drove by in his patrol car. The smirk on his face when he realized what he was seeing could be described with no other word than *evil*. Murray, of course, was blissfully unaware that the man had driven by, but a discovery the following morning would make it maddeningly clear that he had.

From the carwash, he drove home to get ready for a visit from Janet. She was bringing a pan of lasagna, and he was to provide a tossed salad. He parked in the drive, smiling at the relative cleanness of this car, got out and went into the house. By the time she got there, he had the salad ready, the table set and brown-and-serve rolls ready to come out of the oven. She kicked on the door with the toe of her shoe, and he opened it to discover her holding a disposable aluminum pan big enough and flimsy enough that it required both hands.

"Here, let me get that for you," he offered.

"It's hot, Murray," she said. "Better just let me bring it in and set it on the table."

That done, he got the rolls from the oven, and they sat down to eat, both of them wondering if life could get any better than this. They spent the evening talking and watching television.

At a few minutes to ten, Janet stood and said, "I better go. It's just about my bedtime."

Murray grinned. "I've got beds here."

That brought a smile and a shake of her head. "Don't tempt me."

"No temptation," he told her, "only invitation. Anytime you need a place to crash, you're welcome here."

"Janie is expecting me to be home when she gets home, so maybe another time."

She turned in the doorway, and they shared a kiss. He turned on the outside light, watched her get into her car and drive away. *Maybe another time?* Well, it wasn't a never gonna happen, drop dead, and he smiled at the progress he had made.

* * * *

Morning came too soon on Tuesday. Murray had not slept well and was in a foul mood when he went out to his Honda, intending to maybe park it in front of his office rather than leave it on Penn and walk. He opened the door and was about to slip into the driver's seat when he saw the sand.

"Son of a bitch!" he swore.

A liberal dusting of sand covered the entire front seat and was several inches deep on the floorboards. He took a step to the side and looked in the rear window—sand on the back seat and sand on the floor. There was no doubt in his mind who had done it. He even suspected that if he looked around, he might see a patrol car and the man sitting behind the wheel, smirking at him. He didn't look around. Instead, he took out his new cell phone and took photos of the mess. Just what he would do with them he didn't know at the moment. No point taking them to Mayor Banks's office. No doubt he would get the same reaction he had gotten with the slashed tires. Unless he had absolute proof that Hartman was involved, nothing would be done—unless he did it himself. That was becoming more and more obvious and more of a likelihood with each additional insult.

He went back into the house, changed into faded jeans, a t-shirt and an old pair of athletic shoes. He brought out a blanket and spread it over the driver's seat, got in and headed back to the carwash.

It took him more than an hour and a lot of quarters to get most of the sand vacuumed out. Some of it, he figured, would still be in the carpet when the old engine finally died and the vehicle was put into a compactor and turned into a block of crushed metal. From the carwash, he went to his office and parked in the space where Ed Wilson's truck should have been. There were no appointments on the calendar, but he needed some of the antacids from the bottle in the bottom drawer of his desk. A handful of tablets consumed, he was about to lock up and go back to the house to change when Joy Summers walked in the door.

"We need your help," she said, and Murray could tell that she was nearly frantic.

"Help with what?" he asked.

"They've taken my Paul to the Sheriff's Office, and I need you to get him out of there."

"Take a seat, Mrs. Summers," Murray said, taking his own advice and sitting down behind his desk, "and tell me what's going on."

Joy sat down but couldn't relax. "B.J. got served with the divorce papers today and came out to the house in a rage. He said no woman was gonna divorce him. Our daughter married him and promised to love, honor and obey, and she, by God, was gonna do just that. He threatened to drag her out of our house by the hair of the head. That's when her father got *him* by the hair and stuck a three-fifty-seven up under his chin. Told him if he wanted the top of his head to stay where it was, he had best get out of our house and off our property and sign the papers and get on with his life. Then Paul pushed him out the door and onto the porch. He turned around and glared at Paul, and he smashed his head against a porch post and bloodied his nose and made a cut in his eyebrow."

"Your husband smashed the man's head against a porch post?" Murray asked.

"*No!* He did it himself, and then he got in his pickup and he backed it off our property and to the other side of the road and used his cell phone to call the sheriff."

"Why the sheriff? Why not the police?" he asked.

"Maybe he called the police. I don't know. But we live north of town about a mile and a half, and it was Sheriff Kauffman and two of his deputies that came out and took my Paul and B.J. into custody."

"And you saw all of this happen?" Murray asked. "Saw B.J. injure himself?"

"Yes, I did, and so did Cheryl. She was standing in the doorway, crying and begging him to go on and do what he knew was the right thing to do. He looked her right in the eyes just before he whacked his head into the post."

Was her daughter with her, Murray asked, and got an affirmative. Would she be willing to tell the Sheriff what she had witnessed? Her mother was certain she would. He asked Joy Summers to ride with him in his Honda and have her daughter follow them to the Sheriff's Department. If they had made up the story about B.J. injuring himself, keeping them separated might bring about inconsistencies, he thought.

When the three of them walked into the sheriff's office, B.J. was sitting in a chair just inside the door, his head leaned back against the wall, his eyes closed, and Meagan Price, the sheriff's secretary, was holding a bag of ice against the cut in his eyebrow.

"I think the bleeding has stopped," she said, taking the bag away, "but you're going to need stitches," then turning to Murray, "Can I help you?"

"We need to see Sheriff Kauffman. Is he in?"

"Yes, but he has someone in there with him right now."

"Paul Summers?" Murray asked and got a nod. "Mr. Summers is my client, and I need to speak with him before he is questioned any further."

By then, B.J.'s eyes were open, and he was glaring, a smirk on his face. He had them now. Murray glanced at him and his eyes widened in surprise. He had seen that look before. It took him a minute to realize where—on the face of Officer James Hartman.

They weren't in Kauffman's office long. With the three of them testifying to what was going on and what had happened, there was little doubt as to who had caused B.J.'s injuries. When the four of them came out and trooped past Meagan Price's desk and headed out the door, the young man exploded.

"What the hell! You're letting him walk out of here? Look what he did to my nose! Look what he did to my face! This is bullshit!"

By then, the noise he was making had attracted the attention of two deputies, and they came in and put him in handcuffs.

"What the hell?" the young man growled.

"You're under arrest for violating the restraining order that your wife filed against you. You have the right to remain silent..."

The door between them closed, and the rest of it was cut off.

Chapter Ten

Wednesday was quieter, no unexpected clients popping into his office. Murray spent the morning composing an ad for Russell Hockenberry's gun collection and emailing it to newspapers, most of them in the immediate area, but one as far south as Chambersburg, and one as far north as Potter County. In the state of Pennsylvania, hunters were everywhere. He began the ad with: *Janet Hockenberry, the widow of the Deputy Russell Hockenberry of Huntingdon County, is offering for sale her late husband's extensive collection of firearms*, which was followed by a list of the guns available and a number where prospective buyers could call, the number of his new cell phone. No need for Janet to be bothered at work, he figured, when much of his time was spent alone between clients.

The calls did not begin until Friday, on the same day Ed Wilson and his boys showed up to resume work on his apartment. Many of them were just inquiries— what kind of shape was a particular gun in or what was the asking price? If anyone was genuinely interested, Murray invited the individual to come to his office the next day and told them he would have the item there for them to inspect and/or purchase. Nobody used the word *weapon*. To hunters and collectors, guns were just guns.

He spent much of the weekend with Janet. The two of them made a trip out to the homeplace on Saturday and picked up four guns that callers had expressed an interest in. All four of them sold at the asking price, and Janet was elated. With the money they had brought in, she could afford to hire somebody to paint the house.

Sunday was quiet. Few calls came in, and none of the callers were interested in coming to his office on a weekend. Janet wanted to do some shopping, so he rode with her up to the mall in Altoona and stood around while she tried on a mountain clothes, few of which she bought. They ate supper at a fancy Italian restaurant and got back to Huntingdon sometime around seven. Janet made coffee, and they spent the evening together. Life was good. What could possibly go wrong? They would learn the answer to that question the next morning.

* * * *

This time, Murray blew through the outer office like a gale force wind. Stella's mouth dropped open and she started to rise when he barged through the door and headed straight for Mayor Banks's office without slowing down. The mayor looked up but offered no greeting, in fact, had no time to do so before Murray spoke.

"You better get that son-of-a-bitch off my back permanently, or you're gonna be as responsible for what happens to him as I am!" he practically shouted.

Banks rose, a look of fury on his face. "You can't come in here talking to me like that!"

"I just god damn did, and you better god damn do what I'm telling you because I've had it up to here with that son-of-a-bitch!" he said and slashed a hand across his neck.

Banks raised a hand. "Let's calm down and discuss this rationally like two grown men. Have a seat and tell me what he's done now. I assume we're talking about Hartman."

Murray was too agitated to sit, so he paced back and forth in front of Banks's desk while he talked. "I've been seeing Janet Hockenberry."

"Russell's widow," Banks said and nodded.

"She wants to get rid of her late husband's collection of guns, so I made out an ad and sent it to some newspapers, the *Daily News* included. Hartman saw the ad and called her at work this morning, told her if she was going to sell that many guns, she was going to have to get a dealer's license. He threatened to sic the State Police and the FBI on her. She called me in a panic and asked if that was true. You know damned well he's harassing her to get at me, and I've had enough. Stopping work on my apartment, slashing my tires and the sand was bad enough. When he starts going after my friends, something has got to be done, and if nobody else will take care of it, I will."

"What are you talking about, an apartment and sand?" Banks asked, and Murray finally calmed down enough to take a seat and explain.

"I'm having an apartment built in the space behind my office. He came by when I wasn't there a week ago and made the workmen stop, said I needed a building permit when I really didn't. You don't have to have one to build interior walls in an existing structure."

"And the sand?"

"I vacuumed out my car the other day. He must

have driven by and seen me doing it, because when I started to get into it the next morning, there was sand all over the seats and on the floor, I'd say about a five gallon bucketful of the stuff. I know what you're going to ask. Do I have any proof that he was the one who did it? No, but who else could it possibly be? I always lock my vehicle, but it's an older model, and who else would be likely to have a slim jim handy. Sand I can live with, tires I can buy, but this thing with Janet and the guns? He's gone over a line when he goes after my friends, and I won't have it."

Murray exhaled a deep, shuttering breath and dropped his chin to his chest, his eyes on the floor. Banks studied the pose and realized that this was a man at the end of his rope.

"On behalf of the people of Huntingdon," he said, "I want to apologize for the indignities you've suffered. This kind of harassment ends now. I give you my word. I'll have a talk with Chief Coder, and together, we'll work something out."

He stood and offered his hand. Murray slowly pulled himself to his feet and took it. "Thank you," he said quietly, then nodded and turned to leave.

Banks remained on his feet and watched him go. When the door had closed behind him, he reached for the telephone.

* * * *

The adrenaline rush that fueled his anger seemed to dissipate suddenly, and Murray found himself in a deep depression. He drove to his office where Ed Wilson and his sons were hard at work again on his apartment. He gave Ed his spare key and told him to lock up when they left. He was going to work from home today. He would see them in the morning. When he got home, he kicked off his shoes, turned off his phone, hung his suit coat over the back of a kitchen chair, curled up on the sofa and went to sleep.

Janet called him multiple times throughout the day, anxious to know how things had gone with the mayor. His phone always went straight to voice mail. When she got off work at three, she went to his office where Ed Wilson told her Murray was working from home. She got back into her car and headed for his place. Something wasn't right, and she intended to find out what it was. At the back of her mind, there was always the fear that Officer James Hartman might have pulled something really bad this time.

Murray's Honda was in its usual spot in front of his house. She parked her Nissan beside it, got out and looked through its windows. No blood on the seats. So far, so good. On the front porch, she shielded her eyes with a hand and looked through a living room window. There he was on the sofa, apparently asleep. She used the key he had given her to unlock the door (she had not given him one to her apartment as yet), went directly to where he was lying and knelt down.

"Murray?" she asked quietly, "Are you okay?"

He opened his eyes and stared at her for a moment without recognition. Then his vision seemed to clear, and he sat up. Janet knee walked to put herself in front of him.

"Are you okay?" she asked again. "What's going on? Why haven't you been answering your phone? What did the mayor say?"

Murray took a deep breath and exhaled on what amounted to a sigh. "He said he would take care of it."

"Well, that's good news," she said. "Why did you turn off your phone?"

"I shouldn't have talked to him like that" he said. "I used some really bad language. It left me feeling like crap, so I came home and crashed. I'm sorry that I worried you."

Janet put her arms around his neck and drew him forward, pressed his head against hers with a hand. "It's okay. I'm just glad you're all right. Do you think he'll follow through with it, that he'll really do something about it this time?"

"Yes, I think he will," Murray told her. "I made threats, and I think he took me seriously."

"You made threats?" she asked, pushing him back gently.

"He said he would talk to the Chief of Police, and they would work something out together," he said ignoring her question. "We better turn my phone back on and see if anybody called about our ad. It's in the pocket of my coat."

She stood and retrieved it, handed it to him, and he turned it on. In addition to nearly a dozen messages she had left, there were eight from men interested in as many guns. Murray called each of them back and had Janet make a list of their names and the gun that each of them was interested in. He gave them the address of his office and made arrangements to meet each of them there the next day.

"Let's go out to the homeplace and bring them in," Janet suggested.

"Now?" Murray asked. "It's almost suppertime."

"Yes, now," she insisted. "Maybe it'll get you out of this funk you're in. We can stop somewhere and eat on the way back or pick something up and take it to my place if you want to."

He had to admit later that it was a pleasant drive and that it did help his mood. They picked up the eight guns the men were interested in and took them back to town. Janet was a little confused when he drove back to his house instead of stopping at his office.

"I don't want to leave them there overnight," he told her. "We'll put them on the bed in the guestroom, and I'll take them to the office in the morning."

Murray pulled to a stop in his usual parking spot, got out and opened the trunk of the car and each of them picked up two of the rifles. Opening the door with one tucked under each arm proved to be tricky, but he managed to get it done. He led the way up the stairs and across the landing, pushed the bedroom door open and stepped aside so she could go in first. She took one step and came to a halt.

"We can't put guns on that bed," she objected. "We'll get oil on the bedspread. What a beautiful bedroom suite!"

"Vicki was into French Provincial furniture and pink linen," Murray said, stepping past her. "I'm not much on all the cream and gold, and pink is a bit too effeminate for a man, I think. Do you think Janie might like it?

"Janie?"

"Yes, Janie. I'll have to get rid of most of the furniture in this place before I sell it. There's way more than I'll be able to fit into my new apartment."

"I imagine Janie would love it, but I don't know that she would want to buy it."

109

"Who said anything about buying it? If she would like to have it, it's hers." He laid the two rifles he was carrying across the bed.

"Murray!" Janet scolded."

"What?"

"The oil?"

"It'll wash out," he said.

"You get those off of there!" she insisted. "Stand them in the corner. The oil might leave a permanent stain."

Murray did as he was told, feeling a bit like a henpecked husband and loving every minute of it. He relieved Janet of the rifles she was holding and put them next to the ones he had stood in the corner. A trip back to the car and all the guns were unloaded.

"Do you like this entertainment center?" he asked when they got back down to the living room.

"Yes, it's beautiful."

"It would look good in the living room out at the homeplace, don't you think?"

"Yes, but…"

"You can't afford it," Murray interrupted. "Who said anything about buying?"

She gave him a look that was equal parts affection and exasperation.

"We'll talk about it when the time comes," he conceded. "Let's go get something to eat."

* * * *

The rest of the week went well. Murray saw little of James Hartman, in or out of uniform, and no one from the State Police or the FBI showed up to question

Janet or him about selling so many guns. Apparently, Mayor Banks was as good as his word. By Friday, more than half of the guns were gone, and he thought it best to update their ad—same lead in, same phone number, smaller number of items for sale.

The ads were worth what they cost. In another week, all of the guns were gone, and Janet Hockenberry's bank account had increased by a little more than twenty thousand dollars. Some of Russell's "investments" had paid off, and a couple of the guns in his collection had sold for half again what he had paid for them. Painting and making repairs on the homeplace had changed from being just a dream to a possibility.

Chapter Ten

During the first week in June, two things happened almost simultaneously—Ed Wilson and his boys put the finishing touches on Murray's apartment and Harvel Yocum died. The first of those impacted Murray's life immediately, of course. He made plans to move what furniture he would need into his new apartment, and he gave Ed the go ahead to put an overhead door in the north side of the building toward the back. When that was done, there would be no more parking on Penn Avenue. He would simply swing down the alley, hit a button on his remote, pull the Honda into his new garage and walk through a door and into his new home. Fallout from the second event and the situation that followed would have to be dealt with later.

With the use of a U-Haul and the help of Russ Junior (Janet finally got brave enough to introduce them) he moved his bedroom suite, a bookcase and his recliner to his new apartment. Russ Junior turned out to be a six foot-two, one hundred-fifth pound sapling of a man who barely seemed capable of the heavy lifting they had to do, but he proved to be equal to the task. When the house was empty of furniture, Murray figured he could load the dishes, pots and pans, flatware and linens he would need into his car. What he didn't need could be given away or donated. Janet and the homeplace were never far from his mind.

The two of them were unloading the mattress and box springs in front of the office, the doors already propped, when a Huntingdon Police Department unit pulled to a stop on the other side of the street. Hartman sat staring at them through the driver's window, his expression not exactly a glare, but it was far from friendly. Murray set his end of the mattress down, waved for him to come over and asked:

"Want to give us a hand?"

He spoke loud enough for Hartman to hear, and his tone was friendly. The officer put his vehicle in gear and drove off.

"That the one that's been messin' with you and Mom?" Russ Junior asked.

Murray stood staring after the patrol car. "Yep, that's the one. That expression on his face looked like he was in pain, just aching to do something he's evidently been told not to do."

"I don't understand what's goin' on," Russ Junior said. "He killed your son, Mom told me. How's that *your* fault. Why is he harassing you?"

"I filed a wrongful death suit against the city and won. Hartman swore he would get back every penny I got, and he's made a pretty good effort to do so."

Russ let that sink in for a moment and then nodded. "Well, this stuff ain't gonna get unloaded by itself," he said. "Let's get on with it."

Ed and his boys had done a spectacular job. Pass through the door behind Murray's desk and you were in the corner of the living room. His bedroom was to the right, and the bathroom (with shower, vanity and commode) was off of it. To the left was the kitchen, which had enough cabinet space to prepare simple meals and store what dishes, dishtowels and dishrags he would need. A washer/dryer combo sat against the north wall. A door in the back wall of the living room opened into what space remained of the original store building. Ed Wilson and his boys had already opened up a space big enough to drive a car through and were in the process of installing an overhead door, complete with automatic opener.

"This is a nice place you've got here," Russ said when the box springs and mattress had been put into place, "workplace and living space all in one."

Murray smiled and nodded, still trying to catch his breath. Maybe make part of the back space a gym and try to stay in better shape? "Efficient is the word you're looking for."

Russ nodded, and they headed out to bring in the chest-of-drawers.

* * * *

When his apartment had been outfitted to his satisfaction, Murray had Russ help him load the furniture that was left in the house into the U-Haul.

"Where are we taking this?" Russ asked.

"Out to the homeplace."

"What?"

"Out to the homeplace," Murray repeated.

The expression on the young man's face suggested he still wasn't sure he had heard right. "Does Mom know?" he asked.

"We've talked about it some, but nothing was decided. Let's get this stuff out there and unloaded, and then we'll call her and ask her to come out. What do you say?"

Russ was hesitant but finally conceded. "Okay, let's do it."

Murray tossed him the keys and said, "You drive."

The smile of the young man's face as he sat behind the wheel of the truck suggested that he had never driven anything that big before. He kept it a couple of miles under the speed limit until they were out of town and then picked it up only a little. At the homeplace, he eased it down the lane and stopped opposite the end of the front porch as his mother had done on Murray's first visit to the place.

"Be easier to take this stuff in through the front door, wouldn't it?" he asked.

Murray nodded. "Think you can back up to the porch?"

"No problem, but nobody's opened that door in years. Dad might have even nailed it shut. That's the kind of dumb ass thing he used to do if something needed fixed, and he didn't want to mess with it. I'm not sure it will open anymore."

"Won't know until we try," Murray said and swung down from the truck.

115

Chapter Eleven

The door had not been nailed shut. Apparently, the only reason it had not been opened in years was because everyone parked behind the house and always came in the back door. They kicked the old towel that had been used to stop the draft from coming under it out of the way and got it open without too much difficulty. The old lock mechanism required nothing more than a skeleton key, and Russ found one in a drawer of his father's desk.

"What are we gonna do with the furniture that's already in here?" he asked.

"We'll put it out on the porch until we get the truck unloaded," Murray told him, "and then we'll load it into the truck."

"And then?"

"And then we'll wait until we see if your mother is okay with the furniture we brought from my place."

"And if she's not?"

Murray shrugged and smiled. "We'll put the old furniture back where it was and set what we brought from my place out in the yard until she changes her mind."

For a moment, Russ looked confused. Then understanding dawned and he laughed out loud. "You've got a devious mind, Mister McCartney."

116

"Call me Murray, and yes. Yes, I do."

They worked most of the afternoon getting things set up. When all was ready, Russ called his mother and told her to meet him out at the homeplace.

"What are you doing out at the homeplace?" she wanted to know. "I thought you were helping Murray move into his apartment."

"Got that done this morning," he told her. "Need your opinion about some things out here."

"On some things out there? You mean you're already out there?"

"Tell her to bring Janie if she's available," Murray whispered.

"Bring Janie," Russ said. "I'll be waiting."

Curiosity must have gotten the best of Janet. She showed up some twenty minutes later with Janie in the passenger seat. Russ leaned against the battleship gray post at the end of the porch and waited. Murray was nowhere in sight. The two women got out of the vehicle asking questions.

"What's going on?" Janie wanted to know. "Why do I need to be here?"

Janet took one look at the truck backed up to the front door and asked, "What's a U-Haul doing out here?"

"Good afternoon to you, too," Russ said. "Come on inside and look at what we… I've done with the place."

"How did you get that front door open?" his mother asked. "That thing hasn't been opened in years."

Her son didn't answer, just turned and led the way inside. One step into her living room, and she stopped so suddenly that Janie ran into her. There in front of her sat a different sofa, one in much better

117

shape than the one she knew had been sitting there. A familiar entertainment center, sans television, sat against the front wall where a deer head usually hung.

"What...?" she started to ask and then recognized the coffee table and matching end tables as the ones she had seen at Murray's house. "That's Murray's living room furniture. He's here, isn't he? We talked about this. Come out and face the music, mister!"

"Come find me," came a voice from the kitchen, and followed closely by Janie, she went looking.

The table and chairs from Murray's dining room sat where the old, scarred table and four mismatched chairs should have been. Nothing much else seemed different, but then there wasn't much a person could do to hide or change the appearance of the two Hoover cabinets or the cast iron sink.

Murray stepped out from behind the door that led to the basement, and she turned on him. "I can't afford your furniture, Murray, and I won't let you just give it to me. I owe you too much already."

"You don't owe me anything, and by accepting what I can't fit into my apartment, you're doing me a favor. I have to empty out my house so I can sell it. I don't want to spend money on a storage unit."

"Well, I can't let you do this," she objected.

Murray grimaced and looked at Russ Junior. "I guess this means we'll have to set it out in the yard."

Russ's expression matched Murray's, and he nodded his head.

"What do you mean, 'set it out in the yard'?" Janet asked.

"I don't have a place to put it," Murray told her, "so Russ and I will have to carry it outside and set it

118

somewhere. My yard back in town isn't big enough to hold everything and the neighbors would complain."

"You're just gonna leave it out there in the weather and the rain?" Janie asked.

Murray shrugged and Russ tried to hide a grin.

"This isn't fair," Janet complained.

"All is fair in love and war," Murray told her and gave her a lecherous grin.

"Maybe you two should go up and look at your rooms," Russ suggested, trying to break the tension.

"There's more upstairs?" Janet asked.

"Yeah, and it was a bitch getting some of it up there," Russ told her. "I'm not really looking forward to hauling it all back down."

Janet gave Murray a dark look, and the two women headed for the stairs. Russ gave Murray a quiet high-five, and the two of them followed. They were halfway up the steps when they heard an "Oh!" from Janie. When they got to the landing, the two women were standing in the middle of the room with the French provincial furniture and the pink bedspread. Janie looked near tears.

"We'll have to find you a wardrobe to match and get rid of that pipe and those chains," Murray said. "They don't go well with the rest of the room."

Janet nodded. "And different curtains."

"Should have brought the ones from the room at the house," Murray said. "Guess guys don't think of things like that."

Russ offered Murray a palm behind his leg and whispered, "Down low." Murray slapped it lightly, and both men grinned. It didn't look like they'd be carrying any furniture back down the stairs anytime soon.

"Check out *your* room, Mom," Russ suggested, and the men stood back to let the women cross the hall.

There was no, "Oh!" when she saw the six-drawer, mirrored dresser. Janet simply turned and put her forehead against Murray's chest. He hesitated only a moment before he put his arms around her shoulders.

"Okay, you two, get a room," Janie said.

"We're *in* a room," Murray told her. "You kids want to wait downstairs?"

His comment brought a chuckle from Janet, and she raised a tear-stained face and said, "Thank you."

"You're more than welcome," Murray murmured and stole a quick peck on the lips. "Now, what do we do with the old furniture? Is there someplace we can put it out here or do we need to rent a storage space somewhere in town?"

"There should be some room in the barn where Dad used to park his boat and trailer," Russ suggested.

* * * *

Russ drove the truck down to the barn, and Murray walked down with the two women, holding Janet's hand, Janie slightly ahead of them. The men swung the two hinged doors open and Murray just stood and stared. There was adequate space for the old furniture alright, but there was so much junk on either side of it that he felt reluctant to add to it.

"What *is* all this stuff?" he asked.

Russ shrugged. "Mostly junk nobody ever bothered to haul away. It was easier to just toss it in here and close the doors."

"Does any of it have any value at all?"

"There's a thing in the back corner over there that Grandpa used to say was part of an old cotton gin. Don't know why there would be part of a cotton gin in Pennsylvania, but that's what he said it was. It might be an antique. I don't know," Russ said. "And there's some kind of equipment he said his father used to make brooms. It might be worth something if we could find it and knew what it was when we did."

"What's with the chairs that have no backs and the ones that have only three legs and the rusted ironing boards with the bent legs and the rusty bedsprings?" Murray asked. "And how are we going to store the old furniture on this dirt floor? The mattresses will be ruined."

Russ held up a hand and then started throwing junk out of the way until he got down to a couple of wooden pallets. "We'll put the mattresses on these. The floor in here never gets wet, so the legs of the chests and the bedsteads will be okay. Let me get the truck backed around, and we can get it unloaded."

"So, what do we do," Murray asked Janet. "Just put everything in there and close the doors like Russ said?"

"When we get moved back out here, we'll have a yard sale."

"And the junk? You want to just let it all set?" He couldn't imagine it. His father had always kept their home property cleaned up. If something wasn't useful, he got rid of it. If it was and he didn't need it and knew someone who did, he passed it on.

"Maybe I'll use some of the money we got from selling the guns and hire someone to clean it out," Janet suggested, and that seemed to mollify him somewhat.

When the truck was nearly empty, Janie suggested that, since it was past suppertime, she and her mother should go back to town and put something together for their evening meal.

"Can you guys get along without us?" she asked.

"I think we can manage," Russ answered.

Janet went to Murray and put her arms around his waist. "Thanks again," she said, and gave him a peck on the lips. "I'll see you in town."

He stood and watched as the two women walked back to the Nissan she had left beside the house, watched as they got into it and drove away.

"You and Mom getting serious?" Russ asked.

"I not sure about your mom," Murray told him, "but I have been from the get-go."

* * * *

He and Russ got the U-Haul unloaded, closed the doors and headed out. Neither of them said much, Russ processing Murray's last comment, and Murray thinking about how things had gotten to where they were and wondering what direction they would take from here. Both men were tired from the work they had done, Murray especially since he wasn't accustomed to manual labor.

Officer James Hartman pulled out behind them just as they entered the city limits of Huntingdon. For several blocks, he did nothing but follow them. Then he turned on his flashing lights and hit his siren.

"What the hell's he doing?" Russ asked. "I wasn't speeding."

"Just pull over and do whatever he tells you to do,"

Murray said. "He's just being himself, trying to see how close to the line he can get without crossing it."

Hartman had Russ get out of truck and join him in his patrol car. Murray sat still and waited, wondering how far Hartman would take things. Would he have to go see Mayor Banks again? Thinking about their last visit still embarrassed him a little, the language he had used. But it had gotten results (there had been no contact with Hartman until now), so he was beginning to accept what he had said and done as necessary.

After a good five minutes, Russ climbed back behind the wheel, a scowl on his face and a slip of paper in his hand. Murray remained silent and waited.

"The son-of-a-bitch said I was speeding," Russ said "Gave me a warning. I was going five miles under the posted speed limit!"

"This had nothing to do with you," Murray assured him. "He was just using you to get to me. Let's get this truck back to the dealership, pick up our own vehicles and go see what your mother and sister have cooked up."

"I'll need to go home and pick up Kathy and the baby first. We'll meet you there."

Murray nodded, and Russ pulled back onto the road.

Chapter Twelve

Murray did not attend the funeral of Harvel Yocum. He had been next in line for a partnership, had been saddled for years with much of the work that should have been done by junior partners, and had been fired because he filed a lawsuit against the city—a lawsuit he had every right to file—and won. Then to add insult to injury, Yocum had married his ex-wife Vicki, who was now Harvel's widow. She would be at the family visitation the evening before the funeral, Murray was sure, so he didn't attend that either, not that the event was not on his mind.

On that particular evening, he went to Janet's apartment and told her that, once again, he needed a distraction. She seemed glad to oblige—and without hesitation this time. She stepped against him, put her arms around his neck and pressed her lips to his. Janie was off mixing and serving drinks somewhere, so there were just the two of them. They sat on the sofa, holding hands, tilted toward one another until their shoulders and heads were touching, and watched what passed for entertainment on the television. An advertisement for a movie about superheroes who saved the world and the universe brought Officer James Hartman to mind. *They save our entire existence*, Murray thought, *and I can't even save the citizens of Huntingdon from one corrupt law officer.* He was enjoying the evening with Janet and didn't want anything to spoil it, so the thought went unspoken. Occasionally, some mysterious force would turn their heads until his nose would slip past hers and their lips would meet. Then their heads would roll back until they faced the television once again, and they would pretend to be interested in whatever was on the screen. Little was said. Little needed to be said.

It would seem to Murray later that it was some time after the evening news went off that he heard a gentle snore coming from the lady next to him. Taking it as his cue, he muted the television, closed his eyes and joined her in sleep. When he awoke some hour and a half or two hours later, she was still out like a light, and he was in dire need of a trip to the necessary room. He eased himself out from under her, laid her down gently, and made his retreat. Without ever opening her eyes, Janet came awake enough to pull herself up until the entire length of her body rested on the sofa.

A matter of minutes later, she was rudely awakened when someone closed the door to the apartment none too gently and turned on the lights. She sat up, weaving slightly, and tried to remember where she was.

"Mom? What are you doing sleeping on the sofa?" Janie asked. "Why haven't you gone to bed?"

At that very moment, someone flushed the toilet in the bathroom.

"Mom, what's going on?"

"Murray spent the evening with me."

"Are you sleeping with him?"

"I suppose she would have to tell you she was if she wanted to be perfectly honest," Murray said stepping out of the hallway. "We fell asleep on the sofa."

Janet's face turned a little red, and she changed the subject. "Aren't you home a little early?" she asked standing.

"I got off a little earlier than usual. We got the crowd from that viewing for the guy from that law firm that died. My boss cut most of them off long before my shift would have ended. They were having *some* party, I'd say. I couldn't tell whether they were mourning the guy's death or celebrating it."

"Probably a little of both," Murray suggested.

"And how would you know?" Janie asked.

"I used to work for his firm. I was an associate. He had a tendency to condescend to people he thought were beneath him, and in his opinion, most of us were. And also, he was married to my ex-wife."

For a moment or more, Janie was at a loss for words. Then she turned and spoke to her mother. "What are we gonna do for your birthday tomorrow?"

"Tomorrow's your birthday?" Murray asked. "How old will you be?"

Janet grinned. "A gentleman doesn't ask a lady her age."

"It wasn't a gentleman asking," he told her returning the grin. "It was me, and I'd bake you a cake if the oven in my apartment was big enough."

"*You* would bake her a cake?" Janie asked, skepticism in her voice.

"If the oven in my apartment was big enough," Murray repeated.

126

"She'll be forty-eight," Janie said, "and there's an oven here."

"Janie!" her mother scolded.

"Well, you will be, there is, and I'd like to see him do it. You never work on your birthday, and he can come over between clients and bake you a cake."

"You don't think I can?" Murray asked.

For an answer, Janie gave him a wide-eyed look that essentially said, "Prove it."

"Okay, I will be here bright and early tomorrow morning with a cake mix and all the other ingredients I will need. Do you have a cake pan and a hand mixer?" he asked.

"Yes, to both," Janet said.

Murray went to where she stood, took her in his arms and kissed her the way a woman who is about to turn forty-eight should be kissed. "Right now, it's past my bedtime," he said. "I'll see you both in the morning?"

"I'll be here," Janie answered and then turned to her mother when the door had closed behind him.

"Has he been hitting on you?"

"What!" Janet asked. "Murray would have no reason to hit me!"

"Not *hitting* you, Mom, hitting *on* you, trying to get you into bed."

"No! He's been a perfect gentleman."

The look Janie gave her mother was skeptical. "Maybe he's just too old to get it up anymore."

"You've spent too much time in California," her mother told her. "It's late, and I'm going to bed."

* * * *

127

He showed up at her door a little after nine-thirty the next morning dressed in faded kakis and a faded, plaid button-up, ratty athletic shoes on his feet instead of his usual wingtips. He had a grocery bag in one hand and a dozen long-stemmed red roses in a crystal vase in the other. Janet opened the door wearing jeans and a t-shirt, hair pulled back in a ponytail, slippers on her feet. Her eyes got wide and her mouth dropped open. She just stood there stunned, unable to take her eyes off the roses.

"Happy birthday!" Murray said. "May I come in?"

She came out of her trance. "Yes, yes, come on in."

She backed up, he stepped through the door and handed her the vase.

"These are for me?" she asked.

"You're the only birthday girl living here at the moment, are you not?"

"Yes, but… nobody ever brought me roses before."

"Not even your late husband, Russell?" Murray asked.

"Not once in all of our twenty-seven years of marriage."

He leaned past the roses and kissed her. "Well, put them on the table and enjoy them. I've got a cake to bake."

He went to the counter and began to unload his groceries—a chocolate fudge cake mix, half a gallon of milk and a dozen eggs. Janet saw what he had brought and objected.

"I *had* milk and eggs. You didn't need to bring your own."

Murray looked at her and smiled. "This cake is a

128

present from me. You don't contribute to your own present. Where's Janie, by the way?"

"Still in bed."

"Better get her up. If she doesn't see me doing the mixing, she's not going to believe I did it."

Janet grinned, stole a kiss and went to wake her daughter. A moment later, he heard her pounding on Janie's bedroom door and shouting, "Up and at 'em, girl."

She came back into the kitchen smiling, and a few seconds later, Janie followed.

"What the hell, Mom? I worked a late shift last night, and it isn't even ten o'clock yet."

"Murray's here to bake a cake, and he wanted to make sure you were a witness to it. Have a seat and look at the roses he brought me."

"He brought you roses?"

"Something your daddy never did," Janet told her.

Janie's dark expression turned darker. "He wasn't my daddy, he was my father, or if you want to get really exact, my sperm donor."

"Okay," Murray said, "let's not let the past ruin your mother's birthday. Where do I find a mixer?"

Janet looked at him and smiled. "Cabinet door by your knee."

"And the beaters?"

"The drawer right above it."

He found a one-cup measure in the same drawer, emptied the cake mix into a bowl Janet had set out earlier, measured out the milk required, added the eggs and started mixing. Janie sat at the table with a sullen expression on her face until the cake was mixed, poured into a pan and put in the oven.

"Can I go back to bed now?" she asked.

"If you're gonna be this kind of company," her mother told her, "I wish you would."

She got up without a word and disappeared into the hallway. A second later, her bedroom door slammed.

His job done, Murray took Janet by the hand and led her into the living room where he took a seat on the sofa and pulled her down onto his lap. She pressed her lips to his and then said, "Thank you for the roses."

"Didn't you already thank me?" he asked. "I thought you already thanked me."

Her eyes teared up and she hid her face against his neck.

"Hey, now," he said, "none of that. This is supposed to be a *happy* birthday."

"Well, these are happy tears," she said on a sob and let them flow.

Her crying jag over, she went to the bathroom to wash her face. Murray had gone into the kitchen and was checking on his cake when she returned. She walked up behind him, put her arms around him, hands on his chest, her cheek against his back and said, "I love you."

He went perfectly still for a moment, then turned in the circle of her arms and looked down into her face. "Do you really mean that?" he asked.

Tears threatened again and she nodded.

"I love you, too," he told her. "I think maybe I have from the moment you and Janie walked into my office and asked for my help."

"Really?"

"Really."

Janet smiled. "Well, what do you think we should do about it?"

"I think we will just have to bide our time until Janie leaves for her shift this afternoon."

Her smile faded. "Murray, I've had three babies. I have stretch marks."

He framed her face with his hands and studied it carefully. "Well, I don't see any, and this is what I would be looking at if we were to make love. But I don't want you to feel pressured. My libido has never been that strong, and I can wait until you're ready, until you're comfortable with it."

"And if I never am?"

"Then we'll just be friends without benefits."

He pushed her hair back with his hands and brought her lips to his. "Now, after confessions and a revelation like that, I imagine you would be more comfortable if we were somewhere other than in this apartment. We'll have to wait for your cake to come out of the oven and cool so I can ice it, but then where would you like to go?"

"Maybe to the mall in Altoona? I have enough money in my account now that I might even buy some of those clothes I tried on the last time."

* * * *

They took his Honda. For much of the drive, she sat sideways in the seat, a hand on his shoulder and a smile on her face. They walked into and through the mall hand-in-hand. Some of the items she had tried on before were still available and she chose several outfits for herself, one of which Murray paid for over her

131

objections. It was her birthday, he reminded her, and he wanted to buy her a present. She smiled and thanked him, kissed him right there in the store in front of everybody, and then shopped some more and picked up some things for Janie. All in all, what with the roses, the cake and the confessions of love, it was an altogether memorable day. But the incident that would make it totally unforgettable was yet to come.

Chapter Thirteen

They were approaching Huntingdon on Route 22, a comfortable silence filling the vehicle, Janet's hand on his shoulder, when Murray spoke.

"Do you want to stop by Hoss's for supper?"

"After that dinner at Olive Garden? I think not. All I want is a sandwich or a salad for supper and a piece of my birthday cake for dessert. Let's swing by Wendy's."

Murray obliged and, salad and sandwiches in the back seat with her mall purchases, they continued south and crossed the river into town on Fourth Street. He was about to take a left and head for her apartment when she spoke again.

"You know what I haven't had in a long time and I would dearly love on my birthday? An ice cream cone from the Dairy Queen."

"An ice cream cone?" Murray asked. "Not a banana split or a sundae?"

"No, just an ice cream cone."

Without hesitation, he took a right on Penn and headed that way. They passed the courthouse and were making the slight turn that followed when they saw the lights flashing on the hill up ahead, up past the bridge over Stone Creek where the street's two lanes separated beyond Blair Park. A minute later, they were passing Officer James Hartman's squad car and the nondescript Chrysler of indeterminate age that was sitting in front of it.

The driver was a big man, a couple of inches taller than Hartman and possibly a good fifty pounds heavier. He was wearing tan Carhartt Duck Bib overalls and a soiled wife-beater undershirt that left his tanned and hairy arms bare, tan work boots on his feet, burr haircut in need of a trim. He had made it a couple of hundred yards past the place where Hartman liked his victims to pull over. The street had turned into more of a road with a gravel shoulder at that point. There were residences on the other side of it and too much of a possibility for witnesses. The man was standing in the open door of his vehicle, getting ready to duck inside, when Murray and Janet passed. Hartman swung his telescoping baton backhand, likely intending to deliver a glancing blow to the back of the man's head that would have incapacitated him, but he turned and tilted his head at the exact wrong moment, and the blow caught him square on the left temple. He dropped like a rock, down between the door and the chassis of his vehicle.

Murray hit the brakes and pulled as far off the roadway as possible and stopped, getting out of his vehicle and dialing 911 on his new cell phone at the same time. He jogged back to where Hartman was standing, apparently trying to analyze the situation he had just created. Murray passed him and stopped where he could get a good look at the man on the ground. His head was wedged against the car's seat and twisted at an odd angle, and he was bleeding from a wound on his temple. His lower jaw seemed to be somewhat out of line with the rest of his face.

"What the hell do ya think yer doin', McCartney?" Hartman growled, coming out of his trance. "Get back in yer car and get the hell out a here."

"What am I doing?" Murray said. "I'm trying to save this man's life and maybe help you avoid being convicted of murder. I called 911, and an ambulance is on its way."

"Get back in yer damned car and get out a here," Hartman repeated. "I don't need yer help. I'm callin' for backup."

Murray hesitated.

"You wanna get arrested for interferin' with an officer in the conduct of his duty, hang around. I'm sure any one of the guys in the department would give their left nut to slap cuffs on ya and haul you in. Better get yer ass out a here before any of 'em get here. I'll deal with *you* later, personally."

Murray pulled his eyes away from Hartman's latest victim and reluctantly started back to Janet and his Honda. She gave him a wide-eyed stare when he slid behind the wheel.

"You saw that?" he asked.

"Yes, I saw that," she confirmed. "Is that man gonna be alright?"

"I don't know," Murray told her, his hands still shaking and his heart doing double-time. "He doesn't look too good at the moment. I suppose it will depend on how quickly they get him to a hospital. We have to get out of here. Do you still want ice cream from the Dairy Queen?"

"No, let's just go home."

He put the car in gear, drove up the hill and crossed Route 22, turned around in the parking lot of a business and headed back through town. Janet stared wide-eyed through the windshield, and Murray's mind went through a list of possible consequences of witnessing what they had just seen. *I'll deal with you later, personally.* He could think of none that anybody would likely call pleasant.

At "home," which tonight was Janet's apartment, they more or less forced themselves to eat a piece of cake (after all, it was still Janet's birthday) although neither of them seemed to have an appetite for it, and wash it down with fresh coffee. They left their saucers, flatware and coffee cups on the table and moved to the sofa, where they sat side-by-side, staring at a television that had yet to be turned on. Murray reached over and took Janet's hand.

"What are you thinking?" she asked, still staring straight ahead.

What was he thinking? *I'll deal with* you *later, personally.* They had possibly just witnessed Officer James Hartman killing a man. Hartman had broken Janie's taillight and ticketed her because she refused to go out with him. He slashed Murray's tires because he had gotten suspended, stopped work on the apartment just because he could, poured sand in his car just for the hell of it, caused problems with the sale of Russell's gun collection and stopped Russ Junior driving the U-Haul to let everybody know he was still out there. The likelihood of Hartman *not* doing something to keep them quiet, and the possible magnitude of what that something might be, was what Murray had been thinking about. But this was Janet's birthday, and he wasn't about to burden her with any of that.

He slid to the end of the sofa and tugged on her hand. "I'm thinking there's nothing we can do about what both of us are thinking about, so I think we need a distraction," he said. He pulled her closer to him, then turned her around and laid her back across his thighs.

Janet looked up at him and grinned. "So, let the distractions begin."

* * * *

The man's name, they would learn later, was Duane Runk. Why he had been driving through Huntingdon was anybody's guess. His wife didn't even know. At the time of the incident, she thought he was staying in a cheap motel somewhere in the vicinity of Carlisle, Pennsylvania, nearly a hundred miles away, where he was working on construction. He usually made the trip back to their home in Trough Creek Valley only on weekends, sometimes every other weekend. Raising three kids, all of elementary school age, meant money was tight, and they were struggling to make ends meet and to pay off their property.

The ambulance Murray had called arrived on the scene, loaded him up and hauled him across town to J.C. Blair Memorial where doctors determined that he had a broken lower jaw and that the blow to his head had caused a brain bleed, in layman's terms, and put him in a coma. That diagnosis made, he was care flighted to Altoona where a surgeon with the necessary skills to operate might have saved his life if they had gotten him there a little more quickly. Cerebral hemorrhage had created too much pressure inside his skull and his body functions—including heartbeat—had shut down. When attendants lifted him out of the helicopter, he was DOA.

Murray learned all of this piecemeal, kept as much of it from Janet as he could, and wondered if any legal action would be taken against the individual who had caused the man's death—Officer James Hartman. If a grand jury were to be convened, he wondered, would he and Janet be subpoenaed to testify? Maybe this was Fate's way of helping him get the man off the street. Time, and only time, would tell.

Hartman's statement... threat... whatever you might call it—*I'll deal with* you *later, personally*—was ever at the fore of Murray's mind. Not that he would ever be afraid of the man for himself, but Janet had been in the car with him, and he suspected Hartman knew that. Again, time would tell, but at the moment, Hartman apparently had his hands too full with other problems to "deal with" them.

* * * *

Even with the pall that was hanging over them, life went on. The Wilsons finished the garage at the back of Murray's building, and he had them renovate the kitchen out at the homeplace to surprise Janet. The Hoover cabinets and the cast iron sink ended up with the old furniture and other junk out in the barn, and the stainless steel sink from her late husband's private butcher shop became a fixture in the built-in cabinets Ed and his boys built and installed. It sat in front of a window set into the wall between the kitchen and the mudroom and had a light above it. Not an ideal setup but much better than the cast iron sink against the interior wall. He also had them remove the old claw-foot tub from the bathroom and install a modern one with a shower above it. After today, Janet could clean out her apartment in town and move back into the homeplace.

With her help and the help of Janie and Russ Junior, Murray got *his* house cleaned out—right down to the dust in the corners and the assorted junk from the drawer in the kitchen—and put on the market. He thought about making a For Sale by Owner sign, putting it in the front yard and dealing with potential buyers himself but decided instead to enlist the services of Landis Realty, which was now being managed for the widow of Eldon Landis by the man's former secretary, a woman whose name was Janet Staubs.

A Landis Realty sign had been in the front yard for a week and two days and no one had shown an interest. Just before five o'clock on the Friday evening he and the kids were going to surprise Janet with her new kitchen and bathroom, Murray was straightening up his desk when the door got slammed open and Vicki blew in like a gale force wind. She was wearing a silky, button-up-the-front blouse that had a narrow collar and gray pants of some kind of shiny material that were creased so sharply they looked like they could have been used to slice bread. Her gray leather high heels matched her trousers perfectly. Half-carat diamond studs sparkled from her earlobes and a full carat glittered from the ring finger of her left hand. Multiple stones—precious and semiprecious—graced the fingers of her right hand. Her blonde hair had been cut in a bob that framed a face that sported what looked like professionally done makeup. Not a single strand of her silky locks was out of place. Murray had to hide a smile. When the two of them had been married, Vicki would have said someone dressed, made up and bejeweled like she was "looked like money," and she wouldn't have meant it as a compliment.

"There's a For Sale sign in the front yard of our house," she said, anger in her voice, "and the place is empty."

Murray nodded. "Yes, I put it on the market."

"Well, you can't sell it."

"And why not?" he asked.

"Because I might need it to live in. Harvel's kids are contesting the last will he made, and I might have to move out of the house I'm living in soon."

"The house you and your late husband shared?"

"Yes."

"And you want to move into my house?"

"It's not that I *want* to, I might *need* to," Vicki corrected, "and no one's living there, so I know it's available. You can't sell our house. That's the house we lived in when we brought Randall home from the hospital."

"But you divorced me and left," Murray reminded her, "and it's *my* house now, Vicki. It's the house where Randall's spirit haunted you until I had to put some of my *blood money* into a new house for you. Remember? Why can't you live in *that* house?"

"Because we sold it and used the money to take a trip to Europe and to do some other things."

"'We sold it,' meaning you and Harvel, the man

who withheld a partnership from me that was rightfully mine and fired me for winning a lawsuit that I had every right to file?"

He paused to give her a chance to respond, but Vicki just stood there looking just a slight bit sheepish and refused to answer.

"So, the two of you, you and Harvel, used the money you got from the house that I purchased for you with what you called *blood money* because in essence, I got it because of Randall's death—money that Harvel fired me for getting—the two of you used *that* money for your own amusement, taking vacations and such?"

"Yes."

"And now, you think you should be able to move back into the house where we were living when the worst tragedy in our lives happened, and I should just accept it just because your late husband's children are being mean to you?"

"Well, you don't have to get ugly about it," Vicki finally said, her tone still somewhat petulant, and she changed the subject. "And where is all of our furniture? I looked in the windows, and the place is empty! Even my treatments are gone from the windows! What happened to all of them?"

"One minor correction here again," he told her, "it wasn't *our* furniture, it was *my* furniture. It became mine when you divorced me and left it in *my* house. As to where it is, what I couldn't fit into my apartment I gave away."

"Your apartment?" She looked confused.

"I had an apartment built right here behind my office." He indicated where with a gesture of his hand. "It's not very big, but it's plenty big enough for me. I

141

got tired of paying electric bills on a place that had more space that I needed. *Blood money* will only stretch so far."

"But I might need the house," she said, ignoring his sarcasm, "and I'll need the furniture. Can you get it back?"

Murray had been standing behind his desk. Now, he took a seat in his desk chair and pinched the bridge of his nose between a thumb and index finger. Vicki perched her silky-clad cheeks on the edge of one of the armchairs in front of it. The look on her face suggested she thought she was winning. When he finally raised his head, the look on *his* face suggested that he had heard enough, and maybe more than enough, and wasn't about to let her waste any more of his time.

"Let me put this as succinctly as possible..." He paused to get his words in order.

"What does succinctly mean?" Vicki asked.

"It means in as few words as possible." His tone let her know he didn't appreciate the interruption. She sat there, wide-eyed, hands clasped in her lap, and said nothing more.

"You will *not* be moving into *my* house, and I will *not* be getting any of *my* furniture back. There is nothing shared between you and me anymore— *nothing*. That ended when I bought you a house with some of my *blood money* and then discovered you were renting our old place out and pocketing the money when you were supposed to have put it on the market. Oh, and maybe I should mention here, all the while, I was putting more of my *blood money* into an account for you so you would have food to eat. We were married and had a son together, yes, but any commitment I had to you ended when you blamed me for his death and left me and then married Harvel Yocum." Getting up from his chair, he went to the door and opened it for her. Vicki stood but otherwise made no move to leave. "Now, I have someplace I need to be, and I believe we have cleared up what I'll call the somewhat more than a little misunderstanding that brought you here today. It has been… interesting… seeing you again. Best of luck in dealing with the Yocum siblings."

"Would you be my lawyer and *help* me deal with them," she asked, and when he hesitated, "please?"

If anyone had been there to see the look on Murray's face, they would have described him as astounded. His left hand still on the doorknob, he looked down at the floor, closed his eyes and shook his head.

"Does that mean no?" Vicki asked.

"It means I can't believe you just asked me that after… after what I just explained to you. And yes, it means no."

"But what if they take my house and all the money Harvel left me? What am I gonna do?"

"You will just have to get yourself a job and find yourself a cheap apartment, pick up some used furniture somewhere and learn to live like the rest of us again."

His answer turned her face red with anger. He made a gesture with his free hand that essentially said, "Here's the door," and said out loud, "Just go."

She swept by him, obviously in a rage, and the last he heard of her was her high heels clacking on the sidewalk.

Chapter Fourteen

They were waiting on him at the homeplace—Janie, Janet and Russ—out under the tree in the back yard, all three of them dressed in blue jeans and tank tops or t-shirts. The heat and humidity had been stifling all week. The two kids were smiling, and Janet looked confused when he drove up and added his vehicle to the three already there.

"What is going on?" she asked when he got out of his Honda. "The kids told me to meet them out here, but they wouldn't let me go into the house until you got here, and this heat is enough to wilt a body. What have you done now?"

Murray smiled and held out his hand and she took it. The four of them climbed the steps to the back porch and went through the mudroom. He was about to lead her into the kitchen when Russ spoke.

"Hey, let us go in first so we can see her reaction."

"My reaction to what?" his mother asked, and Murray pulled Janet to a stop just outside the kitchen door and let the kids go in first. Then he stepped in ahead of her and turned to watch her face.

Janie and Russ stepped aside, and Janet saw the new cabinets and sink and looked confused. When understanding dawned, her mouth fell open and she put both hands over it. Her face turned red and began to crumple. She turned and hid it against Murray's shoulder, and hers began to shake with sobs. He put his arms around her and pulled her closer.

"Mom, it's a good thing. Don't cry," Janie said. She took a step forward and put her arms around her mother from behind.

Russ Junior just stood there looking confused.

Janet got control of her emotions and pushed herself away from Murray, and Janie stepped back. Russ reached out and flipped the switch that turned the light on above the sink, and the waterworks started all over again. Murray pulled a fistful of tissues out of his coat pocket and handed them to Janet who used them to hide her face for a minute or more.

"Don't you like them, Mom?" Russ asked, and Murray answered for her.

"I don't think it's a matter of not liking them, Russ. I think it's just a matter of being too surprised."

Janet had approached her new cabinets and was running a hand over the white laminate countertop.

"Then I guess we better not show her what's upstairs," Russ suggested.

Janet whirled on Murray. "There's more upstairs?"

She didn't wait for an answer but brushed past him and headed that way. Everybody followed. When they caught up to her, she was standing in the doorway of the bathroom, looking at the new fixtures and not saying a word.

"It's nicer than the one in our apartment in town now, Mom," Janie said. "We can move back out here anytime you want to."

After more than a minute of absolute silence, Janet turned and pushed through Russ and Janie who had been looking over her shoulders and stepped to where Murray was leaning against the opposite wall. When he saw the look on her face, he pushed himself upright and his smile faded.

"You kids go on downstairs," she said, locking eyes with him. "I need to have a talk with Mister McCartney here."

They obeyed their mother without a word and disappeared down the stairs. Janet waited until she was sure they were out of earshot.

"What are you doing, Murray?"

"What do you mean, what am I doing?"

"You've put money into a house that isn't even yours, and I was already in your debt before all of this."

He tried to take her in his arms, and she stepped back.

"I don't need a distraction right now," she said, batting his arms away. "Answer my question. What are you doing?"

Murray shrugged. "I'm helping out a friend. Giving a gift to someone I love. What does it matter? Like Janie said, now you can move back out here to live, and you have a nice, modern kitchen and a nice bathroom. Don't you like what the Wilsons have done?"

For answer, she backed him against the wall and gave him a kiss that left both of their lips puffy. When it was over and she had backed away, he took a deep breath and said something that sounded like, "A-hum," and opened his eyes. Janet was staring at him with the same expression she'd had before the kiss, and it wasn't a smile.

"What was that all about?" he asked.

"Just giving a friend a thank you for helping out a friend," she said. "Giving a kiss to someone I love. Now, let's go down and see what the kids are up to."

Murray stood there stunned, and she disappeared down the stairs. Eyes wide in confusion, he scanned the upstairs hallway for answers and found none. Finally, he heaved a sigh and followed her downstairs.

* * * *

Janet was standing in front of her new cabinets when he rounded the corner at the bottom of the stairs and stopped. While he watched, she tried the light switch her son had flipped earlier and looked up when the light came on. Her back was to him, so he couldn't see her expression, but after her actions in the upstairs hallway, he doubted that she was smiling.

Russ and Janie came through the mudroom and into the kitchen carrying an ice chest full of soft drinks between them. Russ cradled two pizza boxes in his free arm, and Janie carried a bag that contained Styrofoam plates and paper napkins. Apparently, they were all going to have supper before they went back to town. Murray hung back, not quite sure of what his status was.

The kids set about getting supper on the table, placing paper plates and napkins around. Russ used a pocketknife to cut the lids off the pizza boxes, and Janie took charge of the soft drink distribution.

"What would you like to drink, Murray?" she

asked, looking up and realizing he looked like he wasn't feeling included. "Come on and take a place... sit here."

Murray stepped forward and took the place she indicated at what he thought was the head of table (possibly her late father's usual place?) and answered her question. "Diet Coke if you have it, please."

Eventually, everything got sorted out, and he found himself sitting opposite Janet who was at the other end of the table, Janie to his left and Russ on his right.

Janie said, "Dig in everybody," and helped herself to a slice of pepperoni.

Soft drinks got opened and boxes got passed. Russ put two slices of meat-lovers on his plate and passed the box on to Murray.

"So, when do you want to move back out here?" Janie asked between bites of pizza and sips of Dr. Pepper.

"I don't know," her mother answered. "I don't know whether I want to or not. I've gotten kind of used to air conditioning, and it would cost too much to air condition this place."

"We could close off the rooms we're not using and buy us some window units for the rooms we are. Like your bedroom and mine and the living room." Janie seemed eager to make the move, possibly thinking about the new furniture that was now in her old bedroom.

"And the heating bills in the winter are through the roof," Janet countered.

"These old houses have no insulation," Murray offered, "and you're right in a way, most of your heat is lost through the roof. If you put insulation in the attic—say between the floor joists or staple it to the rafters, you would see a lot of difference. Ed Wilson was telling me he knew a guy that did one or the other, and it changed the temperature in his house the next winter so much that all of his wife's houseplants died."

"And what would that cost me?" Janet wasn't buying the idea.

"I don't know," Murray said honestly, "but you have the money from your late husband's gun collection, so why not use some it to do that. Tell you what, you buy the insulation and Russ and I will put it in. How about that, if Russ wouldn't mind helping?"

Russ had his mouth full and nodded emphatically until he could swallow. "Whatever it takes. I love this old house, and I want to see my daughter running and playing in the backyard the way Janie and I did when we were kids."

Mention of her late husband had turned Janet somber, and everybody ate in silence for several minutes.

"Also," Murray said, "Ed told me there's a government program that replaces windows and doors for low income families—what I imagine is an effort to conserve energy. I could look into that for you?"

"What about that, Mom?" Janie asked when her mother failed to respond.

"I suppose it couldn't hurt," Janet said, but her tone was less than enthusiastic.

And so, the evening went. When the pizza had all been eaten and dusk was setting in, Murray pushed back his chair. "Guess I'd better be getting back to town. Thank you for the pizza and the Coke. Next time, it's my treat." He smiled at Janet, expecting her to get up and walk him to the door, possibly to his car. She looked up at him but kept her seat and didn't smile.

"Call you tomorrow?" he asked.

Her answer seemed curt. "If you want to."

He was still looking at her when he said, "Thanks again for the supper. You kids be careful on the way back to town.

Janie said, "You're welcome. Glad you could be with us," at the same time Russ said, "You, too."

Murray turned and headed through the mudroom and out the back door.

"What the hell, Mom?" Janie asked when he was gone. "Why were you so rude to Murray after he's done such nice things for you?"

"I wasn't rude," her mother objected, "and I didn't ask him to do any of this."

"You kinda were, Mom," Russ agreed with his sister.

"It doesn't matter if you asked him or not. He obviously did it because he's in love with you. Did you even thank him for the new kitchen and bathroom?" Janie asked.

"I thanked him when the two of us were upstairs."

"Well, I think you owe him an apology. If you hurry, maybe you could catch him before he leaves."

She took her daughter's suggestion and practically ran through the mudroom and around the corner of the house. She got there in time to see the Honda's taillights turn onto the highway at the far end of the lane. She waved her arms, trying to get Murray's attention but to no avail. His eyes were on the road ahead and his mind on what a reasonably pleasant evening the four of them had just shared, he and the kids anyway. Janet? Well, she didn't seem as happy with her new rooms as he thought she would be. Something was bothering her, something that was his fault, and he wasn't quite sure what it was. When he had exhausted a mental list of possibilities, he turned his thoughts toward other things.

He would have to ask Ed Wilson how to go about contacting the government about getting new doors and windows for the house, he knew, and no doubt Ed would be glad to help. He smiled at the fact that nobody seemed to have given a thought all evening to the situation he and Janet might find themselves in soon, and nobody had even mentioned James Hartman's name. For a few pleasant hours, the man had had no impact on their lives. All of that was about to change when the new week arrived.

* * * *

Murray didn't call her that weekend. In his mind, "If you want to" translated to "Don't bother." Silence from her end of the line seemed to confirm it. He would miss seeing her, miss being with her, he knew, but the ball was in her court now, so to speak. If Janet wanted them to have any kind of relationship, she would have to make the next move.

Monday came, another mundane Monday, with no appointments on the calendar. He spent much of the day in his apartment with the door into his office open. He watched daytime TV from his recliner, the volume turned low so he could hear if anyone were to walk in off the street. The morning and much of the afternoon passed, and no one did.

He finished a cup of coffee, poured himself another cup and went to the bathroom to get rid of the earlier one. "You have got to slow down with this stuff," he muttered to himself. "You're gonna destroy your kidneys, and a man can't live without those."

He had just finished washing his hands and turned the water off when he heard his office door open and close. He dried his hands off quickly, threw the towel at its hanger and stepped to the door into his office. Janet was standing just inside the front door, her eyes wide and uncertain.

"Hi," she said, and it was almost inaudible.

Murray gave her a half-smile and said, "Janet."

She returned the half-smile. "We need to talk."

"Okay," Murray said. "Let me go first. I apologize for having work done on the homeplace without asking you first. I won't do something like that again. Now you."

She took a couple of steps forward, he followed suit, and they were standing close enough that they could have touched. Murray held out his hands, palms up, but she didn't respond, so he dropped them to his sides and waited.

"When we first started… seeing one another, you said no strings attached…"

"And there are no strings," he interrupted.

Janet shook her head in annoyance. "I agree there's no *strings*! It's more like a *web*! A web of steak dinners and favors and furniture that you just keep spinning and spinning and tangling me up in, and now a new kitchen and a new bathroom! When is it gonna stop? I feel like I should do something for you, show my appreciation for all you do, for all you've done, and I'm not ready for that!"

"When we first started spending time together, you asked me where it was going and I told you it was going as far as we could get it to go, as far as *both* of us *wanted* it to go—just friends, good friends, great friends… somewhere beyond maybe. That's all still the same. I do things for you because I like doing things for you. No, that's not right. I *love* doing things for you, and I love *you*. And I thought *you* loved *me.*"

"I *do*!" Janet said, "I *do* love you!"

"The first time you said that to me was on your birthday, and I made a joke about waiting for Janie to leave before we slipped off to a bedroom. You said something about stretch marks and I said I could wait until you were comfortable with it before we made love. Remember?"

Janet nodded.

"You said, 'What if I never am?'" and I said then we would just be friends without benefits. Remember?"

She nodded again, and tears welled up in her eyes, spilled over her lashes and down her face. Murray wanted so badly to wipe them away that his arms ached, but he stood his ground.

"Well, that's still the same, too. I would like to be the one sitting across the table from you, breakfast, dinner and supper, every day. I would like to be the one snuggling up to you every night and going to sleep, and if that is all there ever was to it, I would be okay with that. Since I've met you, I find it miserable being alone, but I didn't mean—and I don't mean—to put any kind of pressure on you. I just want to spend time with you, to be near you as much as I possibly can. Will that be okay?"

Janet stepped forward on a sob and wrapped him up in her arms. "Yes, yes, I'm sorry I acted the way I did about the kitchen and bathroom. I love them and I love you."

Murray's arms went around her shoulders, and he buried his face in her hair. "It's alright. No apology necessary. I love you, too, and we go on from here."

She felt so good in his arms, and he found himself smiling at the contrast between her arrival and reason for being here and the way Vicki had blown in on Friday and the demands she had made—Janet dressed in jeans, t-shirt and athletic shoes, no makeup or jewelry, basically asking that he give her less; Vicki dressed to the nines, bejeweled and made up and demanding his house and furniture. This was the woman he wanted; this one here in his arms.

The office door opened, and Murray looked up. One of the sleaziest lawyers in town stood there grinning.

"Murray McCartney?" he asked, and Murray nodded. The man took a step forward and slapped an envelope on the desk. "You've been served. And who might this young lady be?"

"A client of mine and none of your business," Murray said, releasing Janet and picking up the envelope.

She wiped her cheeks with the heels of her hands and dried them on her jeans. Then she saw the box of tissues on the corner of the desk and pulled a handful out.

"Well, you kids have a nice day," the man said, giving them a lewd grin. He went out the door, closing it behind him.

"What is it?" Janet asked, turning to Murray.

"A subpoena," he said. "I have to testify before a grand jury."

Chapter Fifteen

Janet received her summons at work the next morning. She called Murray, frantic.

"What are we gonna do?" she asked.

"We're going to testify to what we saw and just tell the truth."

"We're not in trouble?"

"No," he told her and found himself smiling. "We're not in trouble. We didn't do anything wrong. We just happened to be at the right place at the right time—or the wrong place at the wrong time, depending on how you look at it—and we saw Officer James Hartman deliver a blow to a man's head that killed him. They will likely just ask us what we saw, and we will tell them."

"Will you be there with me?" Janet asked.

"No, they will take us in one at a time; we will testify and then we'll be dismissed, and life will go on as usual."

She didn't seem to be entirely reassured, but Murray felt he had explained things as succinctly and completely as possible. In his own mind, he found himself wondering again if this was Fate's way of helping him keep his promise to take Hartman off the street. As usual, only time would tell.

She invited him out to the homeplace for supper that evening, kind of an "I'm sorry, forgive me" meal, he thought, but he went gladly. She met him at the kitchen door with a wonderfully soft and heart-felt distraction. When he opened his eyes after it, the smile on Janet's face was the old one that he had been missing, the one that had been on her face when he turned in the circle of her arms the first time she had told him that she loved him.

"Have a seat," she said, "and I'll pour you some coffee. Or would you rather have something cold to drink?"

"Coffee is fine," he told her and sat down at the table.

A window unit hummed in the living room, and someone had hung curtains over the archway into what had been Russell Hockenberry's trophy room. Even with the oven on, the kitchen was semi-cool. Janet saw him looking toward the living room and smiled.

"Russ put them in for us," she said. "There's one in Janie's bedroom and one in mine. They're heating units, too, so I'm thinking about not buying oil for the furnace when winter comes. We want to move out here as soon as we can. I have to make curtains for the bottom of the stairs yet, but things are working out."

A new coffeemaker was sitting on her new white countertop. She poured a cup for each of them, brought them to the table and took a seat to his right. He picked up his cup, blew on it gently, took a sip and set it back down. She put a hand over his on the table and gave him that smile again.

"The lasagna isn't quite ready yet," she said. "I love you."

What her words did to his heart was something he couldn't have described. "I love you, too," he answered.

She began to lean, and he took her cue and leaned toward her. Their lips brushed, and both of them sat back, smiling. And so, the evening went.

When the lasagna was almost done, she got up and took two Corelle plates from her new cabinet, plain white plates that he had never seen before. From a drawer, she gathered new stainless-steel flatware and brought it all to the table.

"Here," she said, "put these where they go. I'll get us some napkins."

He did what he was told, and she came back with some of the paper napkins the kids had brought the Friday before. She went to the oven and brought back a hot pad and a pan of lasagna. Everything in place, she sat down, and they began to eat, smiling at one another and making small talk between bites.

When their meal was over, he helped her wash the plates and flatware in her new sink and wondered if she knew yet that it had come from her late husband's butcher shop. It was doubtful that she would ever go into the place because that's where he and Ross Junior had stored all the mounted deer heads, birds and animals that used to cover the walls of the living room and clutter up the den. Dishes done and put away, they retired to the living room to watch a movie she had rented. They sat on the sofa together as usual, leaning toward one another, shoulders touching and heads together, kissing occasionally. Neither of them said much until the movie ended.

"Well, it looks like it's about dark-thirty," Murray

said. "I'd better be getting on home. Are you staying out here tonight?"

"No," she said, "I'm not quite brave enough to stay out here by myself yet. I want to have the electric company put in some outdoor lighting first."

Janet went into the living room and turned off the window unit. They went out the backdoor together and kissed beside her car.

"I'll follow you," he said, then went to his Honda, got behind the wheel, and they started out. What was it about being in love with her, he wondered, that made even her taillights seem sweet?

When they reached town, she took a street west toward her apartment building, and he hung a left toward his. He hit the remote as he turned down the alley next to his building, the overhead door started to rise and the light inside came on. He swung his vehicle into its spot and started the door back down. It hit bottom before he was out of his car and the overhead light went out.

"I'll have to have Ed's boy do something about that," he said out loud. "Good thing there's a light in my cell phone."

He was using that light to put his key in the door to his apartment when someone spoke out of the darkness to his right.

"Hear ya got a summons to testify at the grand jury, McCartney. Ya best keep yer mouth shut and tell them ya didn't see nothing."

He flinched and dropped his phone but recovered quickly.

"Can't keep my mouth shut and tell anybody anything, now can I?"

"Always the smartass, ain't ya? And you tell that bitch you've been bangin' ta keep her mouth shut, too."

"Don't call Janet a bitch, Hartman," Murray said. "She's not your mother."

There was a blinding pain in the right side of his head, a flash of red behind his eyes and then everything went black.

He woke up sometime later, flat on his back, in the living room of his apartment, his cell phone lying on his chest. The right side of his face throbbed with pain, and the taste of blood was in his mouth. After several minutes, he managed to roll over and get to his hands and knees. The effort made his face throb harder, and he sat back on his heels and rested awhile before he struggled to his feet. With hands on the walls and the furniture, he managed to make it to the bathroom, turn on the light and look at his reflection in the mirror above the sink. The right side of his face was one big, ugly, purple bruise, and the white of his right eye was mostly red.

"Son of a bitch!" he said and flinched at the shot of pain that just speaking caused.

He brushed his teeth to get rid of the taste of blood, using his tongue to see if any of them were loose or missing. None were but there was a cut on the inside of his cheek. He took three 500mg Acetaminophen caplets from the bottle he kept in the medicine cabinet behind the mirror and discovered that swallowing was painful, too. He staggered back into his bedroom, kicked off his shoes, stretched out on the bed, and pretty much passed out again.

The throbbing in his face woke him in the

morning, and he lay there on his back, fully clothed, and tried to analyze what had happened. The voice had spoken to him in a guttural whisper. Was it Hartman, he wondered, or one of his cohorts? Another of Huntingdon's men in blue who thought he was above the law? How had he gotten into the garage? Slipped in under the overhead door as it was closing? And how had he managed to land a punch so perfectly on target in the dark? Night vision goggles?

"What does it matter," Murray muttered. "What am I gonna do? Call the police and make a report? Hello, this is Murray McCartney, and I want to report an assault on my person." Whoever was on the other end of the line would probably laugh so hard they would break a rib. And if anyone were to take him seriously, he had no evidence, no proof of who had assaulted him that would stand up in court. He might just as well tell everybody he had run into a door.

He pulled himself to a sitting position, legs dangling over the side of the bed. The room began to spin, and he leaned back on his arms and braced himself until it stopped. When it did, he staggered out to the kitchen. Breakfast would have to be something soft, something that required little chewing.

It would not be until later in the day that he discovered whoever had waylaid him in his garage had left through the door into his office and the front door, leaving them both unlocked.

* * * *

They were both required to be at the courthouse on Thursday morning. Janet had to take off work, which seemed to upset her, and Murray had to rearrange his schedule. On this rare occasion, he had three appointments on his calendar.

When he got to the courthouse, Janet was already there, waiting in a room with several other witnesses, a couple of them in blue.

"What happened to you?" Janet asked when she saw his face. She reached to touch his cheek, and he flinched.

"I had a visitor waiting for me when I got home Monday evening," he told her. "You might say our visit didn't go well."

An officer sitting on the other side of the room couldn't quite hide his grin.

"Who was it?" Janet asked. "What did they want?"

"We'll talk about it later," he said, sitting down beside her and taking her hand. "It's not important right now."

Several of the people in the room were called, spent their time in the jury room and left. Janet was called in before Murray and spent a scant ten minutes before the grand jury. She came out and went straight to him, smiling sheepishly.

"That wasn't so bad," she told him. "They just asked me what I saw, and I told them the truth."

Before he could answer or she could say anything more, a bailiff appeared at the door. "Mister Murray McCartney?"

"Here," Murray responded.

"You're next." He disappeared back into the jury room, and Murray followed.

* * * *

It soon became clear that the grand jury was not part of Fate's plan to help him get Hartman off the street. Murray was sworn in with the usual, "Do you swear to tell the truth... etc.?," and told to take a seat. The ADA was a young man by the name of Owen Metzler with whom Murray was not familiar. He was a scrawny little runt of a man with curly blond hair, blue eyes and an air of self-importance. His eyes went wide when he saw the bruise on Murray's face, but he chose to say nothing about it. Instead, he got right into the case at hand.

"You were traveling east on Penn Avenue between Blair Park and Highway Twenty-two on the evening of July twenty-eighth when you observed an altercation between Officer James Hartman and one Duane Runk. Is that correct?"

"Not exactly," Murray corrected.

"Then tell us what is. Tell us what you saw."

"We were headed…"

"We being yourself and Janet Hockenberry," ADA Metzler interrupted.

"Yes, myself and Janet Hockenberry were going up to the Dairy Queen. It was her birthday and…"

"Skip the insignificant details and just tell us what you saw."

Murray's expression should have told the man to soften his approach, but Metzler couldn't seem to look him in the eye. Every time the man glanced his way, those blue eyes seemed to focus on the bruise on the right side of his face.

"Officer Hartman had a vehicle pulled over on the

shoulder of the roadway," Murray said, a bit angry in his tone, "and a large man, who was later identified as one Duane Runk, was getting into it, about to slide behind the wheel. Officer Hartman swung his telescoping baton backhanded and struck the man on the left temple, and the man fell down between the door and the chassis of the vehicle."

"And what did you do?" the ADA asked.

"I pulled to the side of the road, called 911 and went back to render assistance."

"And in doing so, you interfered with a police officer in the conduct of his duty."

For a moment, Murray was shocked into silence by the man's statement.

"Were you a witness to what had transpired before your arrival on the scene? The man's argumentative and belligerent attitude? His refusal to cooperate and resisting arrest?"

"Was I a witness to what happened before my arrival on the scene?" Murray asked. "What kind of question is that? No, I didn't see what happened before I got there, and I haven't had my morning cup of coffee tomorrow yet either."

"Watch your tone, and just answer whatever questions I choose to ask you, yes or no. Is it true that you have had a vendetta against Officer James Hartman for the last five and a half or six years because of the death of you son?"

"What? No! If anything, Hartman has had a vendetta against *me* ever since I won a wrongful death suit against him and the city! He wrote *me* more tickets in the first six months after that than all the citizens of Huntingdon got put together."

"Just answer the questions, yes or no," the ADA repeated.

"And lend credence to the way you're trying to cast doubt on my testimony about what I witnessed up on Penn Avenue? I don't think so. Skip the insignificant details, you told me earlier. Well, I have already testified to what I witnessed, and everything you have asked me since then is insignificant to this case. I believe it is time I was dismissed."

"You will be dismissed when I deem it time for you to be dismissed, Mister McCartney, and you are getting dangerously close to being charged with contempt of court. Answer the question, yes or no, have you had a vendetta against Officer James Hartman for the past six years?"

"No," Murray said empathically and then went on a tirade. "I'll tell you what; you should call Mayor Banks to testify here. He could tell you about writing a check to reimburse a young lady for a taillight Hartman broke and then wrote her a ticket for having a broken taillight. He could tell you about Hartman stopping work on my apartment even though I didn't need a building permit. He could tell you about Hartman slashing my tires and dumping sand in my car. He could tell you how Hartman threatened the girl's mother with arrest for selling her late husband's gun collection without a dealer's license."

Metzler kept sputtering, "Mister McCartney... Mister McCartney" in an effort to shut Murray up and glancing at the jurors anxiously to see how they were taking his testimony.

"And this bruise on my face that you seem to find so fascinating..." Murray pushed on, and Metzler finally held up his hand.

"Maybe that's all we need from you, Mister McCartney," he said, loudly and emphatically. "You are dismissed."

Murray hesitated. There was so much more he could tell the jurors, so much more that would enable them to make an informed decision, but it had already become clear to him that the DA's office had no intention of bringing an indictment against James Hartman for the death of Duane Runk. This whole charade was an effort to clear Hartman's name. He nodded at the jurors, got up and left the room.

Janet looked up when he came through the doors and could tell immediately that he was agitated. He held out his hand and she stood and took it, and together, they left the courthouse. Out on the street, he took a deep, shuttering breath and blew it out slowly through this mouth.

"What is it, sweetheart?" Janet asked. "What happened to you in there?"

He told her in as few words as necessary, and the two of them started toward their cars.

"So, he's gonna get away with it," Janet said. "That poor man lost his life, and nothing is going to be done about it."

Murray nodded. "I will be very surprised if the jury brings in an indictment."

"So, what are we gonna do?"

"There's nothing we *can* do. We have done our duty as citizens of this great Republic of ours. Now, we have to let the legal system run its course."

"No," Janet said, "I mean what are we gonna do now, the two of us."

"Oh," Murray said and chuckled. "*You* are going

to leave your vehicle where it is, and *we* are going to take mine over to Hoss's. After what happened back there, I need a steak, something I can gnash my teeth on for a while."

"Wait a minute," she said, taking his arm and pulling him to a stop. She turned him to face her, put her arms around his neck and planted a kiss on his lips, right there in the street for the whole world to see.

"Thank you," he said when he could catch his breath again. "That's a good start. We're on our way to recovery."

Chapter Sixteen

As before, life went on, two ten-ounce rib eyes giving it a jumpstart. Over the next several days, they got Janet and Janie moved out to the homeplace and their apartment cleaned out. Murray spoke to Ed Wilson about the government program that provided new windows and doors and got the paperwork started. He saw a few clients at his office—some old, some new—provided them legal service and was glad for the income. And always, *always*, at the back of his mind was the hope that his house would sell, and he would feel comfortable spending money to make the trip to Louisiana so he could have a talk with Daniel Miller. Recent events seemed to indicate that lives depended on it.

The grand jury *had* failed to bring in an indictment. Officer James Hartman was cleared of all culpability in the death of Duane Runk, and he was once again turned lose on the citizens of Huntingdon, Pennsylvania. He made his presence known to Murray on his first day back on patrol, pulling him over late that afternoon when he was on his way out to the homeplace. Murray decided it was best to go along with whatever the man was bringing and sat staring through the windshield of his Honda until Hartman walked up beside it.

"License and registration," he demanded.

Murray fished his license out of his wallet and the registration out of the glove compartment and handed them to him. Hartman took them back to his patrol car and sat with them a good fifteen minutes.

"I'm letting you off with a warning this time," he said when he finally came back and handed the items to Murray.

"A warning for what?" he asked.

"For bein' a sniveling asshole," Hartman answered and then asked, "How come you didn't go runnin' to Daddy Banks with your black eye?"

"Sir?" Murray said and turned his head to look the man in the eye for the first time.

Hartman gave a snort of derision and walked away, and the tone of the future was set.

* * * *

Janet ordered the insulation that Murray had suggested and called to inform him that the bundles were stacked up on the front porch, waiting to be carried to the attic and put into place. He and Russ had gone up there early one morning, measured the area and discovered that the planks of the floor had not been nailed down. All they would have to do was pick them up and move them to one side—along with what seemed like the tons of miscellaneous junk stored up there—put strips of insulation down, put the planks back in place, move the junk back to where it had been and repeat the process for the other half of the attic.

Murray got out to the homeplace early on a Saturday morning in late-August. Russ was already there and waiting in jeans, a t-shirt and grungy athletic shoes. Janie had gone off shopping in Altoona—or possible Hollidaysburg—her mother wasn't certain.

"You're going to do this in a white, long-sleeved shirt and khaki dress pants?" Russ asked when Murray walked into the kitchen.

"They're all I've got and they're old, so yes."

Janet turned and stepped from where she was working at something on her new countertop, gave him a smile and a kiss and said, "Good morning."

"Okay," Russ said, ignoring them, "let's get the front door open and some of this stuff totted up to the attic. I figure if we get started now, we should be finished by noon."

They carried the insulation up the stairs a bundle at a time and tossed it down among the trunks and boxes and assorted junk until half of it was in the attic. Then they began to pick up the planks and move them aside. That activity stirred up the dust of the ages that seems to collect in all attic spaces, and soon the two of them were coughing and sneezing.

"This is gonna be a bigger job than we thought," Russ said. "I'm thinkin' we might not get it all done today."

"Maybe if we keep at it," Murray suggested, taking a handkerchief from a hip pocket and blowing his nose.

They broke open the first bundle. Russ took hold of the end of a strip and crawled on two of the ceiling joists until he could push the end of it back against the eave. Getting back to the planks that were still down required crawling backwards. The process was slow going, and he had to repeat the process with each piece of fiberglass insulation.

"Damn! This stuff is making me itch," he said when the fifth strip was in place. "I should have worn a long-sleeved shirt like you."

"Let me do a couple," Murray suggested, and Russ did not object.

It was a tedious job, crawling along the joists. A slip to either side might mean falling through the lathe and plaster and making a mess. By the time Murray had pushed his fifth strip into place and gotten back to the plank floor, the attic had heated up under the morning sun, and their shirts were soaked with sweat and sticking to them.

"Let's go downstairs and get some water," Russ suggested, and Murray followed him down the stairs without comment.

"Look at you two!" Janet said when they got to the kitchen. "Are you sure you don't want me to hire someone else to do this?"

"We just need a little water, and we'll get back to it," Murray told her.

After their time in the space under the tin roof of the attic and in their wet shirts, the kitchen felt absolutely frigid. Two glasses of water each and the two of them headed back upstairs.

Before they started dragging insulation again, they opened the windows in the gables at either end of the house. They might as well have left them shut. There wasn't the slightest breeze blowing, and the temperature in the attic didn't drop to any significant degree. In fact, as the day wore on and the sun rose higher in the sky, the temperature in the attic rose accordingly.

"Messing with this stuff the way we are is like

having sex with a porcupine, isn't it?" Russ said at one point.

"Yeah," Murray agreed, "except you have to mount it a little differently."

His answer produced a chuckle from his coworker and the job went on.

When they got the first half of the insulation down and the floor planks back it place, it was eleven forty-five.

"Let's take a break for dinner," Murray suggested. "I think your mother was fixing something for us."

He got no argument from Russ who turned and led the way downstairs.

Janet heard them coming and met them when they turned the corner into the kitchen, a look of concern on her face.

"You two look exhausted. Are you sure you want to finish this today?"

"Positive," her son told her. "If it's not done when the sun sets, it won't ever be done, because I'm not spending another day like this. I'm going home to take a quick shower and get a long-sleeved shirt. Save some of whatever you fixed for me."

Janet turned to Murray when her son had disappeared through the mudroom. Her look of concern had turned into that smile he so loved, and she reached for him.

He took a step back. "You better keep your distance, the shape I'm in," he said.

For answer, she took a half-step toward him and began to lean. He took the hint and leaned toward her. Their lips met briefly in a gentle kiss.

"You taste salty," Janet said straightening up. "Wash your hands and sit down. I made pot roast."

* * * *

Russ was back in thirty minutes, looking somewhat refreshed and wearing a long-sleeved plaid shirt.

"Hartman followed me for several blocks," he told them, "left off at the city limits. I thought he might stop me and give me a ticket, but I wasn't speeding or anything."

Murray had not told them about his latest run-in with Hartman. "He's just an old bull that's found new freedom and enjoys pawing up the ground and snorting."

"More like a jackass farting and braying," Russ countered.

"Russ! Watch your mouth and eat your dinner!" his mother said, but everybody was laughing.

She sat in her usual place and Murray in his, the two of them smiling at one another across the table and watching her son eat. His plate clean, Russ pushed it back and stood.

"Thanks for another excellent meal, Mom," then looking at Murray, "Guess we better get back with it."

They started the afternoon by carrying the rest of the bundles up to the attic. That done, they shifted the trunks and boxes over to the planks that already had insulation under them and began stacking planks from the other half of the floor up in a pile. The heat was stifling, and Russ's new shirt was soon as wet as Murray's.

173

"Do you think if we reached up and touched that tin roof, it would burn us?"

"I imagine it's possible," Murray said, "but I'm not curious enough about it to find out."

They used the same system as they had that morning, each of them dragging five strips to the eaves and then being spelled by the other. It was dusky dark when the last strip had been put in place and the last plank had been laid back down. Both men were exhausted from the activity and the heat to the point of staggering.

"This stuff had damned sure better do some good," Russ said, stamping the last plank into place, "or I'm gonna come back up here and piss all over it. When it's cooler, though."

Murray agreed with the young man in a way and thought his threat was funny, but he was too tired to laugh. He staggered toward the stairs, wishing for a handrail.

When they got to the first floor, Russ didn't even slow down. "Thanks again for the dinner, Mom. I'll see you later." He disappeared through the mudroom again. This time, his mother called after him.

"Thank *you* for all *you've* done today."

Murray sat down in his usual seat at the table with a thump. "Glass of water, please," he said through a throat that was obviously parched. Janet had one in front of him in seconds. He downed the water without stopping, set the glass back down and said, "Thank you."

"Thank *me*?" Janet said, her eyes tearing up. "You're the one who worked himself into exhaustion. Thank *you*!"

She helped him up when he started to stand and walked with him out to his car. She kissed him over the open door, watched him slide behind the wheel, and watched his taillights until he turned at the end of the lane. Then she wiped her eyes with the heels of her hands, dried them on her jeans and went back into the house.

Murray drove in an exhausted daze but made it back to town without incident. When he made the turn into the alley beside his building, a black Dodge Ram pickup was sitting across the street. He had little doubt about who was sitting in it or about why he was sitting there. Something had to be done, he thought, and it looked like he was going to have to be the one to do it.

Chapter Seventeen

By late September, two new doors and two new storm doors had replaced the old ones out at the homeplace. Two-thirds of the old wood-frame windows with their dried-out caulking had also been replaced with pristine white vinyl ones that could be opened and closed easily. Why not all of them? Murray wondered and encouraged Janet to use some of the money from her late husband's gun collection to replace the old ones the government had left behind. A week later, all of the windows in the place were white vinyl.

Finding someone to paint the place proved a challenge. Two-story buildings with end gables required extension ladders that few people had, but Murray finally located a company that had all the necessary equipment and was willing to take on the job. Their bid was a little high, Janet thought, but he talked her into accepting it. The weatherboarding looked like it had never seen paint, and it would likely take at least three coats of paint to seal it properly. On the day the job began, four men dressed in professional-looking white painters' garb showed up in two pickup trucks, unloaded ladders and went to work. It would take them five days, one work week, to get the job done, and when they were finished, the place seemed to sparkle in the sun. Janet was elated, and Murray couldn't have been happier for her.

On the last day of that month, Vicki made another run at him concerning the house they had once occupied together. The Yocum siblings had been successful in their efforts to have her evicted from what they considered their homeplace—although their parents had moved into it after they were all grown and out on their own and not one of them had been born there or had ever lived there. Murray figured it was the appraisal of two million plus that gave them such fond memories of the place.

On this occasion, Vicki pulled to the curb opposite his office in the two-year-old silver Lincoln MKX Harvel had bought her new (she wanted a Cadillac) and had managed to hang on to, up until then anyway. Her entrance into his office was somewhat less blustery than her previous one had been, and she didn't seem as sure of herself as she had back then. It helped a bit that Murray was sitting at his desk and saw her coming and she knew it. She closed the door behind her without saying a word, went to and sat down in one of the armchairs facing his desk.

"I need the house," she said.

"The house is not available," he told her.

"Yes, it is," she contradicted, "I just went by there, and the sign is still in the front yard."

"And what did the sign say?"

"For Sale," she admitted reluctantly, "but I *need* it now. I have to be out of the house I'm in now in two weeks. Harvel's brats have frozen my bank account, and I don't even have money to buy food or pay rent."

"Which changes nothing," Murray told her. "The

house is still mine, and I'm still going to sell it. And," he continued quickly when she sucked in a breath and was about to argue, "it will set empty until it sells, and the new owners move in. The place is not for rent, Vicki, so forget it."

"But what am I supposed to *do*?" she asked, tearing up. "I have no money. How am I gonna *rent* a place with no money? How am I gonna put up deposits for utilities? I can't even buy *food*."

Murray leaned forward and slid the box of tissues he always kept on his desk now toward her and then sat back in his chair. She put the box in her lap, pulled a handful of tissues out and dabbed at her eyes delicately, and he thought, *one cannot ruin one's makeup now, can one?* But he said nothing. He waited until she got control of her emotions again and had sighed heavily.

"Tell you what," he began. "You find an apartment, and I'll loan you the money to pay the first month's rent and to put the necessary deposits down. You can pay me back whenever you find a job."

"And where am I gonna do that?" she asked.

"Why not go back and talk to Henry? Maybe he could use an experienced insurance agent."

"My old boss? You've got to be kidding!"

"You worked for him for nearly fifteen years, and you know the business," Murray reminded her. "He might be glad to have you back."

"But he was mean to me!"

"At that point in our lives, you thought everybody was being mean to you. I think most of it was your imagination," he told her. "Go talk to him. Maybe there was something going on in his life you didn't know about."

She didn't look convinced, but she was getting there. "And you'll give me the money to pay rent and deposits on the utilities?"

"I'll loan you the money," he corrected.

"What about furniture?" she asked.

Murray smiled in spite of himself. "I'll see what I can do."

She gave him a look that was still uncertain, leaned to put the box of tissues back on his desk and then got up and left.

He didn't see her again for two days, and she came in smiling, seemed to be proud of herself.

"I found an apartment," she said, and told him how much her rent was going to be and how much she needed for deposits.

"Where is this place?" he asked and nearly choked when she gave him the address of the apartment Janie and Janet had recently vacated. If she noticed his reaction, she chose not to comment on it.

"And I got my old job back. You were right. Henry was having a problem with his wife when I left. They almost got a divorce, but they're doing okay now. And he gave me a raise!"

"So, how much do you need?" Murray asked, and she gave him a figure lower than he had expected. He wrote her a check for that amount plus a hundred dollars. "You will need to use it to buy food until you get your first paycheck," he explained when she looked at the check and seemed surprised.

"Oh, right," she said. "What about furniture?"

"Will you be in your apartment tomorrow afternoon?" he asked.

"Not until after work, about five-thirty."

"I'll bring you some then." He watched her leave and walk across the street to where she had parked her Lincoln once again, and he smiled. Janet's old apartment was about to be filled with Janet's old furniture, and at the same time, they would be getting rid of some of the junk in the barn.

* * * *

He called Russ and asked him to bring his pickup out to the homeplace when he got off work and help him move some furniture. Using the young man's truck to haul the old furniture out in the barn to Vicki's apartment would be cheaper than renting a U-Haul, he figured, even if they had to make several trips. There were no appointments on his calendar, so he closed the office an hour early and headed out there, picked up a couple of pizzas and a six pack of soft drinks on the way. The day had gone well, he thought, especially the part where he got his ex off his back, and he was looking forward to spending some time with Janet. No telling where Janie might be, and Russ would go home eventually. No doubt there would be "distractions" once they were alone. Murray smiled and mentally put quotes around the word.

He parked beside Janet's Nissan and got out, a little disappointed that she didn't come out to meet him. When he stepped through the door of the mudroom and into the kitchen, she was sitting at the end of the table, hands over her face.

"Janet?" he said.

She dropped her hands and turned to look at him with tears leaking from her eyes.

"What is it? What's the matter?" he asked. He stepped forward, set all of his purchases on the table, knelt down beside her chair and took her into his arms.

When she could get control of her sobs, she answered, "It's Amanda. She's pregnant."

Murray pushed her back until he could look her into the face. "And this is cause for tears because…?"

"She's in Germany," Janet explained, and her tone suggested any idiot would have known what the problem was without asking. "She will have the baby over there, and I won't get to see my new grandchild until it's nearly two years old."

Murray pulled her back against his chest, her chin resting on his shoulder. "Here's a simple solution," he suggested after a couple of minutes thought, "when the baby's born, we'll fly you over there."

Janet pushed herself back until she could look *him* in the face once again. "Fly me over there?" she said. "You mean in an airplane?"

"Well, you're a little too heavy for a kite, and the wind doesn't always cooperate with those things, so, yes, in a plane."

Her expression left no doubt that she didn't like the idea. "Plane tickets cost a lot of money, and I've never flown in an airplane. I'm not sure I would want to."

"You've never flown in an airplane?" he asked. "What about when Janie was living in California all of those years? You never flew out there to visit her?"

Janet shook her head. "Me and the kids had to live pretty much on what I made at the hospital. There wasn't money for airplane tickets."

"So, you didn't see your daughter for what… ten years?"

CHARLES C. BROWN

"More like eleven."

The shock on Murray's face caused her to push on.

"We talked some on the telephone, and she would send a picture now and then. She could have bought a bus ticket and come home now and then if she wanted to. She told me tips were good at the bar where she worked. But she didn't want to while her father was alive."

"And he never drove you out there to see her?"

"She left the day after she graduated from high school, and I never heard Russell mention her name once after that."

Murray frowned, having a hard time processing that—a man being so indifferent to his firstborn that he never even mentioned her name. If Randall was still alive... he let the thought drop.

"Anyway," Janet was saying when he came out of his trance, "we were talking about Amanda being in Germany and pregnant,"

"And flying you over there when the baby's born."

"But I don't think I want to fly," she objected.

"But you want to see your grandchild before it's two years old."

Their conversation was interrupted by Russ coming through the mudroom. He stepped through the door into the kitchen, took one look at his mother's face and asked, "What's goin' on?"

Janet's eyes teared up and she choked on a sob. Murray stood up, moved around behind her and laid a hand on her shoulder.

"Your sister over in Germany is pregnant,"

Murray answered for her, "and your mother's upset that she won't see the baby until it's two years old. I offered to fly her over there when the baby's born, but she says she's never been in an airplane, and she doesn't want to fly."

"Sounds to me like what they call a dilemma," Russ said, "but we can figure it out later. Right now, we need to get some furniture moved, and I need to swing by Walmart on my way home and pick up some diapers and some formula."

"What furniture?" Janet asked.

"Vicki needs some of the furniture we put in the barn," Murray answered. "I thought it would be a good way to get rid of some of it and help her out at the same time."

"Vicki? Your ex-wife, Vicki?" Janet asked.

"Yes," Murray said. "Do you mind if we give her some of the old stuff?"

It took her a few seconds to answer. "I guess not. It's not doing anybody any good out there in the barn."

"Well, let's eat some of this pizza before it gets cold and then get on with it," Murray said. "Time is a wastin'."

When it came to pizza, nobody ever had to ask Russ Junior twice.

Chapter Eighteen

The house sold on Tuesday of the first week in November—brought in most of the hundred and twenty-four thousand Murray had been asking for it—and he immediately began making plans for a trip south. According to the internet, it was just under twelve hundred miles from Huntingdon to Houma, Louisiana, two hard days of driving, he thought. Two days down and two days back, and even if he got tired and decided to take an extra day coming home, he and Daniel Miller would have two whole days to visit. If he could leave on a Monday, he could be home by the end of the same week.

He started by rescheduling the appointments he had on his calendar for the second week of the month. There weren't all that many really but a few more than usual, and they all involved cases that weren't time-sensitive—an older couple wanting to make out a will, a young couple pursuing an amicable divorce, a young man who wanted his marriage annulled and several others. All of them could be postponed until even after the Thanksgiving holiday if it became necessary and that wasn't too inconvenient for his clients. The irony of so many appointments on the calendar when he wanted to be gone for a week was not lost on Murray.

Many weeks when he had nowhere to go, he spent much of his time in his apartment reading or watching TV.

His schedule redone, he made an appointment to take his Honda in and have the oil changed, the tire pressure, coolant level and transmission fluid level checked. The odometer showed fairly low mileage, but the vehicle was old, and there was no point in being careless and breaking down on the side of the road.

When he was satisfied that everything was as ready as he could get it, Murray sent a text to Daniel Miller: *Coming down for a visit. Okay?*

It was several minutes before Miller responded, and the answer surprised him: *Come alone. Use cash. Avoid security cameras. Wear a cap.*

Murray frowned at the screen on his phone. Why all the cloak and dagger? And then the enormity of what he was planning to do—what the sheriff's deputy believed Daniel Miller had already done—hit him, not to mention the penalty he would pay if he were to get caught and convicted. Every day for the rest of the week, he went to the ATM and drew out the maximum allowed. Something in the back of his mind seemed to warn him not to go into the bank and take out a large amount in a lump sum.

He spent as much time as he could with Janet. They had been seeing one another every day for months now, and he wondered how she would take the news that he would be gone for a week. He waited until it was time for him to leave her place on Sunday evening, and he had her in his arms when he told her.

"You're gonna be gone for a week?" she asked, surprised. "Where are you gonna go?"

Taking a cue from what he had come to think of as Miller's paranoia, he said, "I think it might be best if you don't know."

She frowned, suspicion written all over her face. "Are you gonna do something illegal?"

"No, nothing illegal," Murray said, added, "not this trip," and then wished that he hadn't.

"Is it far?"

"Just a two-day drive if I push myself."

"And what will you be doing there?" she wanted to know.

"I'll just be visiting with someone."

"Male or female?" Janet asked and Murray chuckled.

"You've gotten too much information out of me already, so I won't answer that. Suffice it to say, you've got nothing to worry about. I'll be leaving early in the morning, and I'll be back no later than Saturday night, possibly as early as Friday evening."

"You'll come and see me as soon as you get back?" she asked, and he nodded.

She pressed her body against his, tightened her arms around his neck and planted a kiss on his lips that left them wet and puffy and both of them gasping for air.

"There will be another one of those waiting for you when you get back," she said. "Now go."

That said, she turned her back, and Murray slipped out the kitchen door and through the mudroom.

* * * *

He went to bed with his bags already packed, didn't sleep well, and was in his Honda and ready to go before first light. He put his suitcase in the trunk, a tote bag and his overcoat in the back seat. It had turned cold there in Huntingdon, and never having been further south than Luray, Virginia, the idea that it would be warm farther south never crossed his mind.

He started the engine and checked the clock on the instrument panel. It was three minutes after six. He hit the button to raise the overhead door, backed out into the alley and watched the door drop back into place. This would be the longest trip he had ever made, the farthest he had ever been away from home, and although he was looking forward to visiting with Daniel Miller, there was a queasy feeling in the pit of his stomach. He took a deep breath and exhaled slowly, put the car in drive and, with one final stop at the ATM before he left town, was on his way.

Directions he had taken from the internet sent him south on PA 26 to I-70 east which took him to I-81 south. Driving on the Interstate was a bit intimidating at first because he was used to the narrow streets and highways around Huntingdon, and there were so many semis. But traffic was light to moderate, and he soon let himself go with the flow. Some five hours from the time he had left home, after brief stops to buy coffee and others to do what too much coffee made necessary, he found himself passing the exit to Harrisonburg, Virginia, and wondering where he would be stopping for lunch.

Mostly, his mind kept going to the conversation he would be having with Daniel Miller when he got to Houma, Louisiana. How would the man react to questions about what he had supposedly done for Rosalynn Holder? If he were in Miller's place, Murray thought, he would want to deny everything. How could he approach the subject in a way that would put Miller at ease? If what the deputy in the courthouse had said was true and if he could get Miller to open up, the man could help him deal with his Hartman problem and not end up in a cell.

Southern Virginia turned out to look much like northern Virginia, no surprise there, and when he crossed the state line into Tennessee at Bristol, the terrain didn't change. Not until he was farther south and approaching I-40 did the land become a little flatter but not exactly flat by any stretch of the imagination. I-40 took him through Knoxville, and just a little west of the city, he caught I-75, which would get him to Chattanooga sometime around eight P.M., exhausted and ready for a shower and a bed—and a little better than halfway to his destination. He snagged a room at a Hampton Inn just off I-24, took a shower, hit the mattress and slept like a log until shortly before six in the morning.

After a free breakfast, he took I-24 west and caught I-59 south, which took him down through Alabama and Mississippi. The land leveled out considerably the farther south he went, but at some point in the trip, Murray lost interest in the terrain and just wanted to get to Houma, visit with Daniel Miller and get back home. With every stop for a cup of coffee, food, fuel or a restroom break, he became more conscious of just how many security cameras there are in today's world and was always careful to wear the Pittsburg Pirates cap he had borrowed from Russ Junior.

Crossing the state line into Louisiana at last, Murray caught US 90 south and passed the city limit sign of Houma at six forty-five. He found the city intimidating. Highways seemed to be going everywhere, and traffic was heavy. Finding any particular address in a place this big and laid out in what seemed to him to be a haphazard way felt impossible. Had he learned to use his cell phone, he could have typed in any address or just spoken to Siri, and she would have directed him right to wherever he wanted or needed to go. Lacking that option, he drove around until he found a Hampton Inn on Martin Luther King, Jr. Boulevard and rented a room for the night. Then venturing out again, he found a Walmart not too far away and bought enough snacks to hold him until morning. After breakfast, he would call or text Daniel Miller and find out where they could meet and talk.

* * * *

Daniel Miller's office, like Murray's own, was in a storefront, one of several in what appeared to be a mostly defunct shopping strip on Park Avenue, but there the similarity ended. Where Murray's building was made of stone and wood that had been painted multiple times, Miller's building was made of yellow brick, aluminum and glass. A sign not much bigger than the one that had caught Janet Hockenberry's attention months ago was taped to the inside of a large, plate glass window: Attorney at Law. There was no gold gilt lettering on the door, nothing to give a potential client the slightest hint of the name of the young man sitting behind a gray, Army surplus desk in a gray metal desk chair with tears in its green vinyl-covered padding, one arm pad missing entirely. The single visitor's chair sitting in front of the desk was obviously of the same vintage and from the same source, as was the single, Army green filing cabinet pushed up against the back wall.

Miller had answered Murray's text with an address, and upon request, directions on how to get there from the hotel. When he opened the aluminum and glass door and walked in, Miller stood and extended a hand across the desk but said nothing.

"Murray McCartney. Remember me?" Murray asked. "It's nice to see you again."

"I do, Mister McCartney," Miller said, "but I don't understand what is so important that you felt the need to make the trip all the way down here. You could have mailed the rent checks like always."

"Let's let it be just Murray, okay?

"And I'll be Daniel."

"We'll get to the reason for this trip in a little while," Murray said, looking around and taking a seat in the visitor's chair. He crossed one leg over the other, took off his Pirates baseball cap and set it on his knee. "Do you really practice law out of this office?"

"Busted," Daniel said and smiled. "The answer to that question is yes and no, and only when I have to."

"Meaning?"

"This place is mostly camouflage," he said. "You know that Rosalynn left me well-set. I don't have to work if I don't want to, but there's someone in my life that needs to think I have to. So, I studied and passed the bar exam here in Louisiana, and I set up this office, and I come here every weekday, regular as clockwork. Now and then, someone will come in that needs my services, and I do my best to help them. Most people take one look at this place and its furnishings and back away, and that's my intention."

"This person who needs to think you have to work, is it a wife?" Murray asked.

Daniel's smile was a little sad. "No, but she might be someday."

"So, tell me what you've been up to since you left Pennsylvania. How did you end up down here?"

"That's kind of a long story."

"Right now, I've got nothing but time," Murray urged.

Daniel hesitated a moment and then began, "After I came to your office and read Rosalynn's will, I left the States and kicked around Europe for a while, mostly France. I met a girl from here that was kind of stranded over there. A rich boyfriend had taken her over there and then walked off and left her. She was working as a waitress and trying to save enough money for a plane ticket home. I ran into her at a Starbucks, and she reminded me so much of Rose Holder…" he stalled out for a few seconds. "Anyway, I wanted to get to know her better, so I bought us tickets, and we flew back together."

"But you're not together anymore?"

"We are and we aren't," Daniel said. "We'd like to get married, but it can't happen right now."

"Why is that?" Murray asked.

"She was raised Catholic and I wasn't. She has a grandmother that is such a devote Catholic that she would make Rosemarie's life miserable if she married outside the Church."

"So, you have to wait until the old lady dies."

Daniel's smile was completely gone, and he nodded.

"Does she live here in Houma?" Murray asked.

"Grandma lives up in Hahnville, and Rosemarie

191

lives in Thibodaux. We see each other a couple times a week, either at her place or mine. But you didn't come all the way down here to ask about my love life, so let's get to the real reason for your visit."

The moment of truth, so to speak, had arrived, and Murray still had not come up with an approach that he felt comfortable with. He cleared his throat and thought, *just go for it.*

"I've got a problem back up there in Huntingdon, and I need your help taking care of it."

"What kind of a problem are you talking about," Daniel asked, "and how can I possibly help you from down here?"

"There's a police officer up there that needs to be taken off the streets. It looks more and more like I'm going to have to be the one to do it, and I don't want to end up in a cell," Murray explained.

"Again, how can I possibly help you from down here?"

"I know that you did some things for Rosalynn Holder that were very possibly illegal and could have gotten you a death sentence or possibly life in prison, and yet, here you are… a free man. I need you to give me some pointers on how to do what I have to do and get away with it."

The blank look on Daniel's face made Murray smile.

"What makes you think I did anything for Rosalynn Holder that could have gotten me in trouble?" he asked.

"You would make one hell of a poker player," Murray said, and then told him about the conversation he had overheard at the courthouse.

Daniel said nothing. His expression did not change, and he did not break eye contact. If hearing that he was a suspect in four murders shook him at all, there was no evidence of it.

"The man I'm talking about has killed two people already," Murray pushed on, "two that we know of, and nobody will do anything about it. His victims deserve justice, and it has become increasingly clear that if they are to have it, the burden falls on me. I just don't want to end up in a cell, and I think you can help me with that."

Daniel Miller looked him in the eye and remained silent.

"Whatever you tell me will be just between the two of us. You've been paying me a retainer for the past two years, so attorney client confidentiality applies." Murray was practically pleading now.

"Why you?" Daniel asked. "How did you get involved?"

Murray hesitated. "His first victim was my son."

"And you want what, revenge?"

"No." Murray shook his head. "Like I said, I want to see justice done. I want the man taken off the streets. If he isn't, I'm afraid more people will die. He has got to be dealt with."

Daniel finally broke eye contact and looked out the window. "You want to do it with extreme prejudice?" His inflection made it a question.

Extreme prejudice... the expression surprised Murray. Did he want to kill Hartman? He didn't think so. What then? Disable him to the point that he couldn't work anymore?

"No, I wasn't thinking about killing him. I just

want to take him off the streets, so he won't be in a position to kill anymore."

"You would be wise to eliminate him completely," Daniel advised, looking him in the eye again. "Dead men tell no tales."

The look on the man's face sent chills up Murray's spine. "I don't think I can do that."

Miller broke eye contact again and stared over Murray's shoulder and out the window. The two of them sat so long without either of them speaking that Murray was beginning to think his trip had been for nothing. Then, still looking out the window, Daniel spoke.

"Say, hypothetically, someone had done what you heard in the courthouse, and someone was to do what you propose to do."

"Hypothetically is good," Murray agreed.

"He would have to be somewhere else and look like someone else when he did it."

"Be somewhere else?" Murray was confused.

"Have witnesses that could testify he was somewhere else and not at the crime scene when the crime was committed. And if he didn't want to eliminate any witnesses to the crime, then he would have to be careful to do what he intends to do where there weren't any."

That was easy enough to understand, and Murray nodded.

"He would have to be super careful not to leave any fingerprints or DNA behind. Wear latex gloves and take anything he touched at the crime scene away with him. Blow his nose on a tissue, take it away with him. Sneeze and spatter spittle, find some bleach and clean it up. He should leave clues that will mislead investigators, and once he gets the job done, he should discard everything he wore and everything he used, keep nothing that could incriminate him." Here, he looked at his visitor. "Understand?"

Murray nodded, and Daniel went on.

"He would want to have an alibi, witnesses that could put him far away from where the crime occurred."

"You mean like Altoona or Harrisburg?" Murray asked.

"No, farther away than that."

Murray gave it some thought and asked, "Like Philadelphia or Pittsburg?"

Daniel was looking out the window again and he nodded. "Far enough away that he couldn't get to Huntingdon and back in less than several hours. And he would have to have a legitimate reason for being where he is when it goes down."

Murray sat silently for several minutes and considered all that Daniel had said. Then he asked, "Anything else?"

"Yes. When you leave here to go home, don't take the same route you took coming down. Or if you do, don't stop at the same places you stopped at on the way down."

"Why not take the same route?" Murray asked. "I'm just down here visiting a client."

Daniel nodded. "So you say, but given the suspicions they have about me, if they know you've been here, you can be sure they will make a lot more than that out of it when you have done what you intend to do. The authorities up there have to know you have a bone to pick with this Hartman, right?"

"Right," Murray admitted.

"When one of theirs has been assaulted and you're the chief suspect, they will go over your life with a fine-tooth comb, starting with when your mother got pregnant. From this point on, treat everything you do—no, everything you even plan to do—as if there's a possibility that it could be misconstrued and used as evidence against you. Does anybody know you're down here?"

Murray shook his head. "No. Somehow I got the notion it wasn't a good idea."

"Good," Daniel said. "Let's do our best to keep it that way. You texted me on a cell phone. You should take the battery out of it until you get back to Huntingdon or somewhere north of here, and when you get back home, you might want to figure out how to delete this trip from your GPS. The authorities will have a tech go through it when they pick you up for questioning, and they very likely will."

Murray sat silently considering all that Daniel had said. Good advice no doubt and learned from experience. Suddenly, he had a great deal more respect for this young man who was only a little more than half his own age and yet seemed so much older and wiser, calmer.

"How do you feel now that justice has been served for the crime committed against the ones who were responsible for your friend's, your fiancée's death? Any regrets?"

"None," Daniel said without blinking.

"Do you think that... what happened... what you did," Murray asked, searching for the right words, "... changed you in some way? That what I plan to do will change me?"

"Only if you let it," Daniel answered. "The law is supposed to protect us, to punish those who assault us or in some way trespass against us. Sometimes it fails to do so. Sometimes the guilty get away with their crimes because of some minute legal technicality. The legal system *knows* they're guilty but feels its hands are tied because of some infinitesimal word or clause in the written law. When that happens, if justice is to be served, it has to be served in some other way. I believe that I am the same man I was before justice was served in the case you overheard being discussed in the courthouse in Huntingdon. Do what you have to do and don't *let* it change you. Put it behind you and get on with your life."

It was a close to a confession as anything Daniel had ever uttered.

Chapter Nine

At eight-thirty that evening, Murray found himself approaching Birmingham, Alabama, on I-59. Darkness had fallen and his eyes were burning from staring into the pouring rain that had slowed him down to sixty-five, sometimes sixty, miles an hour through most of Mississippi. His visit with Daniel Miller had ended at noon when he suggested they go to whatever was Miller's favorite Cajun restaurant and have lunch on him. Miller's reaction had been negative. The two of them, he said, should probably not be seen together, even way down there in Houma, given what the authorities in Huntingdon suspected him of and what Murray himself was planning to do. By that time, Murray felt that he had all the pointers Miller could give him where his intended actions were concerned anyway. He thanked the man, they shook hands, and he got into his Honda and headed north.

"You sure you don't want to deal with the man with extreme prejudice?" Daniel had asked again at one point.

"I'm sure," Murray had answered.

"Then you will need to be prepared to see than he doesn't die. Take a stun gun and some zip ties with you."

"One of those things that shoot wires?" Murray asked.

"No, one of the kind that you use up close and personal," Daniel said. "You will need to confront him somewhere in close quarters and jab him with the thing before he can get his hands on you."

"And the zip ties?"

"Have some small ones and some large ones with you. Once you have him down, use them to bind his wrists and ankles, maybe put one around his knees. You might need to use one as a tourniquet once the shooting starts. It would be a good idea to get a book on anatomy and refresh your memory where the circulatory system is concerned. You definitely don't want to hit an artery. You could likely pick up a used textbook at a Goodwill store somewhere. Don't check one out at a library, and don't order anything off the internet. In fact, don't use your computer for anything you're planning to do. When you've taken care of your problem, they'll no doubt check it to see what you've been looking at."

Murray had nodded silently and then asked, "Anything else?"

"Don't use the vehicle you usually drive when you make the trip back to Huntingdon to do the job. Get yourself something that's an inconspicuous gray, and make sure it has no scrapes or dents that would make it easily identifiable. Don't let anyone know you have a second vehicle, and like everything else—and I mean everything—get rid of it when the job is done. Wipe it down with bleach before you do. And don't put your real name on the title."

After a pause he had asked, "Any questions?"

That's when Murray had suggested they go to lunch. Now, he found himself once again on I-59 in the middle of Alabama and wondering whether he should push on or find a hotel, get a good night's sleep and start out fresh in the morning. He chose to push on for a little while yet, and his mind kept going back to the first thing Miller had told him: *be somewhere else and look like someone else.* The first part of that was simple enough. He would go out to somewhere near Pittsburg or down to somewhere near Philadelphia and set up an office for six months or so, come back to Huntingdon every other week to take care of his practice there. Philadelphia sounded more appealing for some reason, and he spent a mile or two wondering why. No matter, wherever he chose to go, he would make acquaintances in his new environment that would vouch for his presence there when he was really in Huntingdon doing what needed to be done. Just exactly how he would go about that, he didn't know, but that was a problem that could be worked out in time.

At the moment, *look like someone else* was the problem on his mind. The first time he had ever seen Daniel Miller, the young man had had long hair and a beard. He could let his hair grow, he supposed, maybe pull it up in the back into a little ponytail, but a beard? It would take him months to produce enough whiskers to cover his chin, and they would be sparse, white and scraggly. Wear a fake one maybe? Where would he get one? How much would a really realistic looking one cost? Too many questions without answers.

He began to nod, and his eyes began to close. He realized what was happening and raised his head with a jerk, opening his eyes wide and blinking. A sign showed a Pilot Travel Center to be at the next exit, and he took the ramp gladly. His fuel gauge needle was hovering just above the *E* anyway, and the coffee he had purchased at his last stop was making demands, so much so that he went into the store and used the restroom before fueling up. Tired to the point of exhaustion, he had taken care of his problem, come back out of the store, filled up and returned the nozzle to its place before he realized he had used his debit card. Use cash, Miller had said. Not so easy for someone who was used to using cards, and cards were so much more convenient.

Murray shook his head to clear it and made a decision. He got into the Honda, backed away from the pump and pulled into a slot at the edge of the parking lot and facing away from the lights. A good enough place to sleep for an hour or so, he thought, and he wouldn't have to spend money on a room or deal with hotel clerks. It seemed like a win-win situation. The clock on the instrument panel read 9:02.

* * * *

Murray woke up a little after midnight, went into the store to use the restroom again and made another decision. He wasn't going to stop at any more hotels on the way back to Huntingdon. His only stops would be to get a snack if he got hungry, to refuel when the need arose or to use a restroom. The last, he realized, could be made less frequent if he cut back on his consumption of coffee, and he left without buying any.

He headed north on I-59 again. When he caught I-40 east just west of Knoxville, it was four in the morning. He pushed on, his mind mostly on getting home, getting a shower and getting into bed. Traffic was sparse, and he was making good time. He was taking the same route back north that he had used going south, he knew—something Daniel Miller had advised against—but it didn't bother him. When he eventually did what he was planning to do, this trip would likely be six months or more in the past. Let them check his computer, his checking account, whatever. He would take Miller's advice and use his computer for business only from now on, and if they wanted to know why his debit card had been used in Birmingham, Alabama, on whatever date this was (he had lost track of time) he would think up a reason by then that would send investigators chasing their tails. Six months was enough time to find the answers to whatever questions came up.

He smiled into the darkness beyond his headlights, a smile that suggested grim determination had set in. He would do what he intended to do to end the corruption that was one Officer James Hartman, and then he would put it behind him and get on with his life. Miller had said it wouldn't bother him unless he let it, and he had already made up his mind that he wouldn't let it.

Cities and exits to cities flashed by, and he ignored them all, caught I-81 east of Knoxville and felt like he was finally heading north although the highway actually ran northeast. When he crossed over into Virginia at Bristol, it was after six A.M. The world was beginning to wake up, and traffic got heavier with people heading out to their jobs. An hour and a half later, he took the Grahams Forge exit and stopped at a

Loves to refuel, use the restroom and grab a cheddar sausage and a small coffee for breakfast. Even with the cold water he splashed on his face, he made the rest of the trip home in a kind of mental fog. When the door of his garage descended behind him at a little past 1:30 in the afternoon, he folded his hands on the top of the steering wheel, laid his forehead against them and fell asleep. Some fifteen or twenty minutes later, he woke with a jerk, staggered into his bedroom, tossed his jacket on a chair, kicked off his shoes and fell into bed. A shower would have to wait.

* * * *

It was at least a mildly refreshed Murray who pulled into his usual parking spot behind the homeplace at 8:30 that evening. A quick shower and a fresh set of clothes had done wonders, and the sports jacket he wore, though a bit shabby, was one of his best. Janet's eyes went wide when he stepped through the door of the mudroom. She met him in the middle of the kitchen with the full-body press and the lip-bruising kiss she had said would be waiting when he got back. Then she pulled his head against hers and held him tightly for several minutes.

"I thought you weren't getting back until tomorrow evening?" she said and leaned back far enough to look him in the eye.

"We got finished with our business more quickly than I thought we would."

"We," she said, and he smiled. "Will you be doing business with this person regularly?"

Murray shook his head. "No, just this one time."

203

She studied his face for several seconds, then took him by the hand and led him into the living room. The television was on, and she picked up the remote and muted it, then pulled him down to sit with her on the sofa.

"Anything new going on here?" he asked.

Janet smiled. "Janie's got a boyfriend."

"A boyfriend? Who is he?"

"His name is Charles Bond, and he's…"

"The Chief of Police down in Mount Union," he finished for her.

"Yes. Do you know him?" she asked.

"I know of him," Murray told her, trying to keep the concern he felt from showing. *And he could prove to be a complication,* went through his mind. *Him and his friend Gray Ballard, a man who has been known to find clues where there were virtually none.* Having the two of them connected to the family even remotely would increase the need to be careful considerably, and Murray had come to feel like he was part of the family. He pulled his mind back to what Janet was saying with difficulty. She was telling him how Janie and Bond had met, something about an altercation in the parking lot of the American Legion down there in Mount Union.

"Charles, that's what she calls him, Charles. He got called out to break it up just as she was leaving her shift. From what I understand, she saw him, and he saw her, and it was something at first sight. She hasn't called it love yet. I was surprised that she would have anything to do with a policeman, given the problem she's been having with Hartman. Maybe it's like they said on one of the reruns I watched recently. The heart wants what the heart wants. I've never seen her so happy, and I'm happy for her."

When Murray failed to comment, she asked, "Well, aren't you going to say anything?"

"I'm happy for her, too," he said, "but wasn't this kind of quick?"

"They're not *engaged*, Murray. They've only gone out twice, but it looks to me like it could develop into something. She'll be thirty soon. It's high time she found somebody."

"Like I found you?" he asked and leaned to brush a kiss across her lips.

"I think it was me who did the finding," she corrected and smiled.

"And you're glad you did?"

"And I'm so glad I did."

Her answer made him smile and made him a bit uneasy at the same time. He intended to leave town for a week at a time in the near future and to commit a rather heinous crime before he came back to stay permanently. How would she feel when he informed her of his plans? Worse yet, what would she think of him if she somehow learned of what he had done when the deed itself was in the past?

For the time being, he pushed such thoughts out of his mind. At the moment, he needed a little distraction, and the way Janet was leaning toward him, he knew she needed a little, too.

Chapter Ten

Murray kept his intentions to himself through the rest of November and all of December. He spent Thanksgiving at the homeplace with Janet and the two of her children who were still on this side of the Atlantic and got a little better acquainted with Russ Junior's wife Kathy and baby Madison Louise. Both of them tended to be quite shy, the wife saying nothing more than "Hello" to him all afternoon and the baby hiding her face against her mother's breast every time he spoke to her. And then, of course, there was Janie's boyfriend, Charles Bond, Chief of Police in Mount Union some twelve miles away. Murray had thought he would be nervous around the man, but Bond turned out to be so unassuming and friendly that the two of them got along fine.

In late December, he made several trips down to the Philadelphia area, careful to make sure nobody knew he had ever left town, and finally settled on West Chester, Pennsylvania, county seat of Chester County, as the place he wanted to spend some time. He managed to find an office space for rent much like the one he had there in Huntingdon, laid out the money for a six-month lease and outfitted it with some second-hand furnishings. Going into Philadelphia proper would have been a bit much, he figured, given the traffic and the crime. He caught himself smiling mentally at that last thought, considering the crime he was planning to commit in the not too distant future. His office being where it was, he had easy access to it off I-76, the Pennsylvania Turnpike, for those legitimate trips that would bring him down to do business and take him back home, and also fairly easy access to US 30, the route that he would use when the time came. No way could he ever use the Turnpike when he went back to do the deed. There was too great a possibility of witnesses, to say nothing of security cameras.

* * * *

He spent Christmas alone with Janet at the homeplace. It was Russ Junior's year to spend the holiday with his in-laws, and Janie and Charles Bond had been invited to dinner at Gray and Anna Ballard's home in Mount Union. When Janet told him about the arrangements, just the mention of Gray Ballard's name made Murray feel a little queasy.

He broke the news of his plans to Janet on New Years Day, a Wednesday. They were sitting at her kitchen table having coffee, Murray in his usual place and Janet to his right this time. "I've taken out a six-month lease for office space down in Chester County, and I'll be going down there for a while."

"Where is Chester County?" she asked.

"It's down near Philadelphia, just west of Philly actually."

Her frown told him she wasn't liking the idea.

207

"Why are you renting office space in Chester County? You never mentioned the idea before," she said.

Good question, Murray thought. How do I explain this without really explaining it? He reached to cover her hand where it was resting on the table, and she pulled it back.

"I don't know if I can answer that question to your satisfaction. Things have been going well lately. Life has been good, and I just feel like I need to give something back, and I think there are more people down around Philadelphia that need legal help and can't afford it than there are around here."

"There are plenty of people right here in Huntingdon County who need legal help and can't afford it," she disagreed. "Why can't you stay and help the folks around here?"

All he could do was shrug and say, "It's just something I feel like I have to do."

"So, you're gonna be down there next to a big city helping people who can't afford to pay you. Does that mean you're gonna be working *pro bono*?"

"If I have to, until I can build up a client base or until I can maybe get a position as a public defender."

"And where will you get the money to live on until then?" she asked.

"I still have some of what I got from the wrongful death suit I won against the city when Randall was killed. I've lived frugally. And then there's most of what I got for the house. I'll do alright," Murray assured her.

"What about me?" Janet asked. "What will I do without you here for six months while you're gone?"

"I won't be gone for six months!" he said, and

then, "I'm sorry. I should have been more clear. I'll just be going down there every other week. I'll be leaving on Sunday evening or early Monday morning and coming back on Friday. We will be together every other week."

"So, you'll be leaving on Monday of next week?" she asked.

He answered with a nod.

"And you'll be back Friday evening, and you'll come and see me as soon as you get back?"

Another nod.

"And you'll call me every night while you're gone and tell me how your day went?"

She looked so serious that he was almost afraid to smile.

"I'll call you every night before I go to bed."

"Well, we better make the best of the time we have together then," Janet said, standing and pushing back here chair. She took him by the hand and led him toward the sofa. "You better do some distracting before I get upset and send you back to town for the afternoon."

* * * *

He stayed in Huntingdon for the weekend. Given Janet's reaction to his plans, he thought it best to spend as much time with her as he could before he left. She sent him off late Sunday evening with one of her full body presses and lip-numbing kisses. He backed out of his garage before daylight on Monday morning, took Penn Avenue out to Route 22, caught the 522 bypass around Mount Union and got on the Turnpike at the

Fort Littleton exchange. He couldn't help but feel a little apprehensive, launching this new phase in his life and knowing what he was planning to do at the end of it. Would he have the skills—or the luck—by then to pull it off and still be a free man like Daniel Miller, or would he mess it up and end up...? He left the question unanswered and concentrated on his driving.

Be somewhere else when it happens, Daniel Miller had advised him. That part of the plan was underway. Look like someone else when you do it, now, how to do that was still a mystery to be solved. Leaving Huntingdon on Penn Avenue, he passed the place where he and Janet had witnessed the death of Duane Runk. Something seemed to nag at the back of his mind, but he was too focused on his destination for anything to come clear. It would not be until several weeks later, and with the help of Officer James Hartman himself, that a solution to the mystery would begin to emerge.

His first week in his new office went as well as or possibly a little better than Murray could have expected. He sat and read a John Grisham novel through Monday afternoon and all day Tuesday and Wednesday. It seemed appropriate, a lawyer reading about a lawyer. No one in need of legal aid came in until late Thursday afternoon. Then a mother showed up with a teenage son who had gotten caught with a small amount of meth, not enough to be accused of being a dealer but enough to get him in trouble with the law. She was a single mother and lived on a fixed income and couldn't pay much, she said. Her son was a good boy who had just fallen in with the wrong crowd. She had to have him in court the next day, and she was desperate. Murray agreed to take the case *pro bono*.

"I saw it as a golden opportunity," he told Janet when he got out to the homeplace late Friday evening. With no appointments pending, he had been able to leave for home immediately after his first ever court appearance in Chester County. "I wore my shabbiest pair of pants and my most faded shirt, that sports coat I have with the slightly frayed cuffs and collar. The judge took one look at my clothes and ask me to step back into his chambers when we got my client's case out of the way. You are now looking at a public defender for those indigent individuals in Chester County who break the law and don't have enough sense to get away with their crime or to make certain their crime nets them enough in capital gains to afford an attorney."

Janet's laughter was music to his ears. She had met him at the door of the mudroom and favored him with the full-body press and lip-numbing kiss she had promised.

"How was your week?" he asked.

"Oh, the usual," she answered. "Go to work, get off work, come home and have supper and wait for your call."

"I missed you, too," he admitted and leaned in for a distraction. And so, the evening went.

* * * *

His second week in Chester County, the judge loaded him up with cases until his eyes were burning from reading small print, and he was to the point of exhaustion when the court days ended. After a supper of pizza, which he picked up on his way to his motel room, and a quick shower on Thursday evening, he called Janet and told her about this day.

"I sincerely hope that this week wasn't an indication of what I'll be facing for the next five and a half months."

Janet chuckled. "Poor baby. Did him bite off more than him can chew?"

Murray matched her chuckle. "You're a hard woman, Mrs. Hockenberry."

For several seconds, there was silence on the other end of the line.

"Are you there?" he asked.

"Yes," she said, "but I'd rather be Janet."

"My apologies. Janet it is. How was your day?"

They established a routine. When he was in Chester County, he called her every evening, usually sometime around nine o'clock but sometimes earlier, depending on his mood and how the day had gone. As soon as he got back to Huntingdon, he took care of whatever needed to be done at his apartment and then went out to the homeplace every evening, stayed until bedtime and called Janet when he got back to town. Somehow, his safety and security had become of utmost importance to her. One week in Chester County handling cases that had been assigned to him, and one week in Huntingdon serving clients who had made contact with him and set up an appointment by phone. The routine was interrupted in early February by a snowstorm that closed the Turnpike for two days. Other than that little glitch, things went along fine until Officer James Hartman, apparently emboldened by the grand jury's failure to hand down an indictment, began to harass Janie again.

Now that she and her mother lived at the homeplace, which was north of town, she could no longer take the round-about route up toward Alexandria and down Route 22 and avoid going through town. Hartman seemed to make a habit of waiting for her at the city limits whenever he suspected she would be coming by. During the first week in March, when Murray was in Chester County, he pulled her over three days in a row and accused her of one thing or another—reckless driving, speeding, texting while driving, none of which she was doing—and wrote her out a warning. On Thursday of that week, she had had enough, and he made the mistake of pulling her over and asking her out again.

"You're not my type," Janie told him.

"And what type would that be?" Hartman asked snidely. "Hollywood pretty boys with lots of money and fancy cars?"

The second question surprised her. She wondered briefly if the fact that she had lived in California was common knowledge around town or if he had been checking up on her.

"No," Janie said, looking pointedly at his bald head, "men with hair and a personality. Men who are secure enough in their manhood that they can take no for an answer and don't stalk me when I've turned them down."

There had been no smile on Hartman's face, but her comments definitely brought about a change in his expression. He went back to his unit with her license, registration and proof of insurance and left her sitting by the side of the road for more than fifteen minutes, a ploy he seemed to use often. When he finally returned, he handed her a ticket for a hundred and eighty-nine dollars.

Janie looked at it and said, "I'm not signing this."

"Sign it or I put you in cuffs and take you to the station."

She scribbled her name on the line provided and handed the pad back to him. He tore off the ticket and handed it to her, said, "Have a nice day, bitch," then turned and walked away.

She was furious, and when her shift at the VFW south of Mount Union was over, she showed the ticket to Charles Bond and told him about Hartman's behavior.

"A hundred and eighty-nine dollars, and I wasn't doing anything wrong! I wasn't speeding! I wasn't driving recklessly! And I can't even read whatever it is he scribbled on the line where it supposedly tells what I got ticketed for! When did they pass a law against *in*sulting an officer of the law? Maybe I shouldn't have said what I did, but he had stopped me four days in a row, and I'd had enough. My glovebox is half-full of warning tickets already."

Bond remained calm. "I'll take this up to Huntingdon tomorrow and have a talk with Chief Coder. This can't be right."

But according to Chief Coder, it *was* right. "Tell your lady-friend to drive safely and stay within the posted speed limit, and we'll get along fine. The ticket stands." Then looking Bond in the eye, "I back the men under my command, don't you?"

Murray heard about the incident first thing on Friday evening when he got out to the homeplace. He listened to Janie's version of the story and had no doubt that she was telling the truth. It was vintage Hartman. Something obviously had to be done, and the sooner the better. The question of how to look like someone else still had not been answered, but it would be by the time he headed back to Chester County.

On Tuesday of the following week, Janie spent the night with Charles Bond. Apparently, things were really heating up between the two of them, and since the electric company had put outdoor lights up around the homeplace, her mother was okay with her not coming home at night. Bond had already donned his uniform and left for work when she got into her vehicle to go home and the thing wouldn't start. She called her mother's cell phone.

"I'm at work," Janet told her. "I can't leave now. This is one of our busiest times. Call Murray. If he doesn't have any appointments on his calendar, I'm sure he'll be happy to come and get you."

Murray agreed to help without hesitation. Before he left his office, he made arrangements to have Janie's Malibu retrieved and towed to the dealership across the river. His mind on his mission, he wasn't paying much attention to his surroundings when he passed the courthouse and headed out of town on Penn Avenue. He had crossed the creek east of Blair Park and was a good way up the hill when lights started flashing behind him—Hartman, practically on his bumper. Murray frowned, shook his head and pulled to the side of the road. When Hartman walked up, he wound the window down but kept his eyes straight forward.

"License, registration and proof of insurance," Hartman demanded, and he handed the documents over. Hartman walked back to his unit, and the waiting game began. Murray was surprised when it lasted only a few minutes this time, but the wait was plenty long enough for him to realize that his vehicle was sitting in almost the same spot were Duane Runk's Chrysler had been sitting the night the man died. The thing that had been nagging at the back of his mind every time he passed this particular spot became crystal clear, and he knew the answer to the second question: how to look like someone else when the time came.

"Haven't seen you around much lately, sis," Hartman said when he came back and handed Murray his papers. "Where you been keepin' yerself?"

Murray continued to stare through the windshield and gave him no answer. Hartman gave a snort of derision and turned and walked away. Murray put his Honda in gear and pulled back onto the roadway—and he was smiling. How long would it take to collect the materials he would need? he wondered. No matter. Now that he knew the answer to the question, he was determined to be ready soon. Hartman was obviously out of control, and the sooner the job got done the better.

Chapter Eleven

It had been a wet, miserable morning, and the afternoon hadn't been much better. Damn! He hated April! Bring on the May flowers the teachers all talked about when he was in grade school. His shift finally over, Officer James Hartman lumbered through the front door of the cabin he had built for himself southwest of Huntingdon off Route 26, unbuckling his equipment belt and dropping it on a table just inside the door. The butt of his Glock hit the wood with a thud, adding another dent to the myriad of others that already marred the tabletop, and he began unbuttoning his uniform shirt. The last button undone, he shrugged it off and tossed it at an overstuffed chair. It caught on the arm for a few seconds and then slowly fell to the floor. He stood there in his t-shirt and gave it a mental cussing. Even little things in life were against him, he thought, little things that all added up to a major irritation. In his mind, nothing had gone right for him in years.

He raised his arms high above his head in a stretch, twisted his head from side to side and popped his neck. Arms still raised, he caught a movement behind him out of the corner of his eye. Before he could react, something jabbed him in the lower back and sent a jolt through his entire body that shook him to the core. He toppled forward onto the right side of his face, hitting the floor with enough force to rattle the windows. The impact brought the taste of blood to his mouth. He heard footsteps and wanted to push up and defend himself, but his muscles wouldn't work. A few seconds later, he was hit with the stun gun again, and then things really went south.

A tall figure in tan Carhartt coveralls, gloves, a ski mask and some kind of goggles leaned over him and put the muzzle of his own Glock about an inch from the trigger finger of his left hand which was splayed out on the floor. The big man pulled the trigger, and Hartman watched in horror as his finger seemed to explode and disappear. Blood began to pour out of the stub that was left. He wanted to react, to move, to scream, but he couldn't. His mouth opened wide, but no sound came out. The stun gun hit him in the back again, the next two rounds went through the ball joints of his shoulders, and he heard something that sounded like "Aaaah-ha-ha-ha!" and realized that it was coming from him.

The man in the coveralls laid the Glock on the floor a few inches from Hartman's nose and took a small zip tie from a belt he wore over his coveralls. Another jolt from the stun gun, and the man gathered his wrists together behind his back and bound them tightly. He checked the shoulder wounds he had inflicted, saw that they weren't bleeding too profusely and went about his business. Another jab with the stun gun and the man kicked his legs apart. Hartman felt the muzzle of his Glock against the inside of his left knee and then a bullet tearing through the joint, and he could do nothing but suck air between his clinched teeth.

This couldn't be happening, Hartman thought. This had to be a nightmare and he would wake up soon. But a bullet tearing through his right knee left no doubt in his mind that it *was* happening, and it *was* real, *very* real. Two more rounds, one through each ankle, and his assailant laid the Glock aside again. More zip ties, one pulled tight around each leg just above the shattered knee and one to bind the knees together, one around the shredded ankles. Pain was everywhere, pain like he had never known before, and he couldn't imagine it getting any worse.

His task apparently finished, the man in the Carhartt coveralls returned the Glock to its holster, walked into Hartman's line of vision and just stood there, ten feet away, arms crossed over his chest, the stun gun in his left hand. When the effects of the stun gun wore off enough, Hartman lifted his head and stared at him. In addition to the ski mask and goggles, he saw that the man was also wearing a blue surgical mask, its strings wrapped around large black buttons sewn onto the ski mask, and a New York Yankees baseball cap. There was absolutely no way to tell who the guy was.

"Who the hell are you and why are you doing this?" Hartman demanded.

The man never spoke a word. His only answer was to uncross his arms and hold his hands out to the side palms up, a gesture that suggested, "Why not?"

"You'll never get away with this, you son-of-a-bitch!" Hartman threatened—or promised; he wasn't sure which. "Get me some help before I bleed to death, dammit!" He was beginning to feel faint, whether from shock or from loss of blood, he didn't know.

For answer, the man nodded his head—almost bowed—and walked past him, stopping long enough to bend down and pat him on the shoulder, and went right out the door. The pain from the pat on the shoulder was the last straw. Hartman's eyes rolled back in his head, and he passed out.

* * * *

The 911 call came in some thirty minutes after the assailant left Hartman's place. Someone who sounded like an elderly man or like he had a sore throat said: "Officer James Hartman has been injured. Send an ambulance to his place ASAP."

"What is your name, sir?" the operator asked, "Please, give me your name and current location," but the line had already gone dead.

Through a hasty series of calls, it was determined that James Hartman lived outside the jurisdiction of the Police Department of the city of Huntingdon, so after an ambulance was dispatched, a call went to the County Sheriff's Department. Little was happening at that particular hour, so Sheriff Kauffman himself was notified of the situation, and he showed up at Hartman's place just in time to see the EMTs bringing the injured man out the front door, strapped to a gurney.

"What happened here?" he asked.

"Somebody really did a job on this guy," one of them answered. "He's got bullet wounds in both shoulders, both knees, both ankles, and the index finger on his left hand is gone."

"What!" Kauffman responded. The EMT took it for the exclamation it was and just shook his head.

"I'd say he must have really pissed somebody off to get this kind of treatment."

"Is he awake?" Kauffman asked. "Can I talk to him, ask him a few questions?"

"He's been in and out, and he's in a lot of pain, and we gave him a shot of morphine. I don't know how coherent he'll be, but you can give it a shot if you're quick about it."

So saying, they stopped at the rear of the ambulance and let Kauffman have his time. He stepped up beside the gurney and asked, "Who did this to you, Hartman?"

It had been some forty-five minutes since the last bullet went through his ankle, and Hartman had lain on the floor of his cabin in agony, drifting in and out of consciousness and trying to remember details. He was wearing tan work boots, the man was, about a size thirteen or fourteen, he thought, and tan coveralls. Where had he seen boots and coveralls that color before? Where had he seen a guy that size? And eventually, a vision of Duane Runk came floating up from the back of his mind. Duane Runk, the man that had refused to cooperate and got what he deserved for it, accidentally or not. Now, the tan coveralls and the tan boots and the big guy that was wearing them in his head and the shot of morphine in his veins got all mixed together, and he answered, "Duane Runk."

"Duane Runk?" Kauffman and both EMTs said at the same time.

"Duane Runk is dead," one of them said.

"Duane Runk," Hartman repeated and passed out again.

"We better get him to J. C. Blair," one of the

221

EMTs said, and the two of them shoved the gurney into the back of the ambulance.

* * * *

Chief Alex Coder of the Huntingdon Police Department and several officers, some in uniform, some not, were waiting when the EMTs rolled the gurney into the ER at J. C. Blair Memorial. The lot of them swarmed the gurney and brought it to a standstill. By then, the sheet covering James Hartman had soaked up spots of blood from both shoulder wounds, the knees and the ankles.

"What the hell happened?" Chief Coder demanded. "We were told he had been injured. I expected maybe a gunshot wound, but this... this is ridiculous!"

"Both shoulders, both knees, both ankles and the index finger of his left hand," one of the EMTs offered.

"His trigger finger?" one of the uniformed officers asked.

"If he's left-handed, yes," the same EMT answered.

"Who the hell would do a thing like this?" a second uniform asked.

"That's what I intend to find out," Sheriff Kauffman said, coming into the ER and joining the group. "I've already got my people working on it."

"Like hell!" Chief Coder swore. "Somebody does this to one of ours, the investigation is ours! Thank you, Sheriff, but we'll take it from here."

"The crime scene's out of your jurisdiction," Kauffman reminded him.

"I don't give a damn where it is! The

investigation is ours! Harris, Schueck, head out there and tape the place off," Coder ordered. "I'll be out there as soon as we know whether Hartman's gonna make it or not. Call forensics on the way. Have them dust for prints, look for DNA. You know the drill."

"Okay, it's yours," Sheriff Kauffman conceded, throwing up his hands. He turned and headed for the door. He already had more cold cases in a file back at the office than one man wanted to have in a lifetime, and this crime looked like one of those. Something like this, he thought, had to be carefully planned and executed. Whoever had committed the crime would have been careful to leave no fingerprints or DNA behind, had likely left a few false clues behind and was long gone. Coder and his department had a tough job ahead of them. They wanted the investigation; let them have it.

Two of the uniformed officers broke away from the group and headed for the door.

"We need to get him into an exam room," a young woman in scrubs said, and the rest of the group parted and watched as the EMTs pushed the gurney through the usual double doors.

"Why the hell would somebody do this to him?" Coder asked.

It was obviously a rhetorical question, but one of the younger officers made the mistake of answering it.

"He's not very popular around town. Me and Horne have heard lots of complaints from one place and another. He likes to push things to the limit."

"What?" Coder responded, red-faced and angry. "What did you say, Bilger? You puttin' down a fellow officer that's fighting for his life?"

"Just sayin," the young officer answered.

"And you, Horne? You agree with your partner?"

Horne answered with a shrug, and Chief Coder looked from one of them to the other, his temper rising.

"The two of you, get back out there on patrol. We'll let you know if you need to attend the funeral of one of our own or not."

The two officers hotfooted it toward the door, their Chief glaring after them. Two officers remained, one in uniform and one in civvies. The three of them took seats and waited.

* * * *

By the time Chief Coder joined Harris and Shueck at Hartman's place, the two of them had already discovered all the clues they were going to find—a boot print under a front window and tire tracks that led around to the back of the house.

"Right over here," Officer Erin Schueck said, leading her boss over to the window. "Someone stepped in wet dirt. Looks like about a size fourteen. Has a wedge cut out of the left heel. We find out who owns these boots, and we've got our man."

"Make a cast of it," Coder ordered gruffly.

"Back here," Harris called from the corner of the house and pointed toward the backyard, such as it was. Mostly a smattering of grass and half-dried mud, perfect for leaving tire tracks. The Chief and Shueck joined him.

"Someone, likely our assailant, pulled around back here, likely to hide his vehicle so Hartman wouldn't see it when he got home. I think he usually parks out front where those two ruts are. You can see here," he said pointing, "where a vehicle was parked and then how it reversed and drove away. There's another boot print or two if you think we need to cast them all."

"Do it," Coder said. "Collect everything you can. What have they found in the house?"

"Nothing," Shueck said.

"Nothing?" Coder's tone and inflection suggested that was impossible.

"They dug what's left of the bullet that severed his finger out of the floor, but the others seem to have shattered on impact or have yet to be found. Don't suppose the doctor took any out of Hartman?"

"Just fragments, nothing useful," Coder answered.

"Well, the last time I talked to the guys inside, they hadn't found anything useful either. No fingerprints, nothing to check for DNA, nothing. Whoever did this wore gloves and was very careful not to leave anything behind that we could use to identify him, so careful, as a matter of fact, that we may never know who did this."

"Bullshit!" Chief Coder exploded. "We're gonna find this son-of-a-bitch if it takes all of our time and the Department budget for the next ten years. Keep looking. Go over this place with a magnifying glass if you have to. Find something." He stalked into the house to harass the forensics team.

* * * *

He pulled off the gloves, the ski mask and surgical mask before he left Hartman's yard, tossed them in the passenger's seat along with the Yankees cap. He went south on 26 and turned east on 994. A few miles past the turnoff to the little town of Entrikan, he pulled his Impala to the side of the road, pushed the seat to the full-back position and managed to get the boots and the several pairs of socks that made them fit off his feet. With the distinctive wedge he had cut out of one of the heels, the boots were one thing that could definitely identify him as Hartman's assailant if he was caught with them in his possession. Extra pairs of socks he didn't think would be any problem. He took the .380 semi-automatic he had purchased on the street in Philadelphia, and hadn't needed, out of his pocket and put it in the glove compartment. Then he struggled out of the coveralls, the quilted jacket, the insulated underwear, the extra pairs of pants and the extra shirts he was wearing to give himself bulk and tossed all of it into the backseat. He slipped on a pair of loafers he had brought along, and he was Murray McCartney again, wearing his usual white, long-sleeved shirt and dress pants. One of his better sports jackets waited in the backseat.

He pulled the seat back up to a comfortable driving position, then used scissors he had brought for the purpose and cut out the padding he had sewn to the inside of the ski mask, the black buttons off the outside of it.

He checked his watch and realized it was time to make the call. From the glove compartment, he took a burner phone and dialed 911. When the operator came on and asked what his emergency was, using a guttural whisper he had been practicing, he said, "Officer James Hartman has been injured. Send an ambulance to his place ASAP." She was still talking when he broke the connection, tossed the phone back into the glove compartment and slammed it shut.

He put the vehicle in gear and pulled out onto the road again. By the time he got to the town of Three Springs, the boots were gone, tossed into the woods, one on either side of the road some six or eight miles apart. The dozen or more cardboard inserts he had cut out and stuck into the boots to make himself taller he kept until he could find a dumpster someplace farther on. By the time he got to Orbisonia, the black buttons and pieces of the padding from the ski mask were strewn for miles along the roadway, as was the crumpled-up surgical mask. He chastised himself for littering, and he supposed it was possible that someone might be able to get DNA off them, but they would have to find them first, figure out what they were and link them to him. Somehow, he doubted that would ever happen, and he felt it best that he not be caught with them in his possession. He didn't think the goggles presented a problem, but he intended to get rid of them eventually. When would he ever be likely to need them again?

At Orbisonia, he caught Route 522 and followed it to Burnt Cabins, where he turned off and took some back roads through Cowan's Gap to avoid the mountains. He caught US 30 at Fort Louden and took it into Chambersburg. There he left US 30 briefly, went out Main Street and caught Wayne Avenue where he knew a Goodwill store to be. He threw the coveralls, gloves, extra clothing and socks, the quilted jacket, the

Yankees cap and ski mask into a container at the back of the store and made his way back to US 30.

He had driven the route many times before, practice runs and always in his Honda, but this time it was nerve-wracking. Not so much because of any possibility he might get pulled over but because what happened at the end of it this time was crucial. If somebody saw him going back into his room when nobody was supposed to know he had ever left it, his alibi could be blown in an instant. It would be another two and a half hours until he got through Lancaster and back to West Chester, and he wouldn't know what would happen until he got there.

In Lancaster, he stopped for fuel at a place where he had never stopped before (thank you very much for that bit of advice, Daniel Miller), used the restroom and bought a cup of coffee. As a precaution against witness identification and security cameras, he put on a Baltimore Orioles baseball cap he had bought earlier and kept his head down. He took advantage of the trash can between the gas pumps to get rid of the cardboard insoles and the extra zip ties. After some hesitation, he wiped his fingerprints off the little electric lockpick he had purchased through the mail and discarded it also. He had no intention of ever using the thing again, so why take the chance of getting caught with it in his possession? Which reminded him that he still had the goggles, and he tossed them in on top of the lockpick. Looking around to make sure no one had been watching, he nodded grimly, got back in the Impala and pushed on. He had bought the vehicle several months before from a lady whose husband had died and had been paying her a hundred dollars a month to leave it parked in her garage. The lady was currently visiting her sister and brother-in-law up in Scranton. In his only departure from the advice Daniel Miller had given him, he had put his name on the title. If no one in Huntingdon had ever seen him driving it, how could it be used against him when he finally brought it home? The Honda was old and couldn't have many miles left in it. The Impala had only had one owner before him, and the odometer had less than thirty thousand miles on it—too nice a vehicle to throw away. And he suspected that Janet would love it.

Chapter Twelve

On Thursday morning, at Chief of Police Coder's insistence, the hospital cut back on the amount of morphine they were giving to Hartman and brought him out of his drug-induced fog, brought him out partially anyway. His bed was propped up into almost a sitting position, pillows took the pressure off his shattered shoulders and cushioned his knees and ankles, and yet he was anything but comfortable.

"How are you feeling today?" the Chief asked,

"How the hell do you think I'm feeling?" Hartman responded. "Pissed because I'm missing my tap dancing lessons?"

Coder attributed his surliness to the pain the man was feeling because of the reduction in his medication and let it slide.

"Do you have any idea who did this to you?" he asked.

Hartman frowned. "None whatsoever."

"When they were taking you out of your house, Sheriff Kauffman asked you who did this to you, and you said it was Duane Runk."

Hartman looked at the man like he'd lost his mind. "Duane Runk is dead."

"But that's the name you gave Kauffman when he

asked you who did this. Why would you say 'Duane Runk'?"

Hartman frowned for several minutes and reached back into the still foggy recesses of his mind. "He was a big guy, heavy-set like Runk and maybe as tall as me, maybe not. I was on the floor looking up, so maybe at that angle, he looked taller than he was. I can't be sure. And he was wearing boots and coveralls like Runk was wearing when... when it happened."

"Tan boots and coveralls with suspenders?" Coder asked.

"No, the coveralls had long sleeves, and he was wearing gloves, black leather ones." Hartman closed his eyes and concentrated. "And a black ski mask and some kind of goggles and one of those things doctors and nurses wear over their mouth and nose."

"A surgical mask?" Coder prompted. From a shirt pocket, he had taken out a small spiral notebook and pen, and he began to write things down.

"Yeah. It was blue."

"Anything else you can remember? Was he Caucasian, African American, Asian?"

"Don't know. The ski mask went down into his collar and covered his neck, and the goggles covered his eyes. None of his skin was showing."

Coder looked over the notes he had written and realized he still had nothing. "Did he say anything? Was there anything strange about his behavior?" he asked.

His eyes still closed, Hartman took a while to answer. "Never said a word, just kept jabbing me with that damned stun gun and putttin' bullets in me, and he was left-handed."

"Left-handed?" Coder echoed. "What makes you think he was left-handed?"

"When he emptied the clip and put my Glock back where he got it, he walked over to where I could see him and just stood there with his arms crossed, like he *wanted* me to see him. He was holding the stun gun in his left hand."

Left-handed, Coder thought, and jotted it down in his notebook. Not much of a clue given that ten to twelve percent of the world's population is left-handed. Still no place to start an investigation really.

"How in the hell did he get hold of your Glock?" Coder asked.

Hartman's face and neck turned a little red. "I dropped my equipment belt on the table just inside my front door. He got it out of my holster and put it back when he was finished with it."

"You don't put it in your gun safe when you're not wearing it?"

"Hell no! I never thought anybody would pull something like this. I'm an officer of the law, for god sakes. People are supposed to show us some respect."

Coder regarded the man in the bed silently for several seconds, thinking about the complaints he had dealt with over the years. "Respect is due where respect is given," he said.

"What the hell is that supposed to mean?" Hartman demanded.

"You've pissed off a lot of people over the years."

"Well, tough shit!" Hartman exclaimed. "I was just doin' my job."

Again, Coder regarded him silently for several

seconds. Given the man's attitude and the pain he was obviously in, the tack their conversation had taken was unlikely to get them anywhere.

"Okay, we've gotten off track here. Let's get back to the matter at hand. Forget about the man you saw," he suggested. "Just think about motive. Who do you think might want to do something like this to you?"

"I don't know, maybe some relative of Runk's. Maybe his brother?"

"Duane Runk didn't have a brother," Coder told him.

"An uncle, a nephew, a cousin then."

"No male relatives that live in the area, and none that comes anywhere near the size of the man you described."

Hartman gave the man a glare and remained silent, then closed his eyes.

"Come on!" the Chief coaxed. "Think! Who would do a thing like this? Has anybody threatened you?"

Hartman opened his eyes and cut them toward his boss. "Do you really even have to ask?" He gave the Chief several seconds to think about it, and the two of them said in unison: "Murray McCartney,"

* * * *

The man who had become the chief suspect in the maiming of Officer James Hartman managed to return the Impala to its place in the lady's garage, call an uber and get back into his motel room without being seen. He took a shower and then called Janet, and they spoke briefly. He told her he wasn't feeling one hundred percent, might be coming down with something, thought he'd turn in early. She told him to get well and wished him a good night. He woke up on Thursday feeling relieved and rested, which surprised him. Given what he had done the day before, he had expected to be tense and nervous. What he had done would only change him if he let it, Miller had told him. Maybe his subconscious was already pushing back against any change? Whatever. No time to dwell on yesterday. It was time to put the next phase of his plan into action.

Murray McCartney finished up at the courthouse in Chester County by noon on Friday and headed back to Huntingdon, getting there shortly after five o'clock as had become the usual. A patrol car was sitting across the street from his place, and he chose to ignore it. He swung his Honda down the alley, hit the button on his garage door opener, waited until the door reached its full height and drove in. By the time he had lowered the door and carried his suitcase into his apartment, someone was beating violently on the door of his office.

"It's the police! Open up!" a male voice yelled.

Murray set his suitcase down and opened the door into his office. Two uniformed officers were standing outside his office door, a male and a female, both looking grim.

"Open this damned door before I kick it in," the male growled. He was red-haired, red-faced and looked Irish. His nameplate said: HARRIS.

Murray had barely gotten the door unlocked when it was pushed forcefully inward. The edge of it hit him in the forehead. The world went a bit dark for a second or two and he saw stars. He felt hands jerk him outside, spin him around and press him against the plate glass window. Before he could object, handcuffs closed tightly around his wrists.

"You have the right to remain silent," the female officer began. "You have the right to an attorney…"

"I *am* an attorney," he managed to get out.

"Yeah, a sleazy one," Harris said, jerked him around by the arm and hustled him across the street to the patrol car. The female, a blonde with a short bob, opened the door, and Murray got a glimpse of her nameplate. It said: SHUECK.

"Get in," Harris ordered. Then he put a hand on the back of Murray's head, said, "Watch your head," and rammed it into the roof of the patrol car. Again, things went dark and Murray saw stars. This time, he felt a trickle of blood running from a cut near his hairline down into his eyebrow.

Harris slammed the door, and without another word, the two officers got into the front seat, Harris behind the wheel. Murray half expected him to hit the siren and peel out, but the ride to the police station was almost leisurely. Once there, they hustled him into an interrogation room with the usual two-way mirror in the wall next to the door, and Harris slammed him into a chair so hard the thing almost went over backward with him.

"Don't go anywhere," he said. "We'll be right back."

Murray lost track of time. His arms were cuffed behind him, so he wouldn't have been able to look at a wristwatch if he had been wearing one. He had dropped his cell phone and his keys on the table as the

passed through his apartment. There was no clock on
the wall. When Harris and Shueck finally came back
in, he guessed that he had been sitting there at least an
hour, his head throbbing and blood drying in his
eyebrow. Shueck walked around behind him, pushed
him forward and took off the cuffs.

"I've got one question for you," Harris said.
"What did you do? Tell us what you did."

Murray ignored him and rubbed at the red marks
the handcuffs had left around his wrists. Then he
pulled a small spiral notebook and pen out of the
breast pocket of his sports coat, opened it on the table
and began to write: *OH hb $1,000,000.*

"What the hell do you think you're doing?"
Harris demanded.

Murray ignored him and continued to write: *OH
cuffs $50,000.* And on the next line: *OH hb $1,000,000.*

"I asked you a question," Harris said and
whacked him on the back of the head.

"I'm making a record of what's happening so I'll
know the total amount of the lawsuit I intend to file
against you, the Police Department and the City of
Huntingdon for false arrest, physical and verbal abuse
and mental anguish," Murray told him.

"You ain't making a record of shit!" Harris
slapped the pen out of his hand and swiped the
notebook onto the floor. "Now tell us what you did!"

Murray stared straight ahead and said calmly,
"Pen and notebook, right here, right now." With the
here and the *now*, he stabbed the table with an index
finger.

"Tell us what you did," Shueck spoke for the first
time, her voice rather deep for a woman.

Murray stared straight ahead at his reflection in the mirror. "Pen and notebook, right here, right now," again stabbing the table with the index finger.

"You say that one more time, and I'll bounce you off the wall," Harris threatened.

"I wouldn't advise it," Murray told him. "That would cost you and the city another million." He stabbed the table with an index finger. "Pen and notebook, right here, right now."

Harris drew back his fist and Shueck said, "You'd better give them to him. We're not going to get anywhere like this."

She picked up the pen and notebook and laid them on the table. Murray pulled them over in front of himself and began making notations: *OH nb $50,000*, and on the next line: *OH hw $500,000.*

"What the hell does that mean?" Harris demanded.

"*OH* is you, Officer Harris," Murray explained and continued to write, "*nb* is notebook, just a little something to remind me what just happened here. The *$50,000* is for slinging my notebook onto the floor and the *$500,000* there is for the whack on the head. That's what that little fit of temper just cost you. You want to add some more?"

While he spoke, he was making another notation: *OH cw $5,000.*

"And that means?" Shueck asked politely.

"It means Officer Harris, cussword and what every cussword used from now on is going to cost you. If I, as a lawyer, can't use it in a court of law, you can't use it during this interrogation."

"This isn't an interrogation," Shueck said. "We just want to ask you a few questions."

237

Murray's response was a mirthless chuckle. "I have heard only one question so far and that was: *What did you do?* which was followed immediately with: *Tell us what you did.* I find both the question and the request to be a bit vague. You're going to have to be more specific. For instance, you might ask what did I do at some particular time and in some particular place."

"Alright, where were you on Wednesday of this week and what did you do?" she asked.

"On Wednesday? Let me think," he made a show of concentrating. "I was down in Chester County, this was my week to be down there, and… oh, yes. I woke up at about my usual time, which is between six-fifteen and six-thirty. My sinuses were so stopped up I could hardly breathe, and I had laryngitis. Couldn't utter a peep, which is not good when you're supposed to be representing someone in court at nine. I didn't know what to do, so I decided to just do what I always do in the morning. I made myself a cup of coffee. I have a Mr. Coffee in my apartment here in town, a four-cup that takes those little paper filters. I use Folgers Black Silk, and I have this little silver scoop I measure it with. One scoop makes two cups. The motel where I stay down there in Chester County has a Kurek, one of those things that takes pods and makes one cup at a time."

Officer Harris was beginning to show a little irritation at all the details, but Shueck was doing her best to remain calm.

"The thing doesn't make the coffee as hot as I like it, and the stuff doesn't have much flavor, in my opinion, but the management provides the pods, three a day, mostly something called Breakfast Blend, but I only have to use it every other week, so..." he shrugged and left the sentence unfinished. "Anyway, I get about half of the cup drank on Wednesday morning—that's the day we're talking about, right?—and I start coughing up these big green globs that look like a cross between yogurt and pudding, really nasty tasting stuff. They kind of reminded me of that slimy looking little green cartoon character that's involved in those advertisements for some kind of cough remedy on television. You know, the one the box falls on? You must have seen the commercial."

Here he paused and looked from one officer to the other, Harris standing next to him and Shueck in a chair on the other side of the table, but got no confirmation.

"Anyway, I must have coughed up a pint of the stuff, maybe more, running to the bathroom to spit it out every time I got a mouthful."

Shueck was beginning to look a little green herself and finally threw a hand over her mouth and ran from the room.

"Was it something I said?" Murray asked,

"Very funny, asshole," Harris said and followed her out of the room.

Murray pulled his notebook over in front of himself and made a notation for the cussword. Another $5,000, things were adding up.

Again, he had a long wait, likely another hour, but he had no way of knowing for sure. The room began to heat up, and he was in the process of removing his jacket when they came back in.

"Leave it on," Harris ordered.

"It's getting hot in here," Murray said, and Harris's face twisted into a grin.

"Ain't near as hot as it's gonna be before this is over. Leave it on, and let's hear the rest of your bullshit story."

Murray pulled his jacket back up over his shoulders, pulled his notebook over and made a notation for the cussword, another $5,000. Harris's face turned red and his cheeks bulged in anger, but he said nothing more.

"Now, where was I?" Murray asked when he had finished writing.

"You were about to finish a cup of coffee," Harris prompted, "and we've heard all we need to hear about the green stuff. Get on with it."

Shueck threw her partner a dark look and waited.

"When I finished coughing up… stuff," Murray started, "I found that I could speak after a fashion, kind of a raspy whisper, so when the time came, I went to the court house, met my client and we went up before the judge. I didn't get him off, by the way, but I did manage to get him a reduced sentence. When the judge heard my voice and saw the redness around my eyes, he realized I had a problem. He reassigned my cases to another public defender and told me to go home and take care of myself, get some rest and get well. I'm usually pretty tough, but I have to admit that whatever I had was kicking my butt. I stopped by a pharmacy and picked up a bottle of that green stuff that tastes like licorice and has a lot of alcohol in it. I took a dose when I got back to my room, sometime around eleven, I'd guess. I had a fever and wasn't tracking too well by then. When you have a nine o'clock court appointment, you don't always get up before the bench at nine o'clock, but I'm sure I was out of the courthouse by ten-thirty. Anyway, I took a dose of the stuff, then pulled off my jacket and shoes and lay down on the bed. I didn't know whether I was dead or alive until late that evening. That green stuff is twelve-hour, you know. When I finally woke up, my fever had broken, and my clothes were wet with sweat. I took a shower and got into some pajamas, took another dose of medicine and went back to bed, didn't wake again until seven Thursday morning."

Murray purposely left out the call he had made to Janet, the call he always made before he went to bed during his weeks in Chester County. Mention of her name would likely bring harassment down on her head, and he didn't want that.

"And you expect us to believe that bs?" Harris asked.

Murray grinned at the man. "You're learning," he said. "I bet you didn't mean brown sugar, and yes, I expect you to believe what I've told you. I believe the question was: 'Where were you on Wednesday of this week and what did you do?' Two questions, really, and I believe that I have answered both of them to the best of my ability."

Harris made a noise that sounded like *pisssh!* and began firing questions. What was the name of your client? What was he charged with? Was he guilty? What was the judge's name? What was the name of the person whose case was tried just before yours? What is the address of the courthouse in West Chester? What pharmacy did you stop at?

Murray answered them as quickly as they were

asked, refusing to answer the second and third ones because of attorney-client privilege. The fifth one he couldn't answer because he had been going over his client's file and hadn't been paying any attention to what was going on around him at the time. Six and seven rolled off his tongue like he was used to being asked the questions and answered them every day.

Harris seemed to have wound down, so he looked at Shueck. She was perspiring profusely, wisps of her blonde hair beginning to stick to her forehead. She nodded her head toward the door and headed that way. Harris returned her nod, beads of sweat popping out on his forehead and running down his face as well, and followed.

Murray started to remove his jacket, and Harris said, "Leave it on" as he went out the door.

Again, there was a wait of what he thought was about an hour. So, an hour to an hour and a half of questioning, three hours of sitting there alone and waiting for someone to come in and ask questions. It had to be at least ten P. M., he figured, and the temperature in the room had to be ninety or higher. Murray sat and waited and oozed body fluids into his clothing. Sweat ran down his cheeks and dripped onto his jacket.

When Harris and Shueck came back in, both of them had paper towels and almost immediately began daubing at their faces.

"Can I have one of those?" Murray asked and got no answer. "What is the temperature in here?" he asked.

Harris looked at Shueck and smiled.

"What is the temperature in here?" he repeated

calmly and in a normal tone, this time punctuating the *what* the *temperature* and the *here* by once again stabbing an index finger on the table.

Both officers ignored him, and he repeated the question and the stabbing.

"So, let's start again. Tell us where you were and what you did last Wednesday." This from Harris again.

"What is the temperature in here?" Murray repeated the question and the stabbing.

"It's 95 degrees," Shueck said and got a dark look from her partner.

Murray wrote in his notebook, the sweat on his hand smudging the page: *10 P.M. appox. Temp. 95 deg. $950,000.* "Go turn the air conditioner on now," he said. "Set it at 75 degrees."

Neither of the officers moved.

"Now!" he all but shouted, and Shueck headed out of the room.

"Watch your mouth and your tone," Harris warned.

Murray kept silent, staring at his reflection in the two-way mirror.

In less than a minute, Shueck was back.

"Okay, you got what you wanted," Harris said. "Now, let's start again. Where were you on Wednesday of this week, and what did you do?"

"This was my week to be in Chester County, so that answers the first half of your question—*again*. As for the second half, on Wednesday morning," Murray began, "I woke up at about my usual time, which is six-fifteen or six-thirty, with laryngitis…"

And the farce went on.

Chapter Thirteen

He lost track of the number of times he repeated his story. Harris insisted that he leave out what he called irrelevant details, and Murray insisted on keeping them in, adding even more as he went along. Over a period of hours, Shueck either learned to tune out or got used to hearing about the globs of green stuff that went into the toilet and didn't run from the room again. The temperature dropped considerably, and with the dampness of his clothes caused by the earlier heat, Murray was chilled, and he decided it was time to end the nonsense.

"What time is it" he asked. "Is the sun up?"

"We'll ask the questions here," Harris said.

"No, you will not," Murray responded. "Your time for asking appropriate questions is over. As a matter of fact, the two questions I just asked will most likely be the last two questions anybody asks while the three of us are still in this room. So, you answer them now, and you tell me what this nonsense is all about, or I walk out of here in the next sixty seconds."

Shueck pulled a cell phone out of her hip pocket and looked at it. "It's five-fifteen, A.M., and the sun won't be up for a couple more hours."

"And the two of you pulled me through my office door at about that same time last evening?"

"'Bout that," Harris said. "What of it?"

He got the answer to his question when Murray pulled his notebook over and wrote: *OH & OS 12 hrs. ud $12,000,000.*

"Twelve million dollars?! Yer crazy! And what does that mean," Harris had to ask, "the *ud*?"

"It means *unlawful detainment*," Murray told him. "For the last twelve hours, I've been sitting here, patiently putting up with your nonsense. Now, I'm done with it. I don't believe I heard anybody say, 'You're under arrest,' so it's time for you to get to specifics. All you have ask me so far is where I was and what I did last Wednesday. I've told you multiple times, and nothing I have told you those multiple times would change if you asked me to tell you again. What exactly is it that you want to know?"

"We want to know exactly what you did last Wednes..." Harris began, and Murray cut him off.

"Don't even!"

His shout was so loud that Harris and Shueck both jumped.

"Don't tell us you haven't heard what happened to James Hartman this past Wednesday," Shueck said.

"Something happened to Hartman?" Murray asked. "I was down in Chester County all last week, and I haven't heard anything."

Neither of the officers spoke.

"What happened to Hartman?"

"He was assaulted in his home," Shueck said, and Harris gave her a dark look.

Murray looked from one of them to another silently for more than a minute. "Is he dead?" he finally asked.

"No," Shueck again, "but he's severely injured."

"So why don't you lose the poker face and just admit that you did it?" Harris asked.

"You didn't ask me if I did it," Murray hedged. "You asked me what I did last Wednesday, and I've told you, what?, a dozen or more times? So now you know, and asking me to repeat my answer again won't change a single detail. Again, I ask, why didn't you just ask me if I did it? Why beat around the bush, as it were?"

"Chief Coder told us not to ask specifics, not to give you specific details," Shueck answered. "He said he wanted to hear it from you."

Murray nodded his head and frowned. "He wanted to hear it from me. Is Coder out there behind the mirror? Is Chief Coder in the building?"

"No," Shueck said. "He left sometime after midnight and won't be in for another hour or so."

Harris, who seemed to have lost his voice and run out of energy, plopped down in a chair and said nothing.

Murray stood, stretched, picked up his notebook and pen and put them back in his coat pocket. "So, he will listen to the tape or watch the video you've obviously made of the night's activities. I imagine he will find either entertaining. Give him my regards when he shows up. I'm out of here."

"You'll be out of here when we say you can leave," Harris blustered.

"I've already put a twelve-million-dollar notation in my notebook for twelve hours of interrogation and unlawful detainment. You want to make it thirteen?"

That said, Murray headed for the door.

"Now what?" Shueck asked when the door had closed behind him.

"Now we're done," Harris said and fell into the chair Murray had just vacated. "Now we're done."

* * * *

He walked home through the crisp April morning air, chilled again because of his damp clothing and looking forward to a warm shower. The office door was standing open when he got there, and the first thing he noticed was that his computer monitor wasn't on his desk. It was lying face-down on the floor behind it, and next to it was his keyboard, stomped into pieces. When he turned the monitor over, he discovered its screen had been slashed. The computer tower itself had been kicked over but didn't look damaged. The printer had not fared so well and lay in shards against the wall. The drawers of his desk had been emptied onto the floor; their contents kicked around. Murray stood and looked at the mess for several minutes and then opened the door into his apartment.

They had gone through everything. His suitcase lay on the floor, twisted and ruined, its contents strewn about. He smiled when he saw the bottle of Nyquil with its three doses gone—down the toilet in his motel room, along with the cotton balls he had used to fake a sinus problem, stuffed so far up his nose he had to get them out with tweezers. Thank goodness, the bottle was plastic, he thought, and then wondered why they hadn't thought to pour the remainder of its contents out on the floor and add it to the rest of the mess. His laptop had gone the way of his desktop. The screen had been spared, but it had been torn in half, and its leather carrying case had been shredded. The wireless mouse he used had gone the way of the heel.

Shards of his dishes, coffee mugs and drinking glasses lay in a puddle of the cleaning liquids that had been under the sink. Someone had apparently raked everything out of the cabinet and it fall. Empty plastic bottles dotted the mix. His stainless-steel flatware sparkled in the overhead light, and right in the middle of it all was his cell phone, heel-stomped and useless. *So much for checking my computers and cell phone for evidence, Daniel*, Murray thought. Cushions from his sofa lay in a corner, sliced open and the stuffing pulled out. The seat, back and arms of his recliner had been cut to ribbons, his table and chairs destroyed. Who had done this, and what would it cost them? Murray asked himself. There would be no definitive answer for the first part of the question, but an answer to the second part came easy, another two million dollars, and he hadn't even seen what was waiting for him in the bedroom yet.

He stepped to its doorway and found his mattress slashed open and thrown against the wall, holes punched or stomped in the box springs. His underwear and socks had been dumped out of his chest-of-drawers and his suits, trousers, shirts and ties tossed out of his closet onto the floor, hangers and all, and soiled with footprints. He went into the bathroom and learned that there would be no shower taken here this morning or any time soon. The shower curtain had been torn down and sliced to ribbons. The floor of the shower stall was covered with every towel and wash cloth he owned, soggy and wet, right along with every roll of toilet tissue in the place, not to mention whatever pharmaceuticals had been in the medicine cabinet above the sink, a cabinet that no longer had a mirror.

So, what to do? Pick up enough reasonably decent clothes to make a half-decent change, go out to the homeplace and shower. He gathered up what he thought he would need, went to the garage and discovered that he wouldn't likely be going anywhere in the Honda ever again. Headlights and taillights had been destroyed. Windows had been shattered or knocked out completely. The upholstery was in shreds and all four tires were flat. In a word, the thing was totaled. Murray stood looking at the mess, his jaws bunching in anger, and added a couple more million to the total. All of this just because they *suspected* he was the one. What would they have done if they *knew*?

He took his armload of clothes into his office and tossed them on the desk, sat down in the chair behind it, his mind numb from thinking about the magnitude of the carnage. They had somehow missed slicing up the padding on his desk chair, and the two oak armchairs his visitors used were still sitting upright and in one piece. *Out of respect for their antique status?* he wondered. They hadn't thought to punch or kick holes in the sheetrock walls. He supposed he should be glad of that. Glancing around, he noticed for the first time that his filing cabinet had not been pried open. Another reason for gratitude? *Not by a long shot* went through his mind. *Not by a long shot.*

He slouched down in his chair, elbows on the armrests, and ran a hand over his forehead, felt the dried blood and remembered the cut on his head. Did it need stitches? He went back into his apartment and found a plastic grocery bag that hadn't been destroyed. He stuffed his clothes into it, locked the door behind him and headed for the ER at J.C. Blair Memorial.

* * * *

The gash in his forehead did not need stitches. A nurse cleaned it with something that burned and made his eyes water and then closed it with sterile strips. Murray asked if she would make a phone call for him and gave her Janet's number. She told him she would be glad to and suggested that he should go sit down in the waiting room. The pain caplets she had given him would kick in shortly, she said. She would get him a prescription for more to take at home.

When Janet arrived some twenty minutes later, she found him slouched down as far as he could get in an uncomfortable chair, his eyes closed and a patch at the hairline above his right eye, a plastic bag full of clothes at his feet.

"Murray?" she said, concern in her voice, and when he opened his eyes and pulled himself to an upright position. "What happened to you? Are you alright? I didn't see your car in the parking lot. How did you get here?"

"Long story," he answered somewhat groggy. "Take me home, please. I need a shower. Tell you on the way."

He started to rise, and she pushed him back down.

"You sit right here 'til I bring the car up to the door and I come in and get you."

He settled back down and closed his eyes, too tired to object. She shook him awake minutes later, helped him to stand and prodded him toward the door.

"My clothes," he said and pulled her to a stop.

"Let's get you in the car, and I'll come back and get them."

It took more prodding and some coaxing, but she finally got him into the passenger seat of her Nissan, the seatbelt buckled, and the door closed. When she got back with his clothes, he had nodded off to sleep again. It would not be until she got him out to the homeplace, helped him up the stairs to the bathroom and let him shower that she would begin to get Murray's "long story."

Hair still damp from his shower and in fresh clothes, he lay stretched out on her bed at her insistence, and she sat on the edge of it holding his hand. Word of the assault on Officer James Hartman had not been made public yet, so he started with that.

"Assaulted in his own home?" Janet mused. "How bad was he injured?"

"Don't know. They wouldn't tell me. They took me out of my office almost before I had a chance to set my suitcase down. Took me to the station and kept asking me where I was and what I had done on Wednesday."

"They think *you* did it? But you were down in Chester County all week. You called me from there at nine o'clock on Wednesday evening. Why would they think it was you?" she asked.

"I guess because of our history, Hartman's and mine. Hartman killed my son, and it's no secret that the two of us have been at odds for years. Besides that, I don't think they have any other suspects."

251

"But *you!*" Janet was aghast. "You weren't even in the area when it happened."

"They trashed my office and my apartment," he told her.

"Trashed your apartment?"

Murray nodded. "And destroyed my Honda. That's why I had to have you come and get me at the hospital."

"How did you get to the hospital?"

"Walked," Murray said, still too tired to elaborate.

"Why didn't you call a taxi?"

"Didn't have a phone. They smashed my cell phone and ripped the landline out of the wall."

"Did you call the police?" she asked.

"Couldn't without a phone. Besides, it was the police that did it."

"What?!"

Murray's response was a gentle snore. She shook his hand.

"What do you mean 'it was the police that did it'?"

He came awake with a snort. "They're mad because 'one of their own' was assaulted." He made finger quotes with his hands lying on the bed. "They think I did it, but they can't prove it, so they got back at me the only way they could. They missed the television somehow. Everything else was destroyed, but nothing was taken. Who else would have a reason to do that?"

"Mom? Who are you talking to?" Janie asked from just outside the door.

"I'm talking to Murray, and you can come on in."

"What the hell happened to you?" she asked when she had stepped through the door and gotten a look at the man on the bed.

His story got told again, mostly by Janet, and it got the same reaction from Janie that it had gotten from her mother. How could he have done it when he was down in Chester County all week, and why did they think it was him anyway?

The answers were still the same, and while Janet was giving them to her daughter, Murray drifted off to sleep again.

"Let's slip out and let him rest," she suggested. "He can tell us more when he feels better. What are you doing up so early after putting in a late shift anyway?"

"I was up going to the bathroom, and I heard you talking," Janie said. "I guess I drank too much before I went to bed last night." At her mother's look, she added, "Water, Mom. Water."

* * * *

He slept until late afternoon, and Janet woke him up to eat supper. She had taken the prescription they had given him at the hospital into town and had it filled. The vial was sitting on the table by his plate.

"Thank you so much," Murray told her. "I'll reimburse you, and I'm afraid I'll have to impose on you to take me to a motel when I'm finished eating. Until I can get somewhere to buy another vehicle, I'm gonna be on foot."

"You won't reimburse me for anything after what you've put into this house," Janet told him, "and you

253

won't be staying in any motel. You'll be living right here until you can get your apartment back in shape, which by the way, Charles Bond told me to tell you not to touch until some of Sheriff Kauffman's deputies make a photo and video record of the damage. He didn't doubt for a minute that it was some of Coder's people who did it. And you can use my car until you can get another one."

"How will you get around?" he asked.

"You can take me to work Monday morning and come and get me when my shift is done. Other than that, I won't need it until I have to go get groceries."

Murray took his usual seat at the table and watched as she brought a large bowl of homemade vegetable soup and set it on a hot pad, then went to the cabinet for smaller bowls and flatware.

"What about sleeping arrangements?" he asked. "The sofa is too short for me, and I don't want to put you out of your bed."

"You won't," she said, ladling up soup into their bowls. "We can both sleep in my bed for one night. I'll put some pillows down the middle. You stay on your side and I'll stay on mine."

Murray shook his head and smiled. "And for a second and third night?"

"We'll have you a bed in the spare room by then. You'll need a new one when we get your apartment back in shape anyway. Now, eat your soup so you can take some pain pills. You're still looking a little pale."

"Yes, Ma'am," he said and did what he was told.

* * * *

He passed a bad night and slept most of the day Sunday. Janet got him up for a lunch of cold cuts and cheese sandwiches, made sure he took his medicine, and sent him back to bed. Sunday night through Monday morning went a little better. When the alarm clock went off at five A.M., he found himself with his arm across the pillows and his hand on Janet's back. His head was clear, and he was ready to be about what needed to be done.

After a breakfast of toast and jelly and a cup of coffee, he took Janet to J. C. Blair and was dropping her off when he realized that no stores would be open for a couple of hours.

"Do you have a calculator out at the place?" he asked.

"Should be one in one of the desk drawers in the den," she said. "Why?"

"I've got some things to add up," he told her, "and there's gonna be some big numbers involved."

She looked like she wanted to ask some questions but finally leaned over and brushed a kiss across his lips. "Come and get me about three-thirty," she said and slipped out of the car.

He drove back out to the homeplace and found the calculator where she said it would be. He sat down at the desk with it and his notebook and began punching in numbers. In short order, he had a total of $15,565,000. He laid the notebook aside.

"Okay," he said out loud. "Let's add the damage to my place in town. Office, kitchen, living room, bathroom, garage—five more million? Why not?"

He punched the numbers into the calculator and looked at the screen: $20,565,000. "Twenty million, five hundred and sixty-five thousand," he said out loud. "Let's just add a little for mental anguish and round it up to twenty-two million even."

He had the total. Now he needed a new laptop and a printer to draw up and print the lawsuit he intended to file with the court.

It required a trip to Altoona, the nearest town that had a Staples. Back at the homeplace, he set his purchases up in what Janet was calling the den now and got to work.

Chapter Fourteen

By the time Murray's week at home came to an end, two of Sheriff Kauffman's deputies had made the photo and video records of the damage to his apartment that Charles Bond had suggested, copies of which were sent to Chief Alex Coder. When he had looked at the photos and viewed the video, he called those responsible into his office and ranted at them.

"What the hell were the two of you thinking?" he demanded.

"You told us to tear the place apart, and that's what we did," Bilger said.

"Well, I didn't tell you to destroy potential evidence in the process."

"What potential evidence would that be?" Horne asked.

"Whatever might have been on his laptop and his cell phone," Coder suggested.

"Wasn't no evidence on either one. We checked first."

"And yer both technological experts?" Coder's voice dripped with sarcasm.

"I know my way around a computer and a smart phone," Horne told him. "McCartney's didn't have anything incriminating on either of them, and they weren't even password protected.

Coder's glare shifted from one of them to the other. Neither officer offered anything more. Dealing with the crime against Hartman was beyond their Chief's capabilities, they were coming to understand. If the investigation was to ever get anywhere and the crime was to ever be solved, it was going to require someone less emotional.

Coder glared at the two of them for more than a minute and then shouted, "Get out of my sight!"

Murray's apartment had been cleaned out and the damaged furniture hauled away, thanks to Janie and Russ Junior whom he insisted on paying for their labor. What was left of the Honda had been backed out of the garage on its four flat tires, loaded on a flatbed and hauled to a salvage yard. He would be driving the Impala when he got back from what would be his last week in Chester County, and he would refurnish his apartment, buy new dishes, linens, flatware, whatever he needed then.

A bedframe, mattress and box springs, all king size (all too big for the bedroom in his apartment) had been purchased and installed in the spare room at the homeplace. No more reaching across the pillows and assuring himself that Janet was there. They mounted the stairs hand-in-hand each evening, shared a kiss on the landing and went to their separate rooms. Murray had his new bed all to himself, but something seemed to be missing.

He had drawn up his suit against the Police Department, the Mayor and the City Council, listing in detail the grievances and his reasons for including them. He filed it with the court late Friday afternoon, and he had no doubt that he would be hearing from a representative of or one of the individuals named in the suit when he returned from Chester County at the end of the following week.

They spent the weekend alone, he and Janet. Janie was off to work and then to spend time with Charles Bond. Russ Junior and wife and daughter were spending yet another weekend with his in-laws, an occurrence that happened much too often in Janet's opinion. She seldom got to see her grandbaby.

"And I'll get to see my next one even less," she said, "it being clear across the Atlantic."

Tears threatened, so Murray took her into his arms and administered some distractions. "Don't let things you can do nothing about upset you," he told her and wiped away the single tear that had escaped with a thumb.

"Well, it's just not fair," she declared. "Other grandmothers get to see their grandbabies every weekend, and I'm lucky if I get to see mine a couple times a year."

"Life's not fair," Murray reminded her, "so when it gives you lemons and all of that, you know what you have to do. And speaking of what *I* have to do, can you take tomorrow off work and drive me to West Chester in the morning?"

Janet's smile faded. "You're going back down there after all that's happened here?"

"I need to go back down there for just one more week, and I obviously don't have a car. I need you to drive me. Will you do that?"

"How will you get home?" she wanted to know.

"I'll buy a car sometime during the week and drive myself back. There are always ads in the newspapers, cars for sale, and I need to purchase one anyway. I have left some unfinished business down there, some cases I have to clear, and I'll have to let the court clerk know not to assign any more cases to me. Then I can come back to Huntingdon and never have to leave again. Would that be okay with you?"

Her smile was back. "You know it would."

"So, can you drive me down there tomorrow morning?"

"Let me go make a phone call," she said and ran a hand down his cheek as she left him sitting at the table.

* * * *

They left Huntingdon at seven A. M. Monday morning and caught the Turnpike at the Fort Littleton exchange. They would get into West Chester a little after ten. Janet had never driven on the Turnpike before, and it made her nervous. Small talk didn't seem to help. Sometimes, Murray had to repeat what he had said because her mind was so sharply focused on her driving. Her grip on the steering wheel left her knuckles white. A question he asked just before they reached their destination got her attention, though.

"I called you Mrs. Hockenberry not long ago, and you told me you would rather be Janet. Would you like to be Mrs. Somebody Else?"

"What?" she asked, taking her eyes off the road for a several seconds and looking at him.

"Would you rather..." he began, and she cut him off.

"I heard you." She turned her attention back to the road and was silent for more than a minute. "Is this a proposal?"

"If it was, would your answer be yes?" he asked, trying to read her expression.

"I don't know. Maybe"

"Maybe," Murray repeated, and she took it as a question.

"Yes, maybe. I'll have to think about it."

He let the subject drop and turned his head to stare through the windshield. After that, he said nothing except to give her directions to the courthouse. When she pulled to a stop in front of it, he made no move to get out of the car. They had gotten so close over these past months, and he thought she would already have at least *thought* about the possibility of taking that final step. But it was *maybe*, and that left him feeling a bit depressed.

He opened the door and got out, opened the backdoor and retrieved his new laptop in its new leather case, his new suitcase and his garment bag.

Janet seemed to sense that something was wrong. "I could drop you at your motel?" she suggested. "You could put your things away before you go to work."

"I've got them now," he said. "I'll leave them in the conference room," and he closed the backdoor with his knee. Standing in the open door of the passenger's side, he leaned down and looked at her across the seat, set his suitcase down and handed her a ten-dollar bill. "For the toll on the way back."

"Call me tonight," she said, concern on her face.

"Thank you for driving me. Call me when you get home. You have my new cell phone number."

"I love you," she said, and he thought it had the ring of apology, of desperation, to it.

"Love you, too," Murray said. He stepped back

and pushed the door shut, turned and headed up the steps of the courthouse. He heard her put the Nissan in gear and drive away, but he didn't turn around.

Over the next several days, he thought about the question he had asked her. Would you like to be Mrs. Somebody Else? Maybe it was a string, he thought. He had promised her early on that there would be no pressure and no strings attached. Maybe if he had given her a ring. There was that word again, *maybe*, and no, a ring was just a string without the *s* and the *t*. She had reminded him that she didn't want any strings, and he had promised there would be no strings. He would have to be careful about strings, he decided. He didn't want to burden her with any more strings.

* * * *

His final week in Chester County went as well as he could expect, given the mood he was in. Murray refused to think of it as the mood Janet had left him in. She had called him when she got home as he had requested. He was in court and had his phone turned off, so it went to voice mail. When he had taken care of his last case for the day, he called an uber and had the driver drop him off at the house where the Impala was stored. He backed it out of the garage and then left the key to the house and a hundred-dollar bill on the kitchen table. Smiling to himself, he got into it and drove away. He had his own means of transportation again. When he got to his motel, he opened the glove compartment and checked to see if the .380 was still there. It was.

He called Janet that evening as he had promised. Had he promised? He remembered getting his things out of the backseat. After that, things got kind of blurry, so he wasn't sure, but it had become a habit, so he called her anyway. Their conversation was brief and strained. What do you say to a woman whom you have practically asked if she would like to marry you and she said, "Maybe"? What's more, what does she say to you?

His days were spent at the courthouse, taken up with the cases he had been assigned, and there were quite a few. He began to wonder if they had found out somehow that this would be his last week before he even told them and decided to get as much out of him as they possibly could before his last day. His workload reminded him of what Janet had said the evening he had called her Mrs. Hockenberry and her reaction to it, and he was careful not to say anything about being exhausted when they talked each evening.

Daughter Amanda had her baby in Germany on Tuesday afternoon, and her husband had notified Janet with a phone call, so she was conflicted when they spoke that night. One moment all bubbly because she had a second grandchild—a boy this time—and sounding morose the next because she wouldn't get to see him any time soon, except maybe in pictures. Murray's suggestion once again that she should fly over there and spend some time with her new grandchild was met with a quick negative. She didn't want to get on an airplane and fly anywhere, and definitely not across an ocean.

"Then why don't you do facetime with Amanda?" he asked her.

"What?"

"You have a smart phone, and Amanda has one,

too. The two of you could use them to facetime with one another," he suggested.

"Amanda doesn't have a smart phone," she countered.

"Actually, she does," Murray insisted.

"How would you know that?" she asked."

"Because I sent her one a month ago."

"Murray!"

"Let's not get into the 'Murray, you do too much and I'm already in your debt' thing. If you want to see your new grandbaby, you can facetime with your daughter, and she can let you see the boy."

"But I don't know how to do that," Janet told him.

"Neither do I," he admitted, "but I imagine Janie does. Ask her to help you."

Janet said she would ask, and they left it that way.

By noon on Wednesday, he was counting the hours until he could pick up his last paycheck, pack his things into the Impala and head for home, this time up the Turnpike, and this time for good. His morning hadn't been as busy as some had been, but his caseload for the afternoon was heavy. If things with his lawsuit went as he hoped they would, there would soon be money in the bank back home, so it didn't matter, he felt, if his client list grew or not. He was looking forward to sitting in his Huntingdon office and having a little time to relax between cases.

His conversations with Janet on Wednesday and Thursday nights went well. Janie had shown her how to facetime, and she had actually seen her new grandson, little William Hunter, she told him excitedly, had seen him wave his little hands and heard him cry. Wasn't really fond of the name, but then she thought she could get used to it. She thanked Murray for sending Amanda the smart phone and babbled on about the newest addition to the family, completely oblivious of Murray's subdued responses.

On Friday at noon, he could have made his escape from Chester County, but he procrastinated, having lunch at a diner that had become one of his favorites. Why he wasn't in a hurry to be going, he couldn't have said. He had taken care of everything that needed to be seen too, had a new set of tires put on the Impala that had a different tread pattern from the old ones. He was taking nothing back that could throw suspicion on him again. No reason to be nervous about what Coder and his minions might do. He had made acquaintances here but no friends that he was reluctant to leave. Maybe, he thought, it was the uncertainty of what was waiting for him back in Huntingdon. *Maybe* could lead to any number of unpredictable situations.

Sitting in his usual booth in the diner, he sipped his coffee and smiled. There was that word again— *maybe*. He didn't want to think that, by staying away longer than he had to, he might be punishing Janet. He wasn't that kind of a man, was he?

At one o'clock, he decided that if he wanted to get home in time to buy some furniture before all the stores were closed, he had better get going. His things already packed into the Impala, he slid behind the wheel and started out. He made the three-hour trip in the usual three hours. At a little past four, he walked into Furniture Park, purchased a queen size bed frame, mattress and box springs and a chest-of-drawers. Since it was so late in the workday, he paid a little extra to have them delivered before closing time, then went home to his apartment to wait.

It was not a long wait. The delivery men were knocking on his office door almost before he had set his suitcase and laptop down and tossed his garment bag over the back of his office chair. The bed installed, he made it up with linens that had been washed out at the homeplace, which, of course, made him think of the king size bed he would no longer be sleeping in out there, and started him wondering again how things would go with Janet when he got out there. He emptied his suitcase into the chest-of-drawers and hung the garment bag in the closet. That done, he had no excuse for not going out there to see her—except maybe a quick run out to Walmart to pick up a new coffee maker to replace the one that had been destroyed and some coffee and filters to use in it. And a new shower curtain.

* * * *

It was nearly seven o'clock when he pulled the Impala to a stop beside Janet's Nissan. She was beside the driver's door before he could open it and get out, her mouth hanging open and her brows raised at the sight of his new vehicle. He opened the door, and she took a step back.

"Where did you get such a beautiful car?" she wanted to know.

"Bought it from a lady in Phoenixville whose husband died of lung cancer. She called it a symptom of his mid-life crisis. It has less than thirty thousand miles on it."

"What year is it?" she asked.

"It's a two thousand eight."

"Black or dark gray?"

Murray smiled. "That's what it looks like when it's overcast, but when the sun hits it, it has a kind of bronze glow."

"And it has leather seats!"

"Yes, it does. Would you like to take it for a spin?"

"Maybe later," Janet said. "I thought you would be here earlier. I made you supper, your favorite, lasagna."

There was that word again—*maybe*, and his favorite, lasagna. Sounded like an apology meal.

Murray smiled and said, "Wonderful," and Janet took him by the arm and led him into the house.

It was good lasagna, but then Janet's always was, and she had made sweet tea and yeast rolls to go with it. His hunger sated, Murray pushed his plate back and stood. "Thank you for a wonderful meal, as always. It's getting late, so I best be heading home."

"Home?" Janet said. "I thought this was home?"

"It has been for quite a while," he said, "but I think I've been imposing on you long enough."

"You haven't been imposing. I love having you here. Please, don't go."

She stepped against him and put her arms around his waist, leaned back to look into his eyes.

"I didn't bring any night clothes."

"There's still some here from when we washed your stuff."

He put his arms around her shoulders hesitantly and said nothing.

"Please, stay," she pleaded. "The hours are so long, and this house is so empty when I'm here by myself. I'd do anything to get you to stay."

When she realized what she had said and what Murray might be thinking, her face and neck turned red and she swallowed hard. *No pressure and no strings* went through his mind, and he pulled her more tightly against him, a hand on the back of her head, her chin over his shoulder.

"Could we put the pillows down the middle of the bed again?" he asked, and he felt her smile against his neck.

"We could do that," she said.

"It's a little early for bed, though. Maybe we could have some coffee in the living room first?"

Janet pulled back, smiled into his face and said, "I love you."

"Love you, too.

* * * *

It turned out to be a wonderful weekend. Just the two of them, fixing meals together and sitting down at the kitchen table to eat them. Holding hands on the sofa in the living room and watching *Jeopardy*, reruns of *Law and Order,* whatever they could find that was interesting enough to ignore. They made small talk and smiled at one another, leaned in for a distraction now and then, but the thing that was uppermost in both their minds was never mentioned. They shared the bed in her bedroom again, holding hands across the pillows and talking quietly, while the window unit hummed, until one of them gave a gentle snore and the other one smiled and rolled away and drifted off to sleep.

When Murray woke up at a little after eight Monday morning, Janet's side of the bed was empty, and he realized she had been at work for hours already. Beside a plate on the kitchen table, he found a note:

You were sleeping so peacefully I couldn't bring myself to wake you. It is wonderful to have you back permanently again.
Love,
Janet
P.S. I am *thinking about it.*

It brought a smile to his face and lightened his mood. He wouldn't realize until he had finished his breakfast, was in the Nissan (she had taken the Impala to work) and headed for his office that the meeting he was anticipating with whatever representative the city sent to visit him wasn't nearly as scary as his Friday evening meeting with Janet had been. Failing to win her would change his life much much more than failing to win his lawsuit.

Chapter Fifteen

They did not disappoint him. He was in his apartment, making coffee in his new coffee maker when he heard the door of his office open and close. He finished what he was doing and went to see who it was. Chief of Police Alex Coder and Mayor Arthur Banks himself were standing just inside the door.

"Gentlemen, have a seat," Murray said. "Coffee's on. We'll all have us a mug in a couple of minutes."

"We're not here for coffee." This delivered in an angry tone by Coder.

"I didn't really think you were," Murray admitted, "but have a seat anyway."

The two men took seats in the oak armchairs that had been spared, Banks to his right, Coder to his left, and Murray had to smile.

"Something funny?" Coder asked in the same tone he had used before.

"Funny, no; amusing, maybe. If your people had done a more thorough job, there wouldn't have been any visitors' chairs for anyone to sit in."

"My people?" Coder responded. "If that's and accusation, you better have…"

"Now, let's not get off on the wrong foot here," Mayor Banks, speaking for the first time, cut him off.

"We're here to talk about the suit you filed against me and the City and the Police Department."

"We got off on the wrong foot when this Bozo filed his lawsuit against us," Chief Coder interrupted. "Twenty-two million dollars. You must be out of your friggin' mind."

"I'll ask you to keep a civil tongue in your head while you're here in my office, Al," Murray said. "Can I call you Al?"

Chief Coder's neck and ears turned red. Only those individuals he considered to be his equals were allowed to call him Al. That list was short, and Murray knew he wasn't on it.

"Whatever," Coder said. "You'll never win your stupid suit anyway."

"Probably not," Murray admitted, "but it will cost the city what..." he turned his attention to Mayor Banks... "half a million? Three-quarters of a million to defend against it? That sound about right?"

Banks nodded.

"What?" Coder exclaimed.

"And another half to three-quarters of a million if I lose and appeal. More than that if I appeal it all the way to the State Supreme Court, and I intend to do just that if it becomes necessary."

"Twenty-two million dollars for what? Being taken down to the station and questioned for a few hours?" Coder asked.

"You've read a copy of the suit, so you know for what, but since you asked so nicely, let me refresh your memory. I was pulled out of this office, and had the door slammed against my head in the process, by one of your minions..."

271

"I know what you're pissed about," Coder interrupted. "You don't have to go through it all."

"No," Murray insisted, his tone angrier than any Coder had used. "You asked 'for what,' so you're gonna hear it. I got my face slammed against the window and cuffs put on my wrists so tight they left red marks for days. I had my head rammed into the roof of one of your squad cars and ended up in the emergency room, having a wound closed with sterile strips. I spent twelve hours in your interrogation room, where the temperature was jacked up to ninety-five degrees for an hour or more, being asked the same vague question again and again: Where were you last Wednesday, and what did you do? I understand that was your idea, Al. You wanted to hear it from me. Well, if you watched the video or listened to the audio tape your officers made, you've heard all you're gonna hear. I get back to my office, and I discover that your people have destroyed practically everything I own."

"You can't prove that anyone from the Department destroyed anything," Coder injected.

"Harris and Shueck left that door standing open," Murray nodded toward it, "so if it wasn't your people, they gave access to whoever did it. Everything was destroyed but nothing was taken. Who would think they had reason to do something like that if it wasn't at the orders of someone who thought I had attacked one of their own?"

Mayor Banks, who had been staring at the floor, raised his head and turned to look at Chief Coder.

"Yes," Murray pressed on. "I'm aware that you insisted on handling the investigation yourself, even though Hartman's place is out of your jurisdiction because it involved 'one of our own', to use your exact words. One of your own who has had multiple complaints filed against him, I've come to know, and not just from me."

"Any good officer of the law will ruffle a few feathers now and then," Coder said.

"Well, James Hartman isn't a 'good officer of the law'," Murray used finger quotes. "He's a bully and a coward, and you people gave him a badge. In his mind, that's practically a license to kill."

"Now, wait a minute!" this from Coder.

"A minute won't change the fact that he killed my son in the misconduct of his duty, and the Department looked the other way. It won't change the fact that I won a wrongful death suit against the city, a fact which virtually proved that your 'good officer of the law' was guilty of murder, and he came after me with his ticket pad. Thirty tickets in less than a month, and you told me to take it up with traffic court. Remember that, Al?"

Here, Murray paused to let what he had said sink in. When he continued, his tone was a bit softer.

"More recently, I've made visits to Mayor Banks's office with complaints about slashed tires and sand in my car, among other things. He tried to get some kind of control over your 'good officer of the law' (again the finger quotes), and for that I'm grateful. It worked for a while, and then Hartman was back to his old tricks, harassing me and people close to me."

"He was just doing his job," Coder insisted. "Keeping the streets of Huntingdon safe."

"Oh, yeah?" Murray countered. "Try telling that to Janie Hockenberry. Remember her? Hartman busted

273

her taillight and then gave her a ticket for having a busted taillight. More recently, he gave her a ticket for God and Hartman himself only knows what, because she refused to go out with him. Whatever he wrote down for the reason was illegible, and you backed him up, Al. Was that keeping the streets of Huntingdon safe? Or better yet, try telling that to Duane Runk's widow. Explain to his fatherless children how their father's death makes the streets of Huntingdon safe."

"The grand jury failed to bring an indictment against Officer Hartman," Coder pointed out."

"Because that's what you intended for it to do. I was called to testify, remember? I knew before I left the witness stand that the whole thing was a sham, a charade designed to clear Hartman of his crime. Well, he got away with it and a lot of other crimes and misdemeanors for a long time, but recently, he paid dearly for all of them, didn't he? Do the two of you realize that you are complicit in the death of Mr. Runk?"

"What!" from Coder.

"You can't be serious!" from Banks.

"As far back as Randall's death, you knew you had a rogue on your hands, and you chose to do nothing about it. In the past year, as I said a minute ago, I paid several visits to your office, Arthur, and gave you information that should have made you understand what kind of menace you had preying on the citizens of Huntingdon. I appreciate the effort you made on my behalf, but you didn't take it far enough, and now Duane Runk is dead. His death could have been prevented if either of you had seen James Hartman for the lose cannon he is instead of insisting that he was 'a good officer of the law' and that his actions were 'keeping the streets of Huntingdon safe'. So, yes. Both of you have the blood of Duane Runk on your hands."

Murray seemed to have wound down, and the three of them sat for more than a minute without anyone saying anything. Then the mayor spoke.

"Well, we seem to have lost sight of our reason for being here," he said. "Your lawsuit. Twenty-two million is a bit much, don't you think?"

"Oh, I don't know," Murray said. "Think of what brought us to that number. Three whacks on the head, one that left this scar." He lifted the hair off his forehead and showed it to them. "Twelve hours of interrogation, some of them at ninety-five degrees…"

"It wasn't an interrogation," Chief Coder objected.

"I was detained in a room against my will and asked the same question time and time again. If that wasn't an interrogation, Al, what would you call it?"

Again, Coder's neck and ears turned red, but he had nothing more to say.

"I'll admit you were treated badly," Banks began, "but…"

"Then there's the destruction of practically everything I owned to consider," Murray interrupted. "Some of those things can never be replaced. The photo album that was on the shelf in my bedroom, for instance. It had the only photographs I had of my son Randall in it. We found it under the wet towels and toilet tissue in the shower stall, completely ruined."

"Still…" Banks started but didn't seem to know where to go with it and fell silent.

Murray sat behind his desk and let the silence build. Banks stared at him with a look that could have been interpreted as a plea. Coder's stare could not be mistaken for anything but a glare of hostility.

"Tell you what," Murray said, "you give me your word that me and those close to me will never again be harassed by any member of the Huntingdon Police Department because of our current situation, and I'll drop the amount of my suit to three million."

"One million-five," Banks countered, "and you have my word."

"What?!" Coder exclaimed.

"In writing," Murray insisted.

"In writing," Banks agreed. "I'll have our legal department draw up the contract."

"What the hell?" Coder exploded. "You're agreeing to give this clown a million and a half, so he'll drop a lawsuit he's never gonna win anyway?"

Murray ignored him. "One million-five to be paid into an account I'll set up at Community State Bank at a hundred thousand a year, tax free, over the next fifteen years."

The quickness with which Murray had agreed let Banks know he'd been played, and he smiled mentally. "I don't know about the tax free," he said.

"Have your accountants figure it out," Murray said. "No tax free, no agreement."

"I'm not believing this," Coder muttered.

"We created a situation here," Banks told him. "We let things go so far that someone had to step in and correct our mistakes, and then you and members of your department compounded the problem by adding more. The city is going to be paying out money. Why shouldn't some of it go to a citizen who was treated like he had already been tried and convicted when he should have been treated like nothing more than a person of interest?"

"Oh, and one other thing," Murray said. "I want Randall's Smith and Wesson."

"I doubt that it's still in the evidence locker after six years," Coder suggested.

"Well, if it isn't, you find out who took it and get it back. That's part of the deal or it's no deal. We go back to the twenty-two million and start over."

"Do you know the serial number?" Coder asked. "How will you know if we find the right gun?"

"It's a Smith and Wesson M&P 40 SHIELD," Murray answered. "It was a present for Randall's twenty-first birthday, and I had his initials engraved in the butt of it, RMM. I'll know it when I see it. Find it and bring it to me."

Banks stood and offered Murray his hand. "Can't say it's been a pleasure doing business with you," he said, "but I'm glad we could come to this agreement. I'll have our legal team draw up the papers."

Coder sat sullenly slumped in his chair. "A million-five. The Council will never agree to this."

"Oh, I think the Council is going to agree to this and to a lot of changes I intend to suggest. It's time we made 'to protect and serve' the motto of your department again," Banks told him. "Now, let's be going. I have work to do."

"Hey, Al," Murray asked as the two of them headed for the door, "do you have any leads, or do you still think I'm the one that injured 'one of your own'?" He ended his question with finger quotes.

"No," Coder said after giving it some thought. "We don't have any leads at the moment. And to answer the second part of your question, assaulting one of our officers and then filing a lawsuit against the Department would take balls, and I think that's something you don't have, so you're no longer even a person of interest."

His answer was intended to be an insult, but Murray smiled and thought, Well, good luck finding the man in the Carhart coveralls.

* * * *

Their visit to his office was the only one he was going to get. When the agreement was finally drawn up, Banks insisted that the signing would be done in *his* office. Murray arrived at the appointed time, a minute before five o'clock on a Friday. Kind of appropriate, he thought, at the end of a workday at the end of a week and, hopefully, at the end of an era of police harassment. One look at Stella's face let him know beyond a shadow of a doubt that she knew why he was there and that she didn't approve. He stepped through the outer door, she saw who it was, dropped her eyes to the blotter on her desk, raised an arm and pointed.

"It's good to see you again, Stella," he said cheerfully and headed for the door of Arthur Banks's office.

He found four of them waiting: Banks, of course, Chief of Police Coder, and the Chairman of the City Council, a woman whose name Murray could not remember. The mayor was sitting behind his desk,

Coder and the Chairman in wingchairs in a seating area. Banks's face had the most pleasant expression, Murray thought, but none of them were smiling. The fourth person, who would prove to be a Notary Public, stood behind the Chairman's chair, a hand on the back of it almost protectively. Nobody made introductions.

"Let's get this done before it gives some of us acid reflux," the Chairman (Chairperson? Chairwoman? Murray wondered) said rising from her seat and walking toward Banks's desk. "You've read the copy we sent you, I assume, and you agree with everything in it. The first of your money will be deposited in your account on the first Wednesday in July each year beginning July of this year. The only legal infraction this agreement applies to is the one currently being investigated by our Police Department. Any future infractions you or those close to you might be found guilty of will be dealt with according to the letter of the law. No member of the Police Department will stop, search or question you unless they see clearly that you are in violation of the law. You will disclose the terms of this agreement to no one. If we learn that you have, the agreement becomes null and void."

"As it does," Murray reminded them all, "if any kind of unwarranted harassment from any member of the Department should begin."

His comment earned a grunt from Chief Coder who had followed the others to Banks's desk. A semi-automatic in a plastic bag was lying on the blotter next to a sheaf of paper. Murray picked the gun up, looked at the butt of it and laid it back down."

"A food storage bag, Al? Really! Was that the closest thing to your gun safe at home?"

"That the one that belonged to your son?" Banks asked and Murray nodded. "Then let's not quibble about insignificant details." He spun the contract around and handed Murray a pen, pointed at a line and said, "Sign and date here."

Murray applied his signature, the Chairperson followed suit and then Chief Coder. That done, the mayor himself signed the document and the Notary Public applied his stamp.

"Let this be the last time you extort money from the citizens of Huntingdon," the Chairperson said.

"Extort money," Murray repeated. "You would have done well to keep that accusation to yourself."

"Watch your mouth," Coder cautioned.

Murray turned to face him. "*You*. Watch. *My*. Mouth," he said, "all of you. This has not been extortion. This is reparations for the treatment me, my family and those close to me have received at the hands of representatives of this city over the years, and for the more recent destruction of my property. You want this to be the last of it, hire reputable people. When you discover or are made aware that someone you hired is abusing his position, do a thorough and honest investigation, and if you discover that what you have been told is true, fire them. Otherwise, you will inevitably find yourselves in a situation like this again, if not with me, then with somebody else."

He took a moment to look each individual present in the eye and then turned back to the mayor. "Arthur, would you please have Stella make me a copy of that signed document for my file and have her mail it to me? Or I could come by and pick it up, whichever is more convenient. Just let me know when it's ready."

That said, he picked up Randall's gun and turned and walked out of the mayor's office without a backward glance. Stella watched him pass through the outer office and, as the door closed behind him, gave a snort of anger and turned her head to glare at the wall.

Chapter Sixteen

With the threat of harassment from "good officer of the law" James Hartman neutralized, for the moment if not permanently, and the possibility of harassment from other members of the Police Department a non-threat because of the agreement signed, Murray's life turned into a dull routine. Open his office at nine each morning, whether he had appointments on his calendar or not. Make a pot of coffee with his new coffee maker, which inevitably reminded him of what had happened to his old one and why there was nothing but a bed and chest-of-drawers in his apartment. Make a trip to the courthouse when the occasion required it. Sit at his desk, read a book and wait for a new client to come in when all of his old business had been completed. He thought about investing in a new recliner so he could watch television, but few daytime shows held any interest for him. Seemed like most of them were aimed at women.

Trips to the courthouse became an uncomfortable chore when he realized a number of people he had to deal with or whom he passed in the hallway seemed to be giving him strange looks. Word of his lawsuit had obviously found its way onto the gossip grapevine and had some of them wondering at what stage in the legal process the thing might be. Then to everyone's disappointment, all talk of it, every whisper, ceased. Apparently, everyone involved with the production and signing of the agreement had taken the non-disclosure clause quite seriously.

The only thing that kept Murray's life from being totally boring was the time he spent at the homeplace with Janet. Breakfast with her each morning, an embrace and a kiss before she got into her vehicle and headed off to work. Having supper with her in the evening and enjoying her company until bedtime. Holding hands across the pillows until one or both of them slept and starting all over again in the morning. Just thinking about the brand-new bed that was going unused in his apartment and the row of pillows down the middle of the bed he shared each night with Janet would bring a smile to his face.

On the first Wednesday of July, a deposit of one hundred thousand dollars was made to the account he had set up at Community State Bank. When Murray became aware of it, there was no feeling of elation, no thought to run out and spend it or to celebrate. To him, it was just evidence that what he had done had been right and necessary, evidence of the city's admission of wrongdoing. He would put the money to good use eventually, but for the time being, it was just there, and he gave it little thought.

The subject of his lawsuit came up one evening in mid-July while he and Janet were eating supper.

"You haven't mentioned the lawsuit you filed against the Police Department lately," Janet said casually, her glass of sweet tea halfway to her mouth. "How is that coming along?"

"It's finished," Murray told her without looking up from his plate and said nothing more.

"Finished? What do you mean, finished?" she asked.

"We reached an agreement. Me and the mayor, the Chairman... Chairperson of the City Council and the Police Department."

If he had been watching her expression, he would have known she wasn't happy. "And you didn't think to tell me?"

"I couldn't... can't tell you much. The papers I signed included a non-disclosure clause, so I thought it best not to even bring it up."

Janet sat there silently, watching him twirl the last bite of spaghetti around his fork and lift it to his mouth. When he had laid his fork down and wiped his mouth and chin with a napkin, he looked up and saw her expression.

"I didn't mean to keep secrets. I don't want to keep secrets from you," he said, something like a plea in his voice, "but if I say too much and the wrong people find out, the entire agreement becomes null and void."

"Okay," Janet nodded. "What can you tell me?"

Murray gave it some thought. "I can tell you that I will not be harassed again because of what happened to James Hartman. I can tell you that we will not be harassed by any member of the Huntingdon Police Department unless we are caught committing a crime. We will not be victimized by traffic stops that are intended just to show us someone is watching and is in charge. If we are speeding, driving recklessly or are actually guilty of some other infraction, we will be dealt with according to the law, but the unwarranted and illegal harassment is over."

"Who all does *we* include," Janet asked.

"You, me, Russ Junior and his wife, Janie. Anyone who is close to me."

"And that's it? That's all you can tell me? What about the twenty-two million?"

Murray shook his head. "That's the biggest reason for the non-disclosure agreement. I'm not allowed to say."

"Okay," Janet suggested, "so I'll say it. You didn't get the twenty-two million, but you got some."

He dropped his eyes to the table and nodded. When he raised his head and turned to look at her, he couldn't read the expression in her eyes. He reached out a hand to her, and she took it.

"Are we good?" he asked.

Her smile seemed tentative, but she squeezed his hand and said, "We're good. Now, let's get this table cleared off and find ourselves a seat in the living room."

She started to pull her had away, but Murray held on. "I love you."

Her smile became less tentative. "I love you, too."

* * * *

One hurdle cleared; Murray began to think about another one. He needed to have a visit with "good officer of the law" James Hartman, and he needed to do it without anybody else present, preferably without anybody else's knowledge. Problem was, he didn't even know where they had taken the man, and given his involvement with the case, he didn't feel like he could ask questions. The solution came from an unexpected source.

"They admitted James Hartman to J.C. Blair today," Janet said one evening in late July while they were having a supper of roast beef, mashed potatoes and gravy. "His name was on the dietary list they sent us today."

Murray did his best to hide his surprise. "Where do you suppose he's been?"

"Rumor has it that they gave him new shoulders up in Altoona," she said without looking up, "and now he's here at J. C. to get new knees. They told you he was severely injured, but it sounds like somebody really did a job on him."

Murray kept his head down and kept eating. "Any idea what room he's in?" he asked.

"No, but I can find out. Why?" Janet asked.

"I thought maybe I would pay him a visit, find out how he's doing."

"That would be nice," Janet said. "I don't think he has any family, and given his personality, I doubt that he has all that many friends. He would probably appreciate a visit. I'll get you the room number in the morning and text it to your cell phone."

"I'd appreciate that," Murray told her, and the conversation went on to other things.

The number was in his phone before he left for the office the next day, but he put off his visit until afternoon. Doctors made their rounds in the morning, he told himself. Blood was drawn and other tests were run then, too. He refused to admit to himself that he was putting it off to give himself time to build up courage and figure out what to say when the man he had maimed was lying there in front of him, his legs likely elevated in those apparatuses you see in TV shows and in the movies.

Mid-afternoon, he locked the door to his office and backed the Nissan out of the garage. Janet loved the Impala, and he couldn't bring himself to deny her the use of it. Besides, the people who worked at the hospital had gotten used to seeing it there, and the addition of her old vehicle in the parking lot would likely go unnoticed, both of which, in Murray's mind, were good things. He chastised himself a bit, though, for buying in to Daniel Miller's paranoia.

He wore one of his better pairs of kaki trousers for the visit and a tan, long-sleeved shirt, no tie, a pair of his black wingtips. Still hadn't replaced the brown ones that had gotten destroyed in what he had come to think of as The Raid. Thought about wearing a baseball cap but decided it wouldn't look right with the rest of his attire. He passed few people in the hall, none of whom paid him any mind, and rode the elevator to third floor alone. He checked his phone again to make sure he had the right room, then turned it off and stepped through the door.

Hartman was lying on his back in a bed that had been cranked up to a half-sitting position, his attention on the television that was hung high up on the wall opposite the foot of the bed. Murray could tell at a glance the man had lost a few pounds. For several seconds, he ignored his visitor, likely thinking it was some of the hospital staff, come to empty the trash or do some other annoying chore. When he finally decided to see exactly who was in his room, his eyes left the TV, focused on Murray and went wide for a moment. Then his brow furrowed into a frown. For several seconds, he said nothing, and when he finally spoke, his tone was angry. "What the hell are *you* doing here?"

"Thought I'd drop by and see how you're doing."

"How the hell do you think I'd be doin'?" Hartman asked. "Somebody emptied a clip into me."

"Something like the way you emptied a clip into my son," Murray suggested.

"No," Hartman said, "more like into every joint in my body. What's what happened to your son got to do with anything?"

"I suppose as far as you're concerned it has nothing to do with anything. I hear from the grapevine that you've got new shoulders."

Hartman raised both arms. "Almost as good as new. They're gonna give me new knees in a day or two."

"And then you'll be back on your feet?" Murray asked, knowing the answer before he even asked the question.

"No." Hartman's tone got meaner. "They'll still have to work on my ankles."

"You're ankles?"

"Yeah, my ankles, moron. I took seven rounds," Hartman said, "one here" he held up his left hand to show the absence of an index finger, "two in the shoulders, two in the knees and two in the ankles. After the knees, they'll work on my ankles."

"Well, when that's all done, if by some miracle of modern medicine… hummm, that's really alliterative," Murray muttered, getting off track.

"What?" Hartman asked, his tone confused and irritated.

"Never mind. I was just about to say if they get you back in good enough shape that you think about getting back out on the street, I wouldn't advise it."

"Yeah? And why is that?"

"Because you wouldn't want to risk something like this, or maybe even something worse, happening again."

"Ain't nothin' like this ever gonna happen to me again," Hartman insisted emphatically. "I'll be beyond careful from now on. Nobody's ever gonna sneak up on me like that again, and any asshole that tries is gonna wish he had never been born."

"Just the same," Murray said, "stay off the streets. Don't make me keep my promise a second time."

"What's that supposed to mean? You tryin' to tell me *you* did this to me?" Hartman asked and erupted in a burst of laughter.

"You don't think I could have done it?" Murray asked.

"A wimpy-ass lawyer like you, McCartney?" Hartman glared at him with contempt. "No way. It took somebody with balls to do what they did to me, and that's something you ain't got."

Murray chuckled in spite of himself.

"You think that's funny?" Hartman asked.

'Funny, no" Murray said, "a bit amusing, maybe. I heard the same thing from someone else recently."

"So, somebody out there knows you as well as I do."

"Whatever," Murray said stepping closer to the bed, losing his smile and looking Hartman in the eye.

"The promise I made when you killed my son has been satisfied, whether you believe I'm capable of being the one that satisfied it or not. Now, I'll make you another one. You get put back together well enough that Coder lets you back out on the street, you better abide by the agreement we signed…"

"I didn't sign shit!" Hartman interrupted.

"… or what happens to you next will make what you're going through now feel like a little girl's birthday party. The only way they'll be able to identify your body will be with the serial numbers on the stainless-steel joints they're putting in it, and that will be only if they can find it at all. I've learned some new skills these past few months, and you don't want to find out what they are from experience. We have been bullied enough, me and those close to me. It's not gonna happen anymore, even if I have to put you in the ground. Understand? Now, I've got to go. I promised Janet a rib-eye for supper, and I always keep my promises."

For several seconds more, he maintained eye contact. Hartman's glare softened into something like a look of respect, and Murray backed away, turned and left the room. When the door closed behind him, Hartman turned his head to stare at spot on the wall, the television above it of no interest to him anymore.

Chapter Seventeen

He hadn't realized how much adrenalin it had taken for him to step through the door of Hartman's room and then how much more for him to step up to the bed, look the man in the eye and make the promise he had made. By the time he reached the parking lot, it was fading, and depression was beginning to set in. Not the kind of depression he had experienced after his visit to Mayor Banks's office when he had used such foul language all those months ago, but depression none the less.

He took the keys for the Nissan out of his pocket and stood by the vehicle for several minutes, staring at them and trying to decide what to do. Going back to the office wasn't an option because the bed in this apartment seemed to be calling his name, and he didn't want to let himself collapse this time. Going out to the homeplace was out of the question for a while. Janet would be getting off work soon, and he didn't want to take his foul mood to her.

The thought of Janet getting off work brought to mind what he had told Hartman about the rib-eye. That had been a lie, and it amazed him to realize that lying to the man bothered him more than what he had done to put Hartman in the hospital. He unlocked the car and slid behind the wheel, sat there for several more minutes, undecided. He started the engine, put the car in gear and left the parking lot, driving in a daze, still with no idea where he wanted to go.

A few minutes later, he found himself on Penn Avenue, passing the spot where Duane Runk had died, and then he was on Route 22, heading toward Mount Union, twelve miles away. When he got there, he took the 522 bypass around the north side of town, then swung back onto the main street and pulled into McDonalds. Go inside and sit down or take the drive-thru? He didn't want to be around people, so he chose the latter, ordered a medium coffee, black, and pulled back onto Route 522.

When he got to the little town of Orbisonia, he took a right at the town's only traffic signal and eventually realized that he was tracing the route in reverse that he had taken from Hartman's place after he had done the deed. He didn't want to pass the crime scene, so he took a right onto PA 747 and eventually found himself coming into the southern edge of Mount Union.

"Enough of this," he said to himself. "Time to go home."

* * * *

Janet was leaning against the Impala, her arms crossed under her breasts, when he pulled into the ruts that had become the Nissan's new parking place. There was no smile on her face, and she didn't move when he got out of the car.

"Where have you been, and why haven't you

been answering your phone?" she asked. "I called you half a dozen times."

"I was just driving around," Murray told her, "and I had to turn my phone off when I went to see Hartman. I forgot to turn it back on."

"Why didn't you just go back to your office or come on home?"

"I wasn't in a very good mood when I left the hospital, and it was about time for you to get off work. I didn't want to bring it home to you."

"Your visit with Hartman didn't go well?"

"It went as well, I suppose, as could be expected, given our history," Murray told her. "I just had some things I had to say to him that left me feeling down."

Janet gave his answer a minute's thought, uncrossed her arms and pushed herself away from the Impala. "You don't look like you're in a very good mood yet," she said, "Come here."

Murray did what he was told, and she wrapped him up in her arms. After a minute or more, she stepped back, still not smiling, took him by the hand and led him into the house.

"I had a ham and cheese sandwich and some chips when I got home," she said when they had passed through the mudroom and into the kitchen. "What would you like for supper?"

"I don't know," he told her. "Maybe that would be enough for me, too."

"Sit down, and I'll make you one," she said.

She made the sandwich and set it and a small bowl of potato chips on the table in front of him, brought him a glass of sweet tea.

"Aren't you gonna sit down with me?" he asked.

"No, I'm gonna take an early shower and wash my hair," Janet said. "Get the smell of hospital kitchen out of it." She stepped away and disappeared through the curtains at the bottom of the stairs.

He ate the sandwich and most of the chips, drank the tea and went into the living room, sat down on the sofa, slid down until his head rested on the back of it and closed his eyes. He could hear the water running upstairs, imagined her working shampoo into her hair and thought about how it would smell when they went to bed later, something like coconut. In the bed that still had the pillows down the middle. He had brought up the subject of moving back into the guestroom, and she told him she didn't want him to. The room had no window unit, she said, and she liked the arrangement they had—but the pillows were still there between them. He should bring up the idea of her being Mrs. Somebody Else again, he thought, but her answer had been *maybe*, and he didn't want to take the risk of hearing that again.

Seemingly out of nowhere, Hartman's voice popped into his head. *It took somebody with balls to do what they did to me, and that's something you ain't got.*

Was that the reason for the *maybe*? he wondered. Is that the way Janet saw him, too? He had told her he had never had a strong libido, but he had one, just the same. Did she think she was saving him from embarrassment?

So, somebody out there knows you as well as I do.

Hartman had no way of knowing that he was referring to Chief Coder, but could his comment apply to Janet, too? Was she simply making do with what she

294

had and biding her time until someone more manly, someone that suited her better, came along? After all, her late husband had been a macho, guns and ammunition man and had been in law enforcement. Did she want someone more like that? Would she find him more attractive if she knew about the promise he had kept and the one he had made Hartman this afternoon?

He had committed a crime, what society would call an atrocity even, but everybody still seemed to think of him as just a wimpy lawyer. Did that include Janet? he wondered. Whatever. He had done what he had to do, and he was still the same man that he was before he had done it. Daniel Miller's answer to his question—do you think what I plan to do will change me? —came back to mind. *Only if you let it. Do what you have to do and don't* let *it change you. Put it behind you and get on with your life.*

Get on with his life. And what would that life be like eventually? Living alone in the apartment behind his office? Getting up each morning and eating breakfast alone, having coffee, getting dressed to walk through the door and sit down at his desk? Waiting alone until a client showed up? Of course, there would be the usual trips to the courthouse to file papers and trips to Walmart for groceries. He would run into people he knew, but essentially, he would be alone.

"Murray?"

He opened his eyes and rolled his head toward the sound of Janet's voice. She was standing at the far end of the sofa wearing one of her mid-thigh length night shirts. She held out a hand and said, "Come with me."

"It's too early for bed," he told her. "Come sit down. You can distract me right here."

She smiled. "I just said your name three times before you heard me, sweetheart. You're already distracted. Tonight, you need benefits."

"Benefits?" he echoed.

"Benefits," she repeated, "and the answer is yes. I would like to be Mrs. Somebody Else. Mrs. Murray McCartney to be exact."

He reached and took her outstretched hand. She pulled him up and into one of her full-body embraces, but this time, the kiss was gentle. She leaned back and smiled into his eyes. "If the offer still stands?"

"No more pillows?" he asked.

For a moment, she was confused, and then the light dawned. Her smile brightened and she said, "No more pillows."

Epilogue

Some Months Later

It was bound to happen with both of them living in the Huntingdon area, and it was more likely than not to happen where it did, since everybody seems to find themselves in Walmart now and then. There was one more item on the list Janet had given him, and Murray was rounding the corner into the toilet tissue aisle when he saw James Hartman coming right toward him, a package of that very item tucked under his arm. It would be their first meeting since the one in Hartman's hospital room, and Murray felt his pulse kick up a beat. No telling what the man's attitude would be, but he was determined to keep things casual.

"Hartman," he greeted, doing his best to keep his expression neutral. "How have you been?"

"McCartney," Hartman responded with a nod. "Can't complain, I guess. I'm up and goin'."

"Haven't heard much about you lately. Are you still working for the department?"

Hartman gave his head a negative shake. "They gave me two choices. Ride a desk or take early retirement. I took the retirement. You still bangin' that Hockenberry broad?"

Murray smiled at the man's crude language. "There is no Hockenberry broad anymore. Her name is McCartney now."

"Score one for the wimp," Hartman said and grinned.

Add yourself to that, Murray thought, *and give me a score of two*, but he kept the thought to himself.

"What about that daughter of hers?" Hartman asked. "She still around?"

"Yes and no," Murray told him. "She's engaged to Charles Bond and spends most of her time down in Mount Union these days."

Hartman took his eyes off Murray's face and stared off into the distance. "I really liked that one," he said. "I should a done things different."

Murray nodded agreement, but for several moments, it seemed like Hartman had forgotten he was there. Then he focused on Murray again.

"She doin' okay?"

"She's doing very well," Murray told him. "She's taking online classes and hopes to be a teacher." Some of the money from the lawsuit being put to good use, that and the purchase of a later model Impala much like her mother's to replace her old Malibu.

"Well, tell her I'm sorry for the way I acted, and I hope she does well."

"I'll do that." Murray nodded. "And I hope you get along well, too."

"Have a good one," Hartman said and walked away, heading for the checkout.

Murray eased his basket back to where he could watch the man go. The stainless-steel joints seemed to be serving him well. The smooth, easy swagger was gone, but there was no limp in Hartman's gait, just a steady put one foot in front of the other. For a second or two, Murray wondered if he should feel guilty about the change. Then Daniel Miller's advice came back to mind again: *Put it behind you and get on with your life.*

A lot more than Hartman's gait had changed, he decided, and the change was for the better. The man had actually offered an apology, not to Murray himself but to Janie. Murray had an answer to the question that had been on his mind ever since his visit to Hartman in the hospital: Would Hartman abide by the agreement he and the others had signed? It looked like the answer was yes, and life for the citizens of Huntingdon was going to be harassment free from here on.

About the Author

Charles C. Brown started writing when he retired from teaching high school English after thirty-six years. *Justice as Promised* is his tenth mystery novel, following *Say I Do and Die*, *Dead Man Waiting*, *Cold in the Ground*, *Suffer the Consequences*, *Up From the Grave*, *Best Served Cold*, *Catch and Release*, *Justice Comes Late*, and *Justice by the Numbers*. He lives in Davis, Oklahoma, with his wife of more than fifty years, Carolyn Brown. They have three grown children and enough grandchildren and great-grandchildren to keep them young.

Made in the USA
Monee, IL
06 June 2020